My cat had found something strange, and I could hardly believe it…

Jack and I jogged along the trail behind the cabins just before sunrise the next morning. The sky was lightening, but the mountains blocked the sun's rays, and the path was shrouded in near darkness. Jack trotted along next to me in his harness, his paws making no sound on the soft bed of pine needles that covered the trail surface. We stopped for a breather near the rock I had sat on the previous day, and I noticed Gil about fifty yards away, standing hip deep in the creek in his waders, casting his line upstream and watching it float by. He looked up briefly at me, then he turned away again.

I waited for Jack, who was digging in the dirt next to the trail, no doubt looking for a convenient place for a potty stop. After a few minutes, he was still digging, so I pulled on his leash. "C'mon, Jack. Let's go."

But he resisted and continued digging, growling and becoming more and more agitated. I pulled on the leash again, harder this time, but he wouldn't budge.

I bent over and picked him up. "Okay, if you insist."

I peered down at the hole he had made. Something didn't seem quite right. I squatted to get a closer look, the cat squirming in my arms. I gasped and jumped back, lost my balance, and sat down hard. The taste of adrenaline flooded my mouth as I stared as three fingers protruding from the hole, the bright purple nail polish absurdly out of place among the rust-colored pine needles.

She should have known when she fished that Pink Floyd T-shirt out of the creek that it belonged to that waitress, the one who disappeared...

Kathryn "Ryn" Lowell has escaped the stifling confines of her office at the New York travel magazine she writes for and pulls into Trout Fork, a tiny fishing hamlet in the Colorado Rockies, to write an article about the town. She hasn't been there long when, along with her orange tabby cat, Jack Kerouac, she discovers a T-shirt in the local creek that belonged to the missing waitress. Now foul play is suspected, and Ryn, who has fallen for the quaint mountain town, is determined to find the killer and give her new friends closure. Teaming up with the local police detective, who seems to want more than Ryn can give him, she puts it all on the line—her heart, her job, and her life.

KUDOS for *Death in Trout Fork*

In *Death in Trout Fork* by D. M. O'Byrne, Ryn Lowell is a travel journalist who stops in a quaint little town in Colorado to write a column about it. The first day there, she learns that a waitress from the local café has disappeared, and Ryn takes a job helping out in the café until they can find someone to replace her. Later that day, she finds the missing waitress's favorite T-shirt in the local creek, and the next day she finds the body buried in a shallow grave alongside the creek. Ryn has quickly fallen in love with this little mountain town and the people she has met there, and she is determined to find the girl's killer if it is the last thing she does—as it may well be. A first-class cozy mystery, the story is well written, fast paced, and intriguing. I hope the author is planning a series because I was left wanting more. A great read. ~ *Taylor Jones, The Review Team of Taylor Jones & Regan Murphy*

Death in Trout Fork by DM O'Byrne is the story of a young journalist who writes for a travel magazine. Kathryn "Ryn" Lowell travels around to small towns to do research for her column in the magazine. But when she pulls into the little mountain town of Trout Fork with her cat Jack, Ryn has no idea what she is getting herself into. One of the two waitresses from the local café has gone missing, so Ryn pitches in to help out until they can find someone new. The first day there, Ryn and Jack go jogging by the stream and find a T-shirt that belonged to the missing waitress. Strange as that seems, Ryn is totally unprepared the next day when Jack starts digging beside the path they are jogging on and uncovers a body. Ryn's investigative juices start flowing, and she is determined to stay in town until she finds out who the killer is—

which may be more dangerous than she realizes. O'Byrne has once again demonstrated her marvelous talent for character development, and I fell in love with all the unique characters from Trout Fork. Fast paced, charming, and intriguing, *Death in Trout Fork* is one that cozy mystery fans should love. ~ *Regan Murphy, The Review Team of Taylor Jones & Regan Murphy*

OTHER BOOKS BY

DM O'BYRNE

AND

BLACK OPAL BOOKS

Dangerous Turf

Three to One Odds

DEATH
IN
TROUT
FORK

Ryn Lowell Colorado Mysteries

DM O'Byrne

A Black Opal Books Publication

GENRE: COZY MYSTERY/WOMEN SLEUTHS

This is a work of fiction. Names, places, characters and incidents are either the product of the author's imagination or are used fictitiously, and any resemblance to any actual persons, living or dead, businesses, organizations, events or locales is entirely coincidental. All trademarks, service marks, registered trademarks, and registered service marks are the property of their respective owners and are used herein for identification purposes only. The publisher does not have any control over or assume any responsibility for author or third-party websites or their contents.

DEATH
IN
TROUT
FORK

CHAPTER 1

I should have known when I fished that Pink Floyd T-shirt out of the creek that it belonged to that waitress, the one who disappeared. It was the same shirt she was wearing in the picture Ashley showed me of the two of them in front of Alma's café. As I jogged along the path by the creek that evening with Jack Kerouac, my orange tabby cat, there was no hint of the madness that would threaten my life, the insidious kind of madness that infects whole communities and sets them at each other's throats, the kind that turns fathers against sons and mothers against daughters.

Of course, I didn't know all that when I pulled into Trout Fork, which could hardly be called a town, or even a village. It was just four stores under one shingled roof at the intersection of two winding mountain roads.

"Perfect," I said out loud as I pulled into the parking lot. This was exactly what I'd been looking for all week, an off-the-beaten-path spot I could describe for my column, "Out of My Way."

Cranky old Crenshaw, my editor, had been on my back for days. "This column doesn't write itself, you know, Kathryn," he had pontificated into the phone.

No kidding had been my comeback of choice, but I restrained myself.

I took out my cell phone and started to dial the number of the magazine to assure him he would be receiving another brilliant piece of travel literature in short order, but the No Service message told me Trout Fork wasn't just off the beaten path. It was way off.

I got out of my old Corolla and opened the back door. Jack hopped down and stretched, gazing around with interest, while I put on his harness and leash. The air was typically Rocky Mountain dry and pristine, the kind that makes you grateful you can breathe. The sounds of water rushing over the rocks told me the fork where the creek and the river met was right across the street.

The view of the mountain range to the west was breathtaking, and I stood mesmerized. I had seen the Alps and the Pyrenees, but these Rockies were in a league of their own. Their craggy crests, some still holding onto patches of snow even now in mid-summer, seemed to strain to pierce the sky above. The fourteeners, as the locals call them, challenge the adventurous to scale as many of the fifty-three mountains over fourteen thousand feet as they can.

I had parked in front of Gil's Bait Shop, which was right next to Trout Fork Liquors. A dusty-looking store called Madam Gauzie's Antiques was at one end of the building, with Alma's Café at the other end. The smell of coffee drew me toward Alma's, and as I passed the bait shop, a tall, hawk-nosed man was watching me through a screen door decorated with a huge American flag.

"Afternoon," I said pleasantly. "Lovely day."

He growled something and disappeared back into the store. Apparently helping people murder fish had made Gil a dull boy.

Alma's was a homey little place with blond oak tables and straight-backed chairs in a small dining room with a massive brick fireplace taking up most of one wall.

I joined the line under the "Order Here or Be Seated for Table Service" sign and perused the menu scrawled on the blackboard behind the counter. The sign next to the cash register said, "We don't do fast food. We do good food as fast as we can."

A short, red-faced forty-something woman in a long white apron was taking orders. She rang them up on the cash register, gave the customer a number, and then dashed back into the kitchen. Soon plates of food were being fired through the window in the wall between the kitchen and the counter. "Order up!" she shouted to a harried-looking teenage girl who was delivering plates of food to the customers scattered throughout the room and the patio.

"We don't allow animals in here," the girl said apologetically, gesturing to Jack sitting quietly at my feet. "Sorry. Health Department rules. He's a beautiful cat." She bent down to scratch Jack's head, while he closed his eyes and allowed himself to be adored.

"How about the patio?" I asked. "Would he be okay out there?"

"Sure," the girl called over her shoulder as she hurried away.

The red-faced woman scurried back out to the counter, wiping her sweaty forehead with her sleeve. "What can I get you, honey?"

"A burger, please. Well done, with fries and coffee. And an extra plate."

Her pudgy fingers pounded the cash register keys. "It might be a while. I hope you don't mind. My waitress up and left two days ago. No notice. Nothing. It's just me and my daughter until I can find someone."

"No problem. I'm not in a hurry. I'll be out on the patio."

"Thanks for understanding." She gave me the change

and the number six on a wooden stick shaped like a tall fork with a plastic fish impaled on it. Then she swept back into the kitchen.

On my way out to the patio, the girl gave me a grim smile as she brushed past me. I picked out one of the metal mesh tables with a bright green umbrella providing shade from the bright sunlight.

The railing around the patio was covered with planters of purple and fuchsia flowers cascading over the railing.

I sat down and gazed around at the idyllic setting, wondering how I could have survived city life so long. Jack hopped up onto one of the chairs and proceeded to wash his paws as though he knew lunch was coming.

By the time the girl brought my lunch, I was ravenous.

She plunked the plate in front of me. "Sorry this is so late." Her mannerisms and long chestnut hair reminded me of a Thoroughbred yearling, all legs and energy with the promise of future grace and beauty.

"That's okay. I hear your waitress quit." I cut up some of my hamburger and put it on the extra plate for Jack. He sniffed at it with interest and then began to eat daintily. Two older women at the next table smiled at him.

"Quit? She just bailed, no notice, nothing. Probably rode off on the back of some dude's Harley, the same way she rode in. I just wish she had told someone. We've been slammed, and my mom is freaking out back there."

"Is your mom Alma?"

"Yeah. Alma was my grandmother's name, too. She's dead now."

A family business. More grist for the column. "Do you go to school around here?"

She laughed. "Nah, there's no school in Trout Fork. I

go to school in Pineland Park. Anything else I can get you?"

"No thanks. Oh, I guess there's no cell phone service here?"

"Depends on where you are. There's a cell tower in the area, but it's not close by. The mountains are so tall that it gets blocked. Some places you won't get a signal, or you can get cut off mid-sentence."

"Ashley!" her mother bellowed from the kitchen.

The girl rolled her eyes and hurried off.

I took in the scenery as I ate. The cloudless sapphire sky arched over the pines packed so thick on the rust-colored hillsides that no sunshine could penetrate the darkness under them. A group of motorcycles roared off, leaving only the sound of the rushing water in the creek. I leaned back and smiled. This assignment was going to be a piece of cake.

Jack and I finished our lunch, and on the way out of the café, I noticed a Help Wanted sign had been hastily taped to the cash register. Outside, we ambled along the wooden sidewalk, my Birkenstocks making hollow sounds with each step. I decided the best way to get the lay of the land was to chat up the locals, so I started at the end store.

The sign on the door said, "Enter," so I did. The store was chock full of old stuff on shelves and tables, some of it genuine antiques, but much of it nothing more than garage sale rejects, all of it covered with layers of dust.

An elderly woman dashed toward me with energy that belied her age. She wore a loose-fitting, flowing print caftan that seemed to flutter in the breeze created by her quick stride. Her gray hair was tied up in a bright orange scarf, and necklaces of varying lengths and materials clattered and jangled as she walked. I wondered how she could possibly make a living in this isolated location trying to sell antiques to bikers and fishermen.

"Welcome," she gushed. "Were you looking for anything special?"

If I were, this is the last place I'd find it. "No, just looking," I said.

"Well, I'm Madam Gauzie, the owner. Let me know if I can help you." She pronounced her name "Go-zee," as though it was French. She looked skeptically down at Jack. "Oh, you have a kitty on a leash. I hope he won't do anything he shouldn't in here."

"No. He never does anything he shouldn't."

Jack sniffed around a bit, investigating, and sneezed twice. I wandered through the store, looking for something to use as a conversation starter. If anyone could tell me more about Trout Fork, it might be this old woman.

On one shelf, I noticed a blue and white nineteenth-century Delft vase standing out from among the junk. "Oh, this is a nice piece." I leaned closer. "My mother has one like it in her collection."

"Really? Where does your mother live?"

"New York City. West side." I could see the dollar signs pop up in her eyes, like they do in those old-fashioned cash registers. If only she knew that I had escaped as far from that white-glove society scene as I could with barely enough money to buy gas and cat food. Even my trust fund wasn't really mine until I turned thirty, and that was still two years away.

"What brings you to Trout Fork? Just passing through?"

I offered my hand to her. "I'm Ryn Lowell. I write for a travel magazine, and I'm always looking for out-of-the-way places for my column."

"Ryn? Ryn? That's an unusual name."

"Short for Kathryn." Once again, I was overwhelmed

by the same unwanted vision of my little brother running down the beach, his chubby two-year-old legs kicking up the sand as he ran giggling and squealing, "Catch me, Ryn!" He could never pronounce Kathryn, and his name for me had stuck with the rest of the family. Except for Mother, of course. I would always be Kathryn to her. I forced Davey's image back down into my subconscious. Where it belonged. Where I had to keep it. "Do you live around here?"

She nodded. "My cabin is behind the store."

"A nice quiet little place away from the noisy, crowded city, huh?"

She peered uneasily toward the parking lot where another group of motorcycles had pulled in. "Well, it used to be a lot quieter. Now we get so many of those motorcycle people. They can get quite rowdy at times. Especially the young ones. One night a few weeks ago, a bunch of them had a party right in the parking lot. Loud music from their radios, booze, and God knows what else. I locked my doors and went home early. Disgraceful behavior."

My journalist's instincts were piqued. Now we were getting somewhere. It sounded like a scene from *The Wild Ones*. That angle would never fly for the column, of course, but maybe I could use some of it in the novel.

Madam Gauzie was warming to her subject. "When I got here the next morning, do you know what I found?"

"What?"

"That girl. That waitress from Alma's. Passed out on the bench in front of the liquor store. And her boyfriend, the one she came here with?"

"Yes?"

"Gone. Left her here like so much excess baggage. Took off during the night. She was flat broke, too. If it weren't for Alma taking her in and giving her a job, God knows what would have become of her. Alma, I told her, you've got to be crazy taking that floozy into your home. Her with her pierced lips and nose and whatever else they pierce these days. And she was such a flirt, that one. Making eyes at every man that came into the café. And Alma letting her share a room with Ashley! But she wouldn't listen to me. Too softhearted by half. Took that girl in just like that stray cat of hers. She won't stay, I told her. One day she'll up and clean out the cash register and hightail it down the road."

"Is that what happened?"

"Well, she didn't rob Alma, but she disappeared Sunday. Left Alma in an awful bind. She and Ashley can't run that place without help."

"Didn't anyone see her leave? She must have gotten a ride with someone."

"Who knows? I did see her with some of those bikers that afternoon. You'd think she would at least have said something to Alma before she left. But that's young people today. No consideration." She pulled her loose garment around her more closely. "If I were you, I wouldn't hang around here too long. It's not the same anymore. Not the same…" She moved among the shelves, lovingly caressing some of the items.

Jack and I left her to her faux antiques and headed to the next store in the row. The sign on the door of Trout Fork Liquors said, "We don't serve minors. No ID, no service. No exceptions. Hank Edwards, prop."

I entered the store and nodded to the tall, burly man with bushy red hair and a scraggly red beard standing behind the counter. He frowned at Jack. "I don't allow animals in here. Not sanitary."

I took Jack back outside and tied his leash to the infamous bench. I patted his head, went back inside, and took a bottle of water out of the cooler at the back of the store. I brought it back to the front, where the man was carefully cleaning the counter with Lysol and paper towels.

"This all for you?"

"Yes." I looked around at the boxes of wines and liquors stacked near the counter. "Are you the owner?"

He flashed a wide smile. "Sure am, honey. You here for the fishing?"

"No. I don't fish. I'm a writer."

Immediately, the smile vanished. "What kind of things do you write? Newspaper stuff?" He looked at me as though a bad odor had suddenly wafted in.

I steeled myself for the usual diatribe against the press. "No. I write for a travel magazine. Mostly I write a column about interesting places I find. Like this one."

The smile returned. "Oh. That's okay then. Can't stand those snoopy newspaper reporters. How long you planning to be here?"

"I'm not sure. Is there a motel anywhere nearby?"

"No. People who come here are mostly just passing through to spend the day fishing. There are the houses and cabins that the locals use. But that's about it. Nearest motel is in Pineland Park. About twenty miles south on this road."

"Oh. Thanks." I took my water, and Jack and I sat on the bench. I poured a little water into my hand for Jack to drink from. "Not sanitary. He's got his nerve, right Jack? You wash yourself every day, don't you?"

As I watched him drink, I thought about the waitress. What would prompt her to leave without a word to Alma, the woman who had been kind enough to take her in and give her a job? Was she in trouble of some kind? Running from something? Or someone? Maybe there was a story there I could use, certainly not for the column, but I tucked it away in my memory for the novel.

After about an hour, I wound up back at the café. The lunch rush had subsided, and the dining room was empty, except for Alma and her daughter, who sat at one of the tables. Alma had taken off her sneakers and was rubbing her feet, while her daughter sat engrossed in a book. The woman quickly hid her feet under the table when she saw me.

"Taking a break?" I asked as I approached.

"A short one," Alma said. "Did you want something?" Her bright blue eyes shone from her round red face.

"No. I'm just looking around. I work for a travel magazine, and I'm thinking about writing an article about Trout Fork."

The girl looked up from her book and regarded me as though I had recently escaped from a mental asylum. "You're writing about this place? Seriously?" Without waiting for an answer, she rolled her eyes as only a fifteen-year-old can and went back to her reading.

"This is my daughter, Ashley."

The girl looked at me and nodded.

"I'm Ryn Lowell. Mind if I sit down?"

Alma pulled a chair out. "Not at all. Where's your cat?"

"He's sleeping in his bed in the car." I had pulled my old Corolla into the shade and opened the windows. Jack had kneaded his kitty bed with his paws then curled up with a sigh. Daytime wasn't his thing.

"Not often we get people interested in this place," Alma said.

"You never know what you'll find in a small community like this one. There are often fascinating stories just waiting to be told."

She raised her eyebrows. "Really?"

"Well, I must admit I have an ulterior motive. I'm also trying to write the great American novel, and I'm always on the lookout for interesting characters and plot lines. What I don't use for the column, I can save for the novel."

At the word "novel," Ashley put her book down and regarded me with renewed interest.

"Where is the magazine based?" her mother asked.

"New York. That's where I'm from." I've always found that answering questions isn't as productive as asking them, so I said, "How about you? Your daughter said your mother once owned this place."

"Yes. I grew up here." She leaned over and rubbed her calf. "But it was different then."

I made a mental note. "How so?"

"It had a different feel to it. Then it was mostly the locals and those who came to fish. Now there's the bikers and other tourists. You get all kinds. Some of the locals don't like to stay all year. Most shut up their cabins and go back to the city for the winter. Not that I blame them."

The door opened, and a paunchy, balding, middle-aged man came in. He stopped when he saw the three of us at the table. He wore thick glasses that made his eyes look huge, reminding me of a bug. He was wearing a long-sleeved shirt that must have been uncomfortable on such a warm day.

Alma got up from the table. "Afternoon, Rev. Having a late lunch today?"

"I thought I would," he said in a somewhat high-pitched voice.

Alma went behind the counter and waited for his order.

"I guess the turkey sandwich with salad on the side," the man said.

"Coming right up. Been out fishing today?"

"Follow me, and I will make you fishers of men.

Matthew four nineteen," he intoned seriously.

"Right. Have a seat and Ashley will bring your lunch." She disappeared into the kitchen.

As the man sat down at the other end of the dining room facing us, Ashley snickered. "He does that all the time," she said quietly. "That's why we call him Rev. His real name is Zach something. Heather used to rag on him every time he came in."

"Heather?"

"The waitress who left. She used to tease him like crazy. One time she asked him to explain the word 'fornication,' and he nearly choked on his lunch. It was hysterical."

"Order up," Alma called.

Ashley got up and delivered Rev's plate. "Do you need anything else?"

He gave her a saintly smile. "It is written, man does not live by bread alone. Luke, four, four."

"I'll take that as a no," Ashley said with a smirk and came back to my table.

Alma emerged from the kitchen with a cup of coffee and sat down with us, groaning slightly as she settled into the chair. Something about this place and these oddball characters set my journalist's whiskers aquiver, and I wanted to dig deeper.

I gazed around the café, my eyes resting on the Help Wanted sign. "Having any luck finding another waitress?"

"Not yet," Alma said.

"I'd like to apply for the job."

Ashley looked at me and grinned. "Great. You can share my room in the cabin. It's just behind the café. That's what Heather did. "

Her mother was a little less enthusiastic. "Do you have any experience? I thought you said you're a writer."

"I put myself through college waiting tables." *Much to Mother's horror*, I thought. "I can fill in until you find someone permanent. It will give me time to write while I'm here."

Alma took a deep breath, whether from relief or trepidation I wasn't sure. "When can you start?"

"Anytime."

"Okay. We'll give it a try. Ashley can show you to the cabin. After you get settled in, come back before dinner, and I'll give you some quick training."

"Great. I'll just get Jack and my suitcase out of the car." As Ashley and I left the café, I had the unnerving sensation we were being watched.

CHAPTER 2

Ashley's room in the log cabin behind the café was spare but functional. Twin beds were pushed up against the pine log walls. A small desk, a bookshelf, and one painted dresser completed the furnishings. A lace curtain covered the single window that looked out over the pine trees on the hillside behind the cabin. I was surprised at the lack of posters of boy bands and the usual teenage heartthrobs that papered the walls of my sister's bedroom when she was fifteen. Perhaps I would have more in common with this girl than I thought. I stole a glance at the eclectic assortment of books on the shelf, reminiscent of my collection when I was still trying to figure out who I was and what kind of books could hold my interest.

"You can have that bed," Ashley said, pointing to the one under the window. "That was Heather's."

Lying on the other bed was a pretty black and white tuxedo cat. Her eyes were wide as she stared at Jack, who I'd carried in over my shoulder. I turned around so the two cats could size each other up. Jack always took new situations with a "live and let live" attitude, but you never knew about other animals.

"This is Sasha." Ashley sat down to stroke the cat's

sleek fur. "I've brought you a buddy, Sash," she crooned soothingly. "You're going to be best friends, aren't you?"

Sasha and Jack continued to regard each other. Sasha's eyes were wide, and Jack's whiskers quivered while his tail flicked back and forth. Neither made any aggressive moves, no growling or hissing, so I placed Jack gently on the bed by the window.

He sat up and wrapped his tail around his front paws.

Sasha continued eyeing him warily for a moment then began rubbing her head on Ashley's arm.

"I think they'll be fine," Ashley said. "The litter box is over in the corner."

I lifted my suitcase onto the bed and opened it. I pointed to a small cardboard box on the bed. "Is this yours?"

"That's the stuff Heather left behind. Just dump it somewhere."

I peered into the box. "I wonder why she would leave without her stuff."

"Dunno. She didn't have much with her when she got here. Sunday she walked out after dinner and never came back. There were some bikers around that afternoon. We think she must've found a ride with one and took off. That would be just like her."

I lifted a photo off the top of the few things in the box. It was a picture of Ashley and another girl in front of the café. "Oh, is this her?"

Ashley came over and glimpsed at the photo. "Yeah, that was taken last week. She loved that T-shirt. Hardly ever took it off."

The other girl was exactly as Madam Gauzie had described her, piercings and all. Her hair was short and spiked with purple dye. She wore tight shorts and a black Pink Floyd T-shirt with a bright, multi-colored prism splashed across the front.

She had a somewhat cheeky, devil-may-care expression, her arm draped leisurely over Ashley's shoulders.

I searched through the box. Just a few items of clothing, some toiletries, and some odds and ends. What kind of girl was this who traveled light and moved in and out of people's lives like a breeze? It gave me an uncomfortable feeling to think that people might think of me the same way. Like Heather, I didn't spend long in any one place. I gazed out the window at the sunlit trees. "Is there a good place to jog around here?"

Ashley pointed out the window. "There's a nice path that runs along the creek behind the cabins. It goes through those trees and passes the YMCA camp. Really pretty along there."

"I think I'll take a short run before dinner." I pulled my beat-up running shoes and a pair of socks out of the suitcase and put them on. I ran my hand down Jack's back. "How about you, Jack? Are you up for a run?"

He looked at me through half-closed eyes. Then he yawned and stretched out on his side.

"Apparently not. Ok, maybe tomorrow."

"He jogs with you?"

"When he's in the mood. You should see the looks we get." I took a pair of shorts and a tank top out of my bag and started to change.

Sitting on her bed, Ashley watched me. "Maybe when you get back, we can talk some more about your writing," she said shyly.

"I'd like that. See you in a while."

ひちひ

The trail was easy to find. It wound through the thick pines, following the course of the Trout Creek. Set back from the creek were dozens of cabins made of logs or boards of the same reddish-brown color as the tree trunks. The roofs were treetop green. They were spaced far apart and hidden among the trees as though their owners wanted nothing better than to blend into the forest and disappear. Firewood was stacked high beside each cabin, and most had a pickup or four-wheel drive vehicle in the driveway.

Along the trail, I passed several kids with a guide, each of them wearing a T-shirt with the YMCA logo. The guide was pointing to the birds that skimmed along the creek just above the water. They smiled at me as they passed. The air was filled with a piney smell, and the dappled sunlight danced on the water as it flowed downstream.

I must have run about a mile and was on my way back when I saw a flat rock by the water's edge that seemed the perfect place to rest for a few minutes. I sat down on its warm, grainy surface and took off my shoes and socks. The icy cold water was soothing to my sweaty feet. I closed my eyes and listened to the wind sighing peacefully through the tops of the pines.

"I see you found our trail."

I turned to see the man named Zach from the café standing behind me holding a fishing rod and basket. He was still wearing that same long-sleeved shirt but had traded his slacks for rubber waders.

"Ashley told me about it. Lovely."

He looked wistfully around. "The forest is one of God's most wonderful creations."

I felt uncomfortable having him stand over me, so I asked him to sit down.

"Well, maybe for a minute. I'll have to get back soon. I have Bible study tonight." He lowered himself next to me on the rock.

The religious angle wasn't something I could use for

the column, and the last thing I wanted was proselytizing, but simply to make conversation I asked, "Do you have your Bible study here?"

"Oh no," he said sadly. "The folks here aren't interested in God. I go to church in Pineland Park."

"That's quite a drive, isn't it?"

"Twenty miles. I go three times a week," he added piously, making me wonder how his God felt about the pride that was unmistakable in that statement. He surveyed me through his thick-lensed glasses. "Do you attend church? Wherever it is you come from?"

Visions of Mother and me holding hands with Father Quinn, praying for hours by Davey's hospital bed, rushed unbidden into my consciousness. "I used to. Until I wised up."

"I'm sorry to hear you say that." His sorrowful gaze bored into me. He stood up abruptly. "I must get on. Maybe we can talk again soon."

"Sure."

Zach rose and started down the trail. I sat for a few minutes longer enjoying the scene. Then I heard a soft splash. I watched a speckled trout slip through the water right in front of me. I followed its progress until it stopped and circled in a deep pool near my rock. I peered into the dark water, fascinated by the fish's agile movements, until I noticed something colorful and out of place below the surface. The more I looked at it, the more my curiosity was piqued. I picked up a stick from the bank, plunged it into the pool, and directed it toward the color. The stick snagged on something, and I pulled it up. It was the Pink Floyd T-shirt.

∔ℂ∔

I went back to Alma's cabin to change for my first

shift at the café and found Ashley lying on her bed deep into her book. Lying by her side was the black and white tuxedo cat. She looked up at me curiously and purred as I scratched her head.

Ashley put down her book. "Have a nice run?"

I unfolded the wet T-shirt and held it up. "Does this look familiar?"

She sat up quickly. "That's Heather's. Where did you get it?"

"I found it in the creek. Any idea how it got there?"

Ashley shook her head slowly, her eyes wide.

"Maybe she lost it. Maybe it's not even hers. She can't be the only Pink Floyd fan in the area." I draped the shirt over the back of the desk chair to dry. I didn't want to alarm Ashley, but I was beginning to think there might be more to this than just a selfish girl riding off on a Harley one day. She hadn't told anyone, she had left some of her stuff behind, and somehow her favorite T-shirt had wound up in the creek. It didn't add up to anything good.

I changed, and Ashley and I walked over to the café together. The late afternoon storm clouds were obscuring the sun, and the wind had picked up enough that Alma was closing and tying down the umbrellas on the patio tables.

"Looks like rain," I said as we passed her.

She glanced at the darkening sky. "Let's hope so. We need it. Everything is so dry."

Ashley gave me a tour of the kitchen and some quick instructions.

"Seems pretty easy," I said. "I guess I'll learn as I go."

"It's no big deal. Here's a pad of tickets to use. Hang them on the wheel at the window there, and Mom will call you when the food's ready. The menu never changes. It's all right there on the board."

"Okay. I can handle it."

She nodded toward the door. "Here's your first customer."

It was the man from the bait shop.

Ashley greeted him with a smile. "Hi, Gil. You have your choice of tables tonight."

Gil grunted a reply I couldn't hear and sat at a table by the window overlooking the parking lot. He was tall and thin with a nose like the beak of a bald eagle, brown eyes, and dark hair streaked with gray. He wore a plaid shirt with the sleeves cut off, revealing a US Army tattoo on his bicep. He appeared to be in his early fifties. I remembered him from this morning as the man watching me through his screen door.

I approached with my pad and pen in hand, trying to appear efficient. "Hello. I'm Ryn. What can I get for you?"

As he was about to answer, a group of bikers sailed into the parking lot, their radios blasting, their Harley engines roaring.

Gil glared at them out the window. "Damn biker scum. Just what we don't need around here. Look at them. They make me sick."

I glanced at the group of laughing men and women dismounting their bikes. Most of the men were gray-beards in leather pants and jackets, their middle-aged women perched on the backs of the bikes. They seemed innocent enough to me, if you didn't mind the noise, of course. I identified with their desire to experience the freedom of the open road.

"They do seem to be enjoying themselves," I said.

"Too damn much, if you ask me." His eyes flashed with anger and disgust. "This place used to be for fishermen and maybe a few campers. Now look what we get. Noisy, drunken bikers, townies from Denver, and God knows what else. They wouldn't know a trout from a tire iron. They badmouth their country, flaunt our laws, and bring their whores with them to parade around with practically nothing on."

I attempted a faint smile. "Well, to each his own, I guess."

He gave me a withering look. "Just bring me the meat loaf platter. And tell Alma to go light on the pepper."

"Coming right up."

I went back to the kitchen and put the order slip on the wheel. "Wow. That Gil is one grumpy dude. And he has no use for bikers."

Alma chuckled. "Don't mind him. He doesn't mean anything by it. Gil's a bit of a snob. Anyone who comes here for anything other than the fishing is an invader into his territory. He's one of the few who live here all year round."

I made mental notes for the novel. *This is almost too good to be true. A fish purist.* I puttered around behind the counter while I waited for Gil's dinner.

The door opened, and Hank from the liquor store came in and sat down with Gil. I scurried over to the table. Hank greeted me with a smile, his yellowish teeth nearly lost in his bushy red beard. He reminded me of a mountain man I'd seen in a movie once.

He took out a cloth and wiped the table in front of his place. "Well, here's our little writer. Looks like you made yourself right at home here, huh?"

Gil eyed me with a curled lip. "You're not a newspaper reporter, are you?"

What is it with these people and reporters?

"No. I write for a travel magazine. I thought I'd help out until Alma can find another waitress. Shouldn't be more than a few days. Then I'll be on my way again." I turned to Hank. "What can I get for you?"

"Gil says he's getting the meat loaf. I'll have the same."

"Sure." I made a note on the pad. "Anything to drink? But I guess you have plenty to drink at your place, so you probably don't want—"

His smile switched off in an instant, replaced by an ugly, belligerent glare. "What's that supposed to mean?" he snarled. "What have you heard?"

"No, no, nothing," I stammered, backing up a little. "I didn't mean anything by—"

"Just go order the food." He gave me a dismissive wave.

I hurried away, and I could feel my face flaming. As I hung the ticket on the wheel, a look of concern crossed Alma's face. "What's wrong, honey?"

"Nothing. Doesn't matter."

Ashley joined me and hung a ticket on the wheel. "She's been Hanked," she explained with a grin.

"Pay no attention to his moods, honey," Alma said. "He's harmless."

"All I did was make an innocent remark about him having plenty of things to drink in his own store, and he bit my head off."

Alma grimaced. "Oops. That's a sore subject with Hank. I'll fill you in later." She slid the meat loaf platter through the window. "Here's Gil's dinner. Tell Hank his will be right up."

As I walked back toward the two curmudgeons, I thought of a title for this month's column. Trout Fork: Colorado's Crabbiest Town.

⁓⁓

Later that evening, Alma and I sat in the living room

of her two-bedroom cabin. The interior was rustic with pine log walls, a stone fireplace, a low open-beamed ceiling, and faux suede sofa and chair with puffy plaid pillows. The room was small, but warm, comfortable, and inviting.

Ashley had gone to bed, so Sasha sat on Alma's lap purring. Jack came sauntering out of the bedroom to investigate his new home. He made a leisurely tour of the room, sniffing at the furnishings. Then he strolled to the sofa, hopped into my lap, and gazed at Sasha, who ignored him with classic feline nonchalance.

I sipped the cinnamon tea Alma had made for us. "You were going to tell me about Hank. Why is he so touchy?"

Alma stroked Sasha thoughtfully. "I've known Hank since I was a little girl. He's only touchy about one subject, his drinking. Years ago, he was married to a girl with what my mother used to call a 'roving eye.' I don't think she was ever unfaithful to Hank, but he was jealous anyway. Used to watch her like a hawk. It got so she couldn't do anything right, especially when it came to keeping house. He's a bit of a clean freak. One day she just up and took off. Caught a ride to the bus station with one of the bikers. Not long after, divorce papers came in the mail. That's when he started drinking. He thinks nobody knows he's an alcoholic, but of course everyone does. He's all bound up inside, you know?" She sighed. "I feel sorry for him."

"You'd think owning a liquor store is a bad lifestyle choice."

"It's all he knows. Sometimes I think he stays here hoping she'll come back one day. Of course she won't, but he stays anyway, drinking up all his profits and trying to keep his secret."

"He never remarried?"

"Never. He doesn't have a very high opinion of women since that time. Especially the girls that hang out with the motorcycle crowd."

"Do you think he's dangerous?"

She thought a moment. "I don't think so. But he does have a nasty temper. I guess you saw that today. He can change moods in an instant. That's what we call being Hanked. One time Zach made a remark about booze being the devil's temptation or some such thing. I thought Hank would rip his head off. Gil had to separate them before Zach got hurt."

It made me giggle to imagine the paunchy little bald man putting up his fists. "The Rev? In a fight?"

Alma snickered. "Yeah. Maybe he should have hit him with his Bible."

"Gil and Hank don't seem to have much use for reporters. What's that all about?"

She shrugged. "Gil is a dyed-in-the-wool conservative. He sees reporters as part of the 'left wing media,' as he puts it. Hank is a very private person, and I don't think he trusts outsiders. But they're both okay. Give them time. They'll grow on you."

"Whatever happened to Gil's wife? Did she go off on a motorcycle, too?"

"No. She and Gil had nothing in common. He's a bit of a hermit, and she was a party girl. They only got married because she was pregnant. After Gil, Junior was born, she kind of freaked out. Postpartum depression, they called it. She left the baby with Gil and took off. They've been divorced for years. As far as I know, he doesn't keep in touch with her."

We chatted a while longer, then I stood up and yawned. "What time do you need me at the café in the morning?"

"About six-thirty. We open at seven."

"I'll probably go for a run before that."

"Ok. See you in the morning."

☙❧☙❧

Jack and I jogged along the trail behind the cabins just before sunrise the next morning. The sky was lightening, but the mountains blocked the sun's rays, and the path was shrouded in near darkness. Jack trotted along next to me in his harness, his paws making no sound on the soft bed of pine needles that covered the trail surface. We stopped for a breather near the rock I had sat on the previous day, and I noticed Gil about fifty yards away, standing hip deep in the creek in his waders, casting his line upstream and watching it float by. He looked up briefly at me, then he turned away again.

I waited for Jack, who was digging in the dirt next to the trail, no doubt looking for a convenient place for a potty stop. After a few minutes, he was still digging, so I pulled on his leash. "C'mon, Jack. Let's go."

But he resisted and continued digging, growling and becoming more and more agitated. I pulled on the leash again, harder this time, but he wouldn't budge.

I bent over and picked him up. "Okay, if you insist."

I peered down at the hole he had made. Something didn't seem quite right. I squatted to get a closer look, the cat squirming in my arms. I gasped and jumped back, lost my balance, and sat down hard. The taste of adrenaline flooded my mouth as I stared at three fingers protruding from the hole, the bright purple nail polish absurdly out of place among the rust-colored pine needles.

CHAPTER 3

The yellow police tape and white-coated officials from the Denver coroner's office seemed blasphemously incongruous on that perfect Colorado morning with its crystal sky, slight breeze stirring the pines, and gentle gurgling sounds from the creek. If it hadn't been for the grizzled, sixty-something detective in his rumpled suit standing before me, I could have believed the scene was something I'd dreamed up for a novel.

"Now, Miss…" He thumbed through his grimy notepad.

"Lowell. Kathryn Lowell," I reminded him for the second time. *God help us if it's up to this man to find a killer*, I thought. He appeared disorganized and, worse, disinterested.

He sneezed and wiped his nose with a wadded-up, yellowed handkerchief. "Damn these allergies. Excuse me, Miss…Miss…"

"Lowell," I repeated. I looked down at Jack, who sat patiently at my feet watching the proceedings. It had been hours since I'd pulled him away from the body and dialed 9-1-1 on my cell phone, hoping this was one of those places where service was available.

The Pineland Park Police were the first to arrive, followed by the homicide detectives from the Denver PD. The sirens from the police cruisers and ambulance had attracted the attention of everyone in Trout Fork, and the residents were lined up along the yellow tape, huddling in twos and threes, pointing and whispering.

As gruesome as the scene was, I maintained the journalist's detachment, using all my senses to record the details for future use in some publication or other.

"All right, Miss Lowell, I'm Detective Jenkins, Denver PD. I need to ask you some questions. It shouldn't take long. How did you find the body?"

"My cat found it. He was digging right there, and he uncovered a hand."

"Did you touch anything?"

"No. I just pulled him away and called nine-one-one."

"How do you know the deceased?"

"I don't. Never met her."

He thumbed through his notes again. "The officer said you gave him her name. Heather Blaine. How do you know her name?"

I thought back to my conversation with Ashley about the waitress the previous evening. "Heather Blaine. I refer to her as 'Feather Brain.'" Ashley giggled at her own cleverness.

"I took her place at the café. She used to work there. That's how I knew her name."

"But how did you know it was her?" He eyed me suspiciously. He was right. How did I know?

"I...I don't know for sure. But she went missing two days ago, and I found her T-shirt in the creek yesterday. It was identified as hers by her former roommate, who I'm rooming with now."

He looked around. "Where did you find it?"

"Over there by that rock."

"Show me." I picked Jack up and put him over my shoulder. As we walked carefully around the taped-off area, I glanced at the shallow grave. The girl's body was wrapped in a blood-stained white sheet. As we passed by, the smell coming from the grave reminded me of a swimming pool.

I took Detective Jenkins to the rock where I was sitting when I saw the T-shirt and pointed to the deep pool near the bank. "I saw something colorful in there. I got a stick and pulled it out."

"Reynolds," he called to one of the uniformed officers who stood nearby. "Drag this area and see what you come up with."

The officer nodded.

The detective's rheumy eyes scanned the creek, upstream and down. "Did you see anyone around, Miss Lowell?"

"No. Not when I found the T-shirt." I hesitated for a moment. "I did see a fisherman this morning. But people fish here all the time."

"Can you identify him?"

"His name is Gil. I don't know his last name, but he owns the bait shop in Trout Fork."

He made another note. "Anyone else around?"

"No. Oh, wait. Yesterday, before I found the shirt, another man came by. His name is Zach something. Alma can tell you his last name. He had been fishing, and he stopped to chat for a minute."

He made a note. "Zach something. What can you tell me about him?"

I hesitated, starting to feel uncomfortable talking about people who were essentially strangers to me, especially under these circumstances. "Nothing really. He lives in Trout Fork, and people call him 'Rev.' I guess because he's religious. You really need to talk to Alma from the café about all these people. I've only been here a couple of days."

He put his notepad in his jacket pocket, took out his handkerchief again, and wiped his dripping nose. "What brought you to Trout Fork?"

I explained about my job and my intention to leave as soon as I had enough for the column.

"I'm afraid that won't be possible, Miss Lowell. I'm going to have to ask you to stick around for a while."

"How long a while?"

"Hard to say. At least until the autopsy comes back and we can interview everyone in the area. We'll let you know. My sergeant is doing interviews in that café now."

Another uniformed officer, wearing rubber gloves, approached and handed the detective a dirt-covered wallet. "Found this with the body, sir. There's a cell phone and some other things, but I thought you'd want to see this."

Jenkins held the wallet gingerly by the corners and flipped it open. "Heather Lynn Blaine. Yep. I guess it's her."

⌘⌘⌘

I brought Jack back to the cabin and fed him. By the time I had changed out of my running clothes and showered, he was lying on Ashley's bed with Sasha. The pretty little cat was licking his face. He closed his eyes and purred as she groomed him, like a sultan enjoying the ministrations of his favorite concubine. Jack was willing to accept affection from pretty much anyone, probably a reaction to his upbringing in a back alley near Times Square where I'd found him, a filthy and emaciated kitten living rough.

I left them there and slipped in the back door of the café's kitchen. Ashley was there listening at the door to the dining room. She put her finger to her lips as I joined her.

Alma was arguing with Detective Jenkins. "Like I told your sergeant, I don't care if you use the place to question people, but I have to open the café for breakfast. Did you see that line outside? This is the only eatery around here. Where are these people supposed to go?"

"All right, ma'am," Jenkins responded. "How about if you open the patio."

"Fine, just don't go scaring my customers. There's a rumor that you found a body by the creek. Is that true? Do you know who it is?"

He didn't answer her questions. "We'll get out of your hair as soon as we can."

Alma joined us in the kitchen. "Ryn. You're back. What's going on? Do you know?"

"There's a body buried next to the creek about a half mile upstream. I'm afraid it's Heather."

Alma gasped, and her hand flew to her mouth. Her face blanched as she staggered backward against the counter.

Ashley and I both reached for her.

"Mom! Are you okay?" Ashley held onto her arm as I guided her into a nearby chair.

She burst into tears, rocking and weeping as though her heart would break. I was stunned at what seemed to be an extreme reaction. I had no idea she had become so attached to the girl in only a few weeks. All I could do was pat her shoulder. Ashley was being sympathetic, but there was something else in the girl's eyes that I couldn't quite identify. Was it relief?

It took several minutes for Alma to regain her composure. She wiped her eyes on her apron. Squinting

against the sunlight streaming through the kitchen skylight, she looked up at me, her red eyes pleading. "Why?
How? Who would do such a thing?"

"I don't know. The police are investigating, and
they'll be doing an autopsy. Maybe they'll tell us more
then."

She stared at the floor. Ashley stood close by, her
arms folded tightly across her chest.

After a few moments, Alma got up, headed for the
stove, and began pulling out pots and frying pans from
the drawer beneath it. "Ashley, open the umbrellas on the
patio. Ryn can help you."

"Are you sure you want to open, Alma? You've had
quite a shock." I tried to sound as sympathetic as I could,
but I was still baffled by her reaction.

She came back to us. "I'm sure. We have to feed
these people."

Ashley shrugged and started for the door. I gave Alma one final squeeze on the shoulder and followed.

The patio was deluged with people, both locals and
tourists, all buzzing with the news of a body found in the
woods. Ashley and I took orders as fast as we could and
asked them to give the police some privacy until they
were finished.

At one point, Alma was passing plates out through
the window to me, and she glanced out to the dining
room. "Oh, Garrett is here. I'm glad."

"Garrett? Who's that?"

"Garrett Easterbrook. A local cop. He used to be
with the Denver homicide bureau. Now he works with the
Pineland Park department. Great guy. You'll like him."

Detective Jenkins was standing near the fireplace
with a serious-looking man with thick black hair and a
cut-off shirt that showed his well-developed arms. He
appeared to be in his late thirties. Almost as though he

knew we were talking about him, his piercing blue eyes caught mine. He nodded slightly and went back to talking to Jenkins.

Each time I passed between the dining room and patio, I strained to hear the conversations from the interview table.

Zach was being questioned, and he sat up attentively as though eager to help. "It's a shame," I heard him say as I passed the table. "That poor girl." He sat back with a sigh. "But I guess when you're in that kind of lifestyle, bad things happen."

"What kind of lifestyle is that, sir?"

Zach leaned forward again and narrowed his eyes. "Sinful. A sinful lifestyle. Have you ever seen the way those women dress? It's ungodly, that's what it is. Is it any surprise they come to a bad end? Men have no respect for that kind of woman."

"I see," the cop said. "How well did you know her?"

Zach's eyes widened. "Not—not well at all," he stammered. "I hardly ever spoke to her."

I delivered plates to a group of women at one of the patio tables. I refilled coffee cups and cleared one of the tables of dirty dishes. On my way back through the dining room, I saw that Zach had left, and the cop was now talking to Gil, the bait shop owner, and consulting his notes. "Mr. Acevedo, were you acquainted with this girl, Heather Blaine?"

"I saw her around. Mostly here when I came in to eat."

"What can you tell me about her?"

"Typical biker chick."

"Typical? In what way?"

"You know the type. Pierced lips and nose, purple hair. Pranced around with little on. Like all the biker scum. No morals. Hate their country."

He leaned back and folded his arms, his US Army tattoo plainly visible.

"Piercings? Are you sure?"

"Of course I'm sure. She had them everywhere."

The cop made a note and thumbed through his papers. "It says here that you've made numerous complaints to the Pineland Park Police about the motorcyclists who stop here. Is that true?"

"Yeah."

The cop read from his papers. "Disturbing the peace, public intoxication, littering." He looked up at Gil, his brow furrowing. "Littering?"

"They camp out across the road for a couple of days sometimes. Throw their garbage everywhere. No respect."

The cop continued reading. "You are the registered owner of a 2004 Harley-Davidson. Is that correct?"

"That's my son's bike. Gilbert, Junior."

"Where is he?"

"Damned if I know. He left a couple of years ago. I haven't seen him since."

The young officer's gaze bored in on Gil. "Where were you this morning, Mr. Acevedo?"

"Fishing."

"What time was that?"

"I got there about five. Left about an hour later. I open the store at seven."

"Did you see anyone while you were fishing?"

"Right before I left, I saw that new waitress with her cat. That's all. Are we about done here? I need to get back to my store."

"Yes, we're done. But don't go anywhere, please."

"I'm always here. Anything I can do to help."

The detective ushered Hank in next and led him to the interview table. As I passed them on my way to the patio with two breakfast plates, I could see that Hank's eyes were red and he was a bit unsteady as he sat down.

"Now then, Mr. Edwards," the young cop was saying, "did you know the waitress named Heather Blaine?"

Hank stared at the cop owlishly. "Who?"

I didn't hear the answer. I delivered the order to a couple of bicyclists who had stopped in Trout Fork. Then I went back to the counter, where I busied myself, staying close enough to hear the interrogation with Hank. I glanced toward the table and noticed that Hank seemed to be having trouble concentrating, and the cop was becoming agitated with him.

"Have you been drinking today, Mr. Edwards?"

Hank glared at the cop, his face reddening. "No."

"You seem to be slurring your words. Are you feeling all right?"

"Just fine."

The cop looked somewhat skeptical, but he cleared his throat and continued. "When was the last time you saw the girl?"

"I dunno. Maybe a couple of days ago. Sunday, I think."

"And where was that?"

"She was coming out of Gil's."

"The bait store?"

"Yeah."

"Was she into fishing?"

Hank scoffed. "Not for fish."

"For what then?"

"Pretty much anything she could get. Like most women."

"Do you know anyone who would have a reason to kill her?"

"Nope. What does it matter, really? I mean, those biker gangs are always killing each other, aren't they?

Why not do the rest of us a favor and let them get on with it?"

Even coming from Hank, that seemed pretty harsh.

A look of disgust appeared on the cop's face. "All right. You can go, Mr. Edwards. If you think of anything else after you…when you're feeling better, give us a call. The number is on this card."

Hank put the card in his pocket and wove unsteadily toward the door.

Detective Jenkins ushered in Madam Gauzie, who settled herself in the chair, arranging her flowing garments demurely around her legs.

Before the cop could ask a question, she began. "I knew it. I told Alma that girl would come to a bad end. Now here she is buried in a hole like so much garbage. Alma, I told her, that kind is nothing but trouble. Don't get attached to her. You've got your own daughter to see to. But did she—"

"Yes, thank you, Mrs. Gauzie. Now—"

"It's Madam, not Missus," she said, lifting her chin.

The young cop sighed. "Right. Sorry. Now, when was the last time you saw the deceased?"

"Couple of days ago. Sunday it was. She was with one of those motorcycle groups in the parking lot that afternoon."

"And that was the last time you saw her? Sunday afternoon?"

"Then I saw her again when I was putting the trash out in back of my store. She was heading toward the trail."

"What time was that?"

"Oh, in the evening. After the café closed."

"Was she alone?"

"I suppose. I didn't see anyone else."

Alma called to me to pick up my orders, so I missed

the rest of the interview. When I came back in from the patio, I collided with Detective Garrett Easterbrook on his way out of the café. The tray I was carrying tipped, and several plates slid off it and crashed to the floor.

"I'm so sorry," he said. "Here. Let me help you."

We both bent down and our foreheads bumped.

"Sorry again." His smile showed his perfect white teeth. "Today must be my day to be clumsy."

The noise of the dishes clattering to the floor had drawn everyone's attention, and my face grew warm, but whether it was from their stares or the effect of his smile, I wasn't quite sure.

"That's okay. No harm done."

We stood up, and he said, "I'm Garrett Easterbrook." He offered his hand but smiled when he saw me trying to juggle the tray full of dishes. "We can shake hands some other time."

"I'm Kathryn Lowell. Ryn."

"Nice to meet you. Will you be working here for the summer?"

"No. Only until Alma finds someone and I finish my column. I write a column for a travel magazine. So really, I'm just passing through."

"Well, it was nice running into you. We'll have to do it again sometime." He made his way across the patio and disappeared around the corner.

Ashley passed me on her way to a table with a tray of food. She grinned at me. "Cute, isn't he?"

"Very nice looking."

"I bet he'd be a lot more fun to cuddle up with than a cat."

"Maybe. But cats are a lot less trouble."

CHAPTER 4

The rest of the breakfast rush kept me too busy to hear much of the other interviews. Several local fishermen and a few tourists were questioned briefly. I had no idea whether they offered any pertinent information.

As I worked, I kept wondering about Heather. Who was she really? Where did she come from? Did anyone notify her parents? What must that be like, being told your daughter has been found murdered and buried in some lonely spot in the Rocky Mountains?

I decided it had been too long since I'd last called home. No matter what differences I had with my mother, she was still my mother, and I had a sudden longing to hear her voice.

I stood at the window waiting on my orders, when I heard raised voices coming from the kitchen.

"I don't know why, Ashley," Alma's said, her tearful voice cracking. "It just does."

"I mean, it's not like she was part of the family. She was only here a couple of weeks."

"You wouldn't understand."

"No. I'm too stupid to understand anything," Ashley said, her voice becoming shrill. She started to leave the kitchen.

Alma stopped her by taking her arm. "That's not what I meant."

Ashley pulled her arm away and looked at her mother with a mixture of anger and hurt. "What I don't get is why you took her in at all. We could have found another waitress. Look how easy it was to get Ryn."

Alma sighed. "Like I said, you wouldn't understand." She came to the window and set three plates on a tray. She snatched the ticket from the wheel and tossed it on the tray with the plates. "Order up," she said, not really noticing my presence. Her eyes were red and swollen, and her mascara was smudged. She turned back to Ashley. "Please go bus the patio tables. I'm running out of dishes in here."

Ashley rolled her eyes and flounced past me, nearly colliding with Detective Jenkins as he was on his way into the kitchen. I delivered my orders and came back to the window. Jenkins was munching on a dinner roll and following Alma around the kitchen as she worked. "My men are going to have something to eat. Then we'll be on our way."

Alma turned to him, drying her hands on a dish towel. "Are you finished already? That didn't take long."

"There's not much more we can do here. Once the autopsy is done, we'll know more."

"I trust you will find whoever did this."

"Umm." He brushed the crumbs off his wrinkled shirt. "Good roll. Thanks."

Alma eyed him. "You *do* think you'll catch the guy, don't you?"

The detective cleared his throat. "We do our best, but in these cases, where the victim has a dubious lifestyle, it's not easy."

"Dubious lifestyle? She lived with me and worked for me. It wasn't like she was homeless."

"Of course. And you are to be commended for taking her in. But I have to tell you we see plenty of cases like this."

"Like what?"

"Drifters, mostly girls, who get hooked up with the biker gangs. It's a dangerous life among dangerous people. Drugs, violence, extortion. She may have run afoul of one of them. They kill for the fun of it, some of them. Not all bikers, of course. Most are law-abiding. But the ones on the fringe are real rotten apples. If she was involved with them, well…" He shrugged. "I'll be going now. Thanks for your help."

I saw the sorrow and anger in Alma's eyes as she watched him leave. The detective nodded as he passed me and left the café.

Ashley came in from the patio to join me at the window. She clipped two order tickets onto the wheel. "Mom, that Malone guy is here again. He said to tell you he wants to talk to you."

Alma snatched the tickets from the wheel. "Not again. That man won't give up. Tell him I'm busy."

"I did. He said he'll wait."

"Fine. Let him wait." She hurried to the refrigerator at the back of the kitchen.

"Who's Malone?" I asked.

Ashley rolled her eyes. "Some guy who keeps asking Mom to sell the place to him. He comes in all the time. Never gives up. I'm like, dude, seriously? What part of 'no' don't you get? She doesn't want to sell."

"He wants to buy the café?"

"The café, the stores, the cabins. All of it. A couple hundred acres, I think."

"Your mom owns all of it?"

"Yeah, my grandpa left it to her when he died."

"Huh." *Another tidbit for the column.* I went back

out to the patio and started cleaning the tables. The breakfast rush had pretty well subsided, so most of the tables
were empty.

A pasty-faced man in a bright green shirt sat near the
door, as though trying to avoid the sun. His thinning
blond hair was in a comb-over, and he reeked of cheap
aftershave. He looked up and flashed a wide smile at me,
but it was one of those smiles that don't include the eyes,
reminding me of a shark I had seen once on a *National
Geographic* special.

I approached his table.

"Well, hello. You're new here." Before I could answer, he stood up and put his hand out to me. "Dave
Malone."

I shook his hand, wincing as I heard the bones and
tendons in my hand crackle. He didn't seem to notice.
"Uh, hi. I'm Ryn."

"Rin? Like in *Rin Tin Tin*?" He guffawed at his own
joke, his mouth open and his well-polished teeth flashing.

"No. Ryn, as in Kathryn."

He was still pumping my arm. "Well, nice to meet
you, Ryn as in Kathryn. How long have you been here?"

"This is my second day." I gently extricated my hand
from his grip.

Ashley came through the door. Malone called across
the patio to her in a booming voice. "Did you tell your
mother I'm here?"

"Yeah. She said she's too busy."

"Too busy." He looked back at me. "Can you ever be
too busy to make money?"

That seemed a rhetorical question that didn't merit
an answer, so I shrugged and kept cleaning the table.

"Tell her I'm out here waiting, will you?" he boomed
to no one in particular.

"She knows," Ashley said.

"Order me a hamburger, Ryn as in Kathryn. With a Coke. Plenty of ice."

❧❧❧

That evening, I lay on my bed with Jack by my side. The café had closed at eight, after the busiest day Alma had ever seen. Apparently a murder was good for business. I had left her counting the proceeds for the next day's bank deposit and taken my weary body back to the cabin. I had forgotten how hard waitress work could be. My feet were swollen, and my hips felt like they had been stomped on by a rhino.

As I scratched Jack's ears, he rolled over, his eyes begging for a belly rub. I obliged him and thought about my column, which I hadn't even started yet. Guilt began to emanate in waves from my laptop on the desk, its dark screen reminding me I hadn't written a word since leaving Denver. Crenshaw was bound to be hounding me soon, spouting the usual clichés he was so fond of. "Deadlines, Kathryn. Deadlines." Or his favorite, "Time, tide, and the printers wait for no man."

Ashley came out of the bathroom wrapped in a towel. I had a lot of admiration for this fifteen-year-old kid who had done the work of two people today.

"You did great today, Ashley, even after getting such awful news about your friend. You should be proud of yourself. You're amazing."

She pulled on her pajamas and stood before the mirror brushing her long, auburn hair. "Too bad Mom can't see it. To her, I'm nothing but a screw-up."

"I'm sure that's not the case. She knows how hard you've been working."

"Not like her precious Heather, though. No one can compare to little Miss Perfect." She tossed the brush on the dresser and sat on her bed. She slid a book with a pen clipped to it from under her pillow. She opened the book and, gazing thoughtfully out the window for a moment, began to write, her long hair hanging over one shoulder.

"You have such pretty hair. Maybe I'll grow mine out one of these days," I said, knowing I'd never do it. Not conducive to my lifestyle. "What are you writing? Do you keep a journal?"

Her cheeks took on a slight pink tinge. "Yeah. It's nothing, really. Heather kept one too. But she never wanted to talk about what she was writing. Said she was just taking notes." She put air quotes around "taking notes." She regarded me for a moment. "I'd love to do what you do. Travel around, write about different places. Not stuck in a hole like this."

"I'd hardly call this a hole. You should see some of the rattrap motels Jack and I have stayed in over the past year."

"But you're free. You can come and go whenever."

"I'm not all that free. I have deadlines and responsibilities to my editor. And I'm not free to write anything I want. There are libel laws, journalistic standards, advertisers to please."

Sasha strolled in and hopped on Ashley's bed. She curled up next to Ashley, who stroked her as she leaned back on her pillow. "You know, sometimes I watch those motorcycle clubs come and go and wish I could join them. I know why Heather was part of one. She used to talk about her time on the road with her boyfriend."

"That detective called it a dangerous lifestyle. Violence, drugs, that kind of thing."

She sat up quickly. "I just remembered something. Heather mentioned something about meth once. She said she was going to make a bundle on it."

"You mean like selling it?"

"No. She was totally against that. Never used it either. But when I asked her what she meant, she just smiled."

"Did you tell your mom?"

Ashley rolled her eyes. "Like she would believe me. Anything Miss Perfect Heather did was always cool with her."

"You underestimate your mom. She adores you."

"Whatever." She went back to her journal.

I was staring into the black abyss of mother/teen daughter relationships, a place where reason and logic go to die. I thought about my own mother and the battles that had raged in our upper Westside apartment all those years. I could still see Mother's face of thunder when she found me on the balcony setting all her parakeets and budgies free. Her expression as she silently closed the doors of the empty cages and took them back inside was one of pure disgust. Or was it merely disappointment I mistook for disgust? Either way, she didn't understand my explanation. My eight-year-old conscience simply couldn't reconcile wings with cages. I think she lit a candle for my sanity in church that night.

The incident with the parakeets, along with my sitting for hours in the park feeding the pigeons, led my older brother, Jarrod, to dub me the Bird Girl, which I thought was somewhat flattering. I'd rather watch birds than the fluctuating price of gold on the Nikkei exchange, but then I wasn't the one trying to follow our father into the world of Wall Street.

By the time I graduated from college with a degree in journalism, I think Mother had hopes I might not bring total disgrace upon the family. Even the episode at the cotillion was forgiven, if not entirely forgotten. My father thought it was mildly amusing, but Mother's sense of humor was in a different league. One did not dance barefoot in the ballroom of the Waldorf-Astoria, no matter how tight one's shoes were. It simply wasn't done.

Of course, I had no doubt Meghann more than made up for Mother's disappointment with me. Her youngest daughter's straight-A record at Vassar was a constant source of delight for Mother and made up for her middle daughter's unfathomable wandering ways. "Really, Kathryn," she was fond of saying, "what's wrong with a secure job in a newsroom? Perhaps at the *Times*? I'm sure your father could use his influence with the editors." She was somewhat mollified when I landed the job at the travel magazine, but she should have known I wouldn't be able to tolerate a desk job for long. Even having a magazine column all my own, with my byline, couldn't make the constant traveling acceptable to her.

Alma knocked on the door and poked her head in. "Anyone for a cup of tea?"

"I'd love one." I slid Jack off my lap. "How about you, Ash?"

"No. I'm good."

Alma's face fell slightly. "It's all ready," she said to me.

I left the room, followed by Jack, who was always up for a bit of socializing. The tea tray was waiting on the coffee table, and I sat down with Alma.

She handed me a cup and nodded toward the bedroom. "She's still mad at me."

"Ashley? I don't think she's mad, exactly. To tell the truth, I think she's a bit jealous."

"Jealous? Of what?"

"Of your affection for Heather. She saw how upset you were today, and I think it scared her."

"What does she have to be scared of?"

"She's afraid you loved Heather more than you love her. All kids are naturally afraid of losing their parents' love. Especially teenagers. She sees Heather as a rival. Her living and working here made her part of the family. A perfect scenario for sibling rivalry. Now that she's gone, Ashley has no way to compete for your affection. She sees herself as having lost the battle."

Alma leaned back and looked up. "She asked me today why what happened to Heather hurt so much. I couldn't explain it. I still can't. She doesn't understand why I took her in in the first place."

Lectures from my Psych 101 class echoed in my brain. "You're the mothering type, Alma. Madam Gauzie said you took Heather in the same way you took in the stray cat. You see someone or something in need, and you just have to help. It's in your DNA."

"So I have a mothering gene?"

"It's a wonderful thing to have. Not all women have it." *Was I referring to Mother or to myself? Maybe both of us.* "The problem is that teenagers, especially girls, are conflicted. They want independence, but they still need their mothers. And they hate themselves for that neediness. When you mother her, she sees it as smothering. Then Heather comes along and your mothering her threatens Ashley, and she lashes out."

"Does she know how hurtful it is?"

"I'm sure she doesn't. Teens are completely self-absorbed. They have a hard time empathizing with adults on any level. Don't worry. She'll grow out of it."

Alma sipped her tea and stroked Jack, who had curled up between us. "Poor Heather. Who would do such a thing?" Her eyes widened. "Do you think whoever did it is still here? My God, it could be anyone. Half the time, we don't even lock our doors."

"I wouldn't worry. The Denver Police are on it."

She scoffed. "Detective Jenkins as good as said they might never find out who did it. And he didn't seem all that concerned, either. I think they're blowing it off. Just another biker chick. Heather deserves better than that." She regarded me pensively. "Ryn, I know you're a travel writer, but have you ever done any investigative reporting?"

"Not professionally, but in college, I was on a team that investigated corruption in a small town in upstate New York. We uncovered a whole lot of government graft, misuse of tax money, and corruption."

"How did you do it?"

"Asked a lot of questions and did a lot of digging. You'd be surprised how much you can learn by watching people's reactions to questions. I think journalists develop a sixth sense about people from questioning them."

Alma turned to me, her eyes bright and eager. "Why can't you do the same thing here? I mean, ask questions and watch reactions. You might be able to find Heather's killer that way."

I tried to refuse her request gently. "Alma, I'm not a detective."

"But you have the same skills a detective needs." She appeared to grow more excited. "And you don't have the same restraints they have. And you don't have a prejudice against her, like that Jenkins does. What do you say? Will you try? Please?"

I hesitated, not wanting to let her down but knowing the police wouldn't need, or want, my help. "I don't know, Alma. I won't be here that long. As soon as my column is finished, I'll have to go somewhere else."

"But as long as you're here, you can look into it, can't you?" Tears began to form in her eyes, and her voice rose. "She has no one else, no one in her corner. She wasn't my daughter, but she may as well have been. Isn't it bad enough she died a horrible death and was buried like so much trash? We can't just forget her. We can't!" She burst into tears, and I held her while she sobbed.

"All right," I soothed. "I'll look into it as much as I can while I'm here." I held her at arm's length. "Okay?"

She sniffed and whispered, "Thank you."

We sat for a few more minutes, while I wondered what I was getting myself into. Then Alma stood up and started to clear the tea tray.

"I'll do that, Alma. You go to bed."

She yawned. "Thank you, dear. See you in the morning." She trudged wearily off to bed.

I sat alone with Jack, sipping my cold tea and growing more irritated with the cops. Yes, Heather did deserve better than that. So did the people of Trout Fork, oddballs though they might be. I thought about the intensity of Alma's feelings for Heather and felt a longing for that kind of mother love I had never known. If nothing else, I rationalized to myself, there might be something in this story I could use in my novel.

I took the tray to the kitchen and washed the cups. Then I picked Jack up and headed for the bedroom. Ashley was asleep, her arm around Sasha. A sudden rush of affection washed over me for her, for all of the people of Trout Fork, and a desire to help them, especially to help ease Alma's sorrow. But I was there to write a column, I reminded myself. Once I had enough to complete the column, I would have to move on. That was the life I had chosen. But in the meantime, I would do what I could to find Heather's killer.

As I was getting ready for bed, I heard the sound of a twig snapping outside the window. I turned off the light and pulled the curtain aside. The trees were bathed in silvery moonlight, their branches rustling gently in the slight breeze. I caught a glimpse of something moving away from the cabin into the shadows, but I couldn't see what it was. Wildlife is abundant in Colorado, especially in the mountains. It could have been a deer, black bear, moose, or even a mountain lion. I only hoped that whatever predator was out there was the four-legged variety.

I let the curtain fall back in place and turned around. It was then I realized Jack wasn't on my bed. I looked in the bathroom, the closet, then under the bed, where I found him huddled in the corner, his eyes wide and his tail bushed out to twice its normal size.

CHAPTER 5

Before the alarm went off at six the next morning, Ashley was already up and writing in her journal. She raised her eyebrows at me as I sat up and groaned. "You're sounding like an old lady," she teased.

My good intentions for an early morning jog had fallen victim to sore feet and fatigue. "I guess I'm not in shape for this kind of work." I stretched my stiff back. "Too many months sitting at a desk.

"Yeah, that'll kill you," she said in mock seriousness. She slid her journal under her pillow and headed for the bathroom. "Mom went over early. I think she's making waffles."

Waffles, which I rarely eat, seemed like the most marvelous of all possible breakfasts. I was unusually ravenous. Maybe it was the mountain air. I pulled the curtain aside and studied the landscape. The early morning sunlight was dappled on the leaves and pine needles under the trees. The sky was the kind of sapphire blue you only see at altitudes where the air is thin. A few white puffy clouds drifted by. A Rocky Mountain magpie landed on the windowsill, its iridescent blue-black wings glistening in the sun. Jack crept to my side to watch the bird with me, his whiskers quivering, and the tip of his tail switching back and forth. The bird saw him and began aggressively scolding him through the screen while Jack answered in that chattering voice cats use when they see prey.

I stroked his back. "You know the rules, Jack. No chasing the birds. Besides, those magpies are bigger than you are."

The bird strutted along the windowsill, peered in at us haughtily for a moment, then took off and soared to the top of a pine tree.

Ashley came out of the bathroom. "Let's go. I can smell those waffles from here."

By the time we'd fed both cats, emptied the litter box, and gotten dressed, it was past six-thirty, the time we were supposed to be at the café preparing to open at seven. We hurried out of the cabin and in the back door of the café, where we found Alma putting waffles on two plates for us. Her eyes were swollen from crying, but she seemed to be more upbeat this morning. Ashley and I sat at the kitchen counter.

"Wow. Thanks, Mom. They look great."

"Yeah, thanks, Mom," I teased. The first bite was pure heaven. "Delicious."

"Never mind buttering me up, you two," Alma scolded. But her eyes mirrored her pleasure. "Hurry up and eat. And get the patio set up. The starving hordes will be here soon."

We wolfed down our breakfasts and spent the next fifteen minutes making pots of coffee, setting tables, opening umbrellas, and sweeping the patio. It couldn't compare to the joy of writing, but I was surprised how much I relished the physical activity. I actually looked forward to interacting with the characters in Trout Fork— so different from the people I had grown up around in New York.

Alma unlocked the door, and the crowd gathered outside began to file in. Hank and Gil were the first in line at the ordering counter, followed by Madam Gauzie, Detective Garrett Easterbrook, and at least a dozen fishermen, including a scruffy-looking old man the locals referred to as "Sarge." He sat by himself in a corner of the patio.

Ashley frowned when she saw him. "I hate waiting on that old geezer. He smells bad."

I eyed the man. "Fishing has that effect on people."

"He doesn't smell like fish. He smells like...I don't know what. Something funny."

Ashley took the orders, and I brought the cups of steaming coffee to the tables.

Madam Gauzie placed her order then fluttered over to Garrett's table and began questioning him. "Do you know any more about that poor girl they found yesterday?" she asked with wide eyes. Without waiting for an answer, she sat down to pour forth her theories about the murder. "I told that detective I had a feeling she would cause trouble around here. Know what I think? That gang of hoodlums she rode with came back to get her, and she refused to go with them. So they killed her and dumped the body."

Garrett nodded patiently. "Anything is possible."

She peered out the window, her brow furrowed. "Have you seen how many people are coming around since they found that body? Ghouls, that's what they are. Ghouls."

"Well, people are curious about crimes like this. It's human nature."

"Human nature, humph. We need a little less nature and a little more humanity, if you ask me. How can people do things like that to one another?"

Garrett sipped his coffee and set the cup down. "I've

often asked myself the same question."

"This generation, no morals, no standards. It's shameful. Just shameful." She got up and went to find a table on the patio, shaking her head and mumbling to herself.

Hank and Gil occupied their usual table by the window, where Gil was drawing what looked like a poster on a yellow pad. I saw the word "barbeque" on the pad. He showed the drawing to Hank. "What do you think of this?"

Hank seemed absorbed with wiping the table in front of him with a paper napkin. He hardly looked at the drawing. "Looks good to me. Pretty much the same as last year."

Gil looked up at me as I set the coffee down in front of him. "Ryn, are you going to be around for the bash on the Fourth?"

"What bash?"

"Gil throws a Fourth of July barbeque every year," Hank said. "The stores close down, and we all celebrate. Biggest party around. Gil cooks the best steaks you've ever tasted."

"That's awfully nice of you, Gil," I said, "to do that for your neighbors."

Gil shrugged slightly. "People need to celebrate living in the greatest country in the world. Men have fought and died for the freedoms we take for granted. Patriotism has become a dirty word since the liberals have been in charge. But not in Trout Fork." He rapped his finger on the poster with emphasis. "Not if I can help it."

"Are you still going to be here on the Fourth?" Hank asked.

"What is that, about a week from now? I'm not sure. As soon as my column is done and Alma finds another waitress, I should be on my way." I approached Sarge's table with the coffee pot to ask if he needed a refill.

He regarded me warily, his watery blue eyes having difficulty focusing on me. "You're new here," he said gruffly.

"Yes. I'm Ryn. I'm helping Alma out for a while."

He narrowed his eyes at me. His thin gray hair and mottled, sunburned skin gave him the appearance of someone who had spent his life outdoors. "Better be careful."

"I guess you heard about the murdered girl who worked here."

He grunted something unintelligible.

I poured his coffee. "Do you live in Trout Fork?"

He looked up at me suddenly as though he had forgotten I was there. Then he stared out the window and shook his head. "Can't be too careful around here. There's stuff going on..."

"Okay," I said, reluctant to get into a conversation with him.

An odd smell wafted from the old man, one I couldn't identify. Like Ashley said, he smelled funny.

At about eight-thirty, Zach came in. He was dressed in slacks, a long-sleeved shirt, and a tie. He asked Ashley to tell Alma he was waiting.

"Good morning, Zach," I said. "Did you want to order anything?"

His buggy eyes regarded me through thick glasses. Then he looked at his watch. "No time. I have to be at my men's group at the church at nine, and I have to stop at the bank first." He peered anxiously at the kitchen door and looked at his watch again. "Does she have the deposit ready? I can't be late."

Alma came out of the kitchen with a small canvas bank bag. She handed it across the counter to Zach. "Here you go, Rev."

Zach reached for the bag, and as he did, the long sleeve of his shirt pulled up slightly, showing several fresh, angry-looking red marks on his wrist and lower arm.

"What did you do to your arm?" I asked.

"What?"

"Your arm. Did you cut yourself?"

"Poison oak. These woods are full of it. Thanks, Alma. I'll bring you a receipt."

"Bring me one, too," Gil called from his table. "And Hank, too. We can't have you running off to Vegas with the funds." The two men guffawed at their joke.

"I always bring you receipts," Zach replied stiffly as he hurried out the door.

"You shouldn't tease him," Alma said. "He's doing us a service."

I watched Zach through the window as he pulled out of the parking lot in his immaculately clean Ford hybrid. I turned to Alma, who was standing at the cash register. "He does your banking for you?"

"He goes into Pineland Park three times a week for church, so we all give him our deposits. Who better to give them to? If we can't trust the Rev, who can we trust?"

Gil laughed. "I still think he's going to run off with the dough one of these days."

"I don't think he could stand the guilt," Hank added.

"Alma, you gonna pitch in at the barbeque again this year?" Gil asked.

"Of course. The barbeque wouldn't be the same without my potato salad and baked beans now, would it?"

"Do you have fireworks too?" I asked as I set their cheese omelets in front of the two men.

"Fireworks are illegal in this area, ever since the big fires a few years back. Ain't that right, Garrett?"

Garrett Easterbrook looked up from his newspaper. "Correct." He caught my eye and smiled. "Could I get a refill, Ryn?" He held up his coffee cup.

I brought the coffeepot and began filling his cup, trying not to focus on the snug T-shirt he was wearing that showed off his well-muscled chest and arms.

"Do you have time to sit down for a while?" he asked.

It certainly wasn't the first time I'd been chatted up by a good-looking guy, but something about his deep blue eyes, his warm manner, and the way his thick black hair fell over his forehead warned me there was a risk here I needed to avoid. "Not really. Maybe after the breakfast rush is over. Around ten? But you probably have to get to work."

"It's my day off. I can wait." He went back to his paper.

Ashley grinned at me when I joined her at the ordering window. "That's a new one."

"What's a new one?"

"Garrett coming on to someone. I've never seen him with any women. Have you, Mom?"

Alma slid several plates across the counter. "Nope. And he's been coming here for a few years."

"I wouldn't make anything of it. He probably just wants to ask questions about finding Heather. Maybe he has some information from Denver."

Ashley raised one eyebrow at me. "In only twenty-four hours? Nah. Face it, girl. He's hot for you."

"Right. I'll keep that in mind." I walked away with my order for a table on the patio. The rest of the morning I avoided looking at Garrett as I passed by his table, but I could feel his eyes following me. It was after ten when the place finally emptied out. I had cleaned all the tables and restocked everything I could think of, so I couldn't put it off any longer. I wanted to get to know him better but didn't want to seem too eager. I approached his table with my glass of iced tea.

He stood and pulled out a chair for me. "Nice of you to join me."

"Nice of you to ask." I cringed inwardly. *That sounds like bad dialogue from a soap opera.*

We both sat a bit awkwardly. "So, you're a policeman."

At the same time, he started to say, "So, you're a writer."

We both laughed.

"You first," he said.

"Alma tells me you used to be with the Denver Police."

He nodded. "Homicide bureau."

"What brought you to Trout Fork?"

His face clouded a bit. "Big city policing got a little too intense for me. Too many murders. Too much violence. It started to get to me. Couldn't sleep. Don't get me wrong, I like being a detective. Solving crime is like solving a puzzle, but I couldn't divorce the puzzle from the human toll. The misery, the carnage. So I moved down here and hired on with the Pineland Park department. The slower pace suits me. They've only had two murders this year. Three, if you count the one you found. But that one's really Denver's jurisdiction."

"I saw you talking to Detective Jenkins. I thought maybe you were on the case."

"Only in an advisory capacity. They have all the facilities up there. We don't have a decent lab or a coroner here."

"Will they tell you what they find?"

"If I ask, sure. Why?"

I thought about the girl whose short life had come to

such a brutal end, the shock of finding her, and the effect it had had on Alma. "No reason. It's just that I noticed something that I've wondered about. As a journalist, you know."

"Like what?"

"This is going to sound weird."

"Go on."

"When they uncovered her, there was a smell."

"There usually is," he said gently.

"I don't mean that. This smell reminded me of a swimming pool."

"Swimming pool?"

I nodded. "I can't stand that smell. Ever since..." I paused, overwhelmed again with those images. Davey face down in the pool at our home in the Hamptons, his tiny body floating among the pool toys. Mother screaming. My father frantically trying to revive him with CPR as the paramedics rushed in. The wailing siren of the ambulance racing him to the hospital.

"Ryn. Are you okay?" Garrett's hand was on my arm.

I cleared my throat. "Fine."

We chatted about police work and his background. He was so easy to talk to.

When I glanced at the clock, I could hardly believe it was nearly noon. "I'd better get back to work. I have to help get ready for lunch."

"Okay. But I've told you about me, and I still don't know about you."

"Some other time." I stood up and pushed my chair in.

He stood and the deep blue of his eyes and his nearness were disconcerting. "Are you doing anything Saturday night? After the café closes? How about if I cook dinner for us? I make a mean lasagna."

Did I want to get something started when I knew I'd be moving on soon? I decided that was the very thing that made it safe. I'd be moving on. Besides, if I was going to try to find out who killed Heather, a detective would be a valuable asset. "Sure. I love lasagna."

"I'll pick you up at eight."

I went back to the ordering window, where Ashley gave me that impish grin again.

"Don't say a word," I said.

She pantomimed zipping her lips, but she continued to give me teasing looks the rest of the day.

∽∾∽

Later that evening, I sat on my bed with Jack, who was chewing on his toy mouse. Sasha hopped onto the bed and strolled over to join the fun. Soon the two were rolling around in mock battle, swatting each other, and chewing on each other's ears. As I moved my purse out of their way, my cell phone dropped out. It lay there staring at me, reminding me it was time I called home. I picked it up on an impulse and pressed two on the speed dial, hoping to see the No Service message again. But it rang the New York number. Usually, I had to prepare myself for a conversation with Mother, blocking my emotions and steeling myself for the inevitable sound of disapproval in her voice.

I knew it was two hours later there and hoped for a moment they were in bed.

But Mother's cool voice answered. "Hello. Lowell residence."

"Hello, Mother. I hope I'm not calling too late."

"Oh, Ryn dear. How nice to hear from you." The subtle message was unmistakable— why hadn't I called sooner?

"How are things at home?"

"We're fine. Where are you calling from? Somewhere civilized, I hope."

"It's a small place in the Rocky Mountains called Trout Fork. I'm doing my next column about it."

"That's nice, dear. Is there a decent hotel there?"

I nearly burst out laughing. No doubt she was envisioning me ensconced in a Radisson or Hilton. "No. There are no hotels here. I'm staying with the lady I'm working for. I'm sharing a room with her daughter." I explained about the waitressing job at the café and heard her sniff in that way she had of disapproving without words. I didn't dare mention the murder.

"That can't be very comfortable," she said.

"Well, you know what Kerouac said, 'Better to sleep in an uncomfortable bed free, than sleep in a comfortable bed unfree.'"

"Really, dear, must you always be quoting Jack Kerouac? It can be tiresome."

Is it Kerouac she finds tiresome? Or just my quoting him?

"Will you be coming home once the column is done?" Without waiting for a response, she continued, "I met Mr. Crenshaw at the Winstons' cocktail party last weekend. He seemed pleased with your work so far. I'm sure he would be happy to have you back in the office when you return from your travels."

There was no use trying to explain to her how I felt sitting at a desk eight hours a day. The suffocating sensation of drowning in the recycled air of the office, the inane chatter of my colleagues spouting the same sociopolitical clichés as they scratched and clawed their way to the top of their sphere.

Of course she wouldn't understand my aversion to it. How could she?

I took a deep breath and decided not to take the bait. "How's Dad?"

"You know your father. Work, work, and more work. He's hardly ever home. He and Jarrod are working together on a deal, as he calls it. Something to do with China's financial markets. It's such a shame that Jarr—" She took a deep breath.

"What about Jarrod?"

"Well, I wasn't going to mention it, but he and Meredith have separated. He's living here with us. I'm sure it's only temporary until they can get into counseling."

"That's too bad. I hope they can work it out. I always liked Meredith." I remembered my big brother's wedding and the 500 guests that filled the ballroom. I had to hand it to my parents. They never did anything halfway, especially when it came to impressing their society friends. "How's Meghann?" Anything to keep the conversation off the wandering black sheep of the family.

"She's taken a summer internship at the Guggenheim museum. Quite prestigious. There were hundreds of applicants. Oh, and she's going to spend a semester in Florence next year. Isn't that wonderful?"

"Wonderful." *Apparently traveling isn't a problem as long as it's to some place like Florence.*

"Do you still have that cat with you?"

"Yes. Jack is sitting here with me now. He says hello."

Jack looked at me at the sound of his name.

"Just be sure he doesn't pick up any diseases. I've heard of something called Rocky Mountain tick fever. One can't be too careful."

I wondered how she would react to the news that Jack had dug up a corpse the day before. "I'm always careful with him, Mother. He only goes out on his leash."

She said something that sounded garbled, and I knew we were about to be cut off.

"Phone service is a bit spotty here, Mother, so I'll say good-bye. I'll call again from my next stop."

There was silence from the other end. I clicked off and put the phone in my bag. I sat there stroking Jack, listening to Alma and Ashley laughing and joking in the kitchen. Whatever had come between them was now forgotten in their love for one another. I closed my eyes, trying to enjoy the sounds of the summer night and ignore the familiar ache in my spirit.

CHAPTER 6

At six the next morning, I slipped quietly out of the bedroom with Jack. Ashley was cuddled up with Sasha, and the little cat watched me through half-open eyes as I closed the door. The living room of the cabin was bathed in golden sunbeams from the skylight. The remains of Alma and Ashley's tea and scones from the night before cluttered the coffee table, along with Alma's notes for the Fourth of July barbeque. I glanced at them briefly and noticed she had listed the names of guests, including the regulars from Trout Fork, along with some names I didn't recognize. She had even listed Dave Malone, which was a surprise. I was irritated with myself for checking to see if Garrett's name was there. It was.

Jack was eagerly pulling on his leash and leading me to the door. We left the cabin and scooted down the slight incline to the trail along the creek. I did a few stretches and started off at a slow jog, with Jack padding along beside me. The air was crisp and cool, unlike the heavy, muggy East Coast atmosphere I had always found so oppressive. There was something about Colorado that made me feel like I had come home, even though this was my first trip to the Centennial State.

After jogging and walking for about a mile, I stopped and sat down on my usual rock. I let Jack prowl around in the leaves and pine needles at the end of his leash. Hopefully, he wouldn't uncover any more dead bodies. The rippling stream at my feet murmured and splashed over the rocks and around the tree stumps protruding from the water. A solitary oak leaf floated downstream, catching momentarily on a twig near my rock. I watched it intently, hoping against hope it would be able to remain there indefinitely, but, of course, the current dislodged it and forced it downstream. A feeling of loneliness and melancholy washed over me.

I sat for a while, wondering where I would be a week, a month, a year from now. Oddly enough, the thought of leaving Trout Fork felt too painful to contemplate. I knew there were stories here that, once developed, could add immensely to my novel. But using these people—their secrets, their disappointments, their pain— seemed obscene, and I was overcome by a desire to be of use to them in some way. Alma's genuine grief over Heather's death, and Ashley's insecurities and jealousy of that grief, seemed to cry out to me for relief that I might be able to provide. Then there were the two men, Gil and Hank, drawn together by some secret shared anguish I couldn't identify, and Zach and his Bible-thumping that could mask some insecurity. Madam Gauzie's lonely, fearful prophecies of doom also echoed in my mind. As reluctant as I had been to try to find out who killed Heather, I was surprised to now find myself equally dedicated to doing exactly that.

I thought about that poor confused girl whose wanderings weren't all that different from my own, except I had an education and a purpose to my wandering. I could no longer rationalize my feelings as simply wanting to write a good column or novel. As much as I might not like to admit it, this place, these people, had gotten under my skin, not just as a journalist, but as a human being longing to connect with other human beings. I especially longed to be of use to Alma. Perhaps I could ease her sorrow in a way I was powerless to help my own mother when she lost her baby boy.

Jack stepped carefully onto my rock and sat down by my side. His amber eyes peered at me questioningly as I stroked his head. He watched a blue jay soar over the creek and disappear into the pines. Then he settled down on the warm rock, tucked his front paws under his chest, closed his eyes, and sighed.

ভসেভ

Ashley and I had cleared the tables after a fairly quiet lunch hour. She sat at a table with her book, while I decided to stroll down to Hank's for a bottle of Evian. I found Hank feverishly spraying Lysol all over his counter and cash register. He greeted me with a nod when I went to the back cooler. I stood at the cash register, paying for the water out of my tips, when we heard the roar of a group of motorcycles pulling into the parking lot.

Hank glanced out the window with what I thought was a hopeful look. "I can hear Gil now, 'damn biker scum.'" His bushy red beard wobbled as he shook his head.

I watched the group of five men dismount and pull off their helmets and gloves.

Like most of the groups, they were in their fifties and sixties, with gray beards and long gray hair pulled back into ponytails. Their denim vests were decorated with patches of all colors, military insignias, and American flags.

"What's Gil got against the bikers, anyway? They

seem harmless enough. I bet some are even former soldiers, like him."

Hank peered out the window at the group. "These guys do look pretty harmless. Not all gangs are like that, though. Some are the one-percenters."

"The what?"

"One-percenters. That's what they call the outlaw gangs. Some really bad dudes."

I remembered what Detective Jenkins told Alma about Heather's dubious lifestyle among the dangerous motorcycle gangs. But these guys looked anything but dangerous. The one who had led the group into the parking lot came toward Hank's. As he opened the door, I looked for an excuse to eavesdrop. If motorcycle groups were a regular part of the Trout Fork landscape, that could make a fascinating slant for the column.

"Maybe I'll get a couple more bottles of water, Hank." I returned to the tall cooler at the back of the store where I could eavesdrop.

The man greeted Hank. "Warm day, isn't it?" he said in a gentle voice.

"Yeah. Cold beer's in the cooler over there."

The man smiled. "Thank you. I'll just get some water."

I busied myself, pretending to peruse the water bottles in the cooler. The man opened one of the doors near me. "Excuse me, please, miss." He reached into the cooler for several bottles.

I glanced at him briefly and did a double take. I had never seen him before, yet his face caught my attention. His smile crinkled the corners of his eyes, the clearest hazel eyes I had ever seen, set in a face bathed in a glow of absolute serenity. His expression so startled me that I stammered something incoherent and moved slightly out of his way.

"Thank you," he said quietly. Then he headed for the counter to pay for the water.

I followed him and stood nearby as he paid and left the store. He crossed the lot to distribute the water to his friends.

Hank took a bottle of Lysol from under the counter and wiped the place where the biker had placed his money. "Were you going to get some more water, Ryn?"

"Huh? Oh, yeah. No. Maybe later." I left Hank's, sat on the bench in front of Gil's store, and watched the man as he lounged next to his bike, gazing at the sky as though he hadn't a care in the world. I couldn't stop thinking about the man's expression. What was it about his face that made me keenly aware of the inner turmoil that so often overwhelmed me?

After a while, one of the men called to him. "Duane. Hey, Duane. Let's hang here for a while."

Duane nodded, and the group took their bikes to a clearing at the far end of the parking lot and sat down under the shade of the trees there. Several of them lay back in the grass, their heads on their folded jackets. What kind of men were these who exchanged the creature comforts the rest of us spend our lives pursuing in order to be absolutely free? Their lifestyle seemed at once strange and inviting.

I left the bench and returned to the café. Ashley and Alma were laughing about something in the kitchen, where Alma was preparing a pot of soup. They looked up when I came in.

"Can you do without me for a while?" I asked.

Alma said, "Sure. We're not busy. Going for a run?"

"No. I have to stop procrastinating and get busy writing my column or my editor will have my head."

"No problem."

I went through the kitchen and out the back door.

Once in the cabin, I went into the bedroom and sat down at the desk. As soon as I opened my laptop, Jack took that as his cue to begin his usual routine of pacing back and forth between me and the keyboard. I stroked his back on each pass, knowing he would tire of the game eventually.

I opened a new Word document and typed the heading: Trout Fork by Kathryn Lowell. Then I stared at the blank page. Nothing. How should I begin describing the area? Maybe I should emphasize the fishing. Or the winding mountain roads. But no angle about this idyllic spot could wipe away the memory of those purple nail-polished fingers protruding from the dirt.

After about twenty minutes, I sighed and closed the laptop. It would have to wait another day. Nothing like a looming deadline to get the creative juices flowing. Or so I hoped.

Ashley came in and flopped on the bed with Sasha. "How's the column going?"

"It isn't." I got up and eyed my clothes hanging in the closet. What was I going to wear for my date with Garrett tomorrow night? There was nothing even remotely appropriate for a dinner date, but then again he usually wore casual clothes, so maybe he wasn't expecting anything different from me. I noticed one of Ashley's tops hanging there, a burgundy short-sleeved blouse with a round neck and batwing sleeves in a delicate, feminine material. Maybe she'd let me borrow it. We were both slim, so it would probably fit. I held it up in front of me and looked in the mirror. Perfect. I showed it to her. "Ash, would you let me borrow this tomorrow night?"

"Sure. Going somewhere?"

"Garrett is having me over for dinner. I guess he likes to cook."

Her face broke into its impish grin. "Oh—h—h. At his place?"

"Yeah. Where is his place, anyway? In Trout Fork?"

"No. He has a house about halfway between here and Pineland Park. You shouldn't have any trouble finding it."

"He's picking me up here."

She grinned again. "O—h—h."

"Oh what? Is that unusual?"

"We've never seen Garrett with any girls, not since we've known him."

"Maybe he dates people from Pineland Park, and you just don't see him. I mean, who brings dates to Trout Fork?"

"True." She went back to playing with Sasha.

As I was posing in front of the mirror, holding the blouse in front of me, she said, "Are you playing tonight?"

I turned. "Playing?"

"Yeah. The weekly poker game at the café."

"You play poker?"

"Not me. Mom, Gil, and Hank. Sometimes they invite some of the other locals, too."

"Zach?"

Ashley snorted. "Rev? Play cards? Not even. He thinks a lightning bolt from heaven would zap him."

I wasn't much of a poker player and hadn't played since college, but listening to the locals talk while they played might give me an idea for the column. "I'll ask your mom if I can sit in. What time do they start?"

"As soon as the café closes."

⌘

The four of us sat at one of the tables in the café dining room that evening.

Gil dealt the cards while Hank refilled our glasses

with beer and wine from his store. Hank had obviously gotten a head start on us while waiting for the café to close.

His eyes were already bloodshot and his hands unsteady. He always gave me the impression of an explosive device that needed only a nudge to go off.

Madam Gauzie hovered in the background, her necklaces dangling as she leaned over the table. "Who wants a sandwich? I've made ham and tuna. There's plenty more chips and dip, too."

The men ignored her, deep in contemplation of their hands.

"No thanks," Alma said. "Maybe later."

"C'mon, Alma," Gil said. "How many cards?"

She sighed. "I'll take three, I guess."

I had been watching the players and listening to the conversations most of the evening.

Whenever there was a lull, I tossed in a question and was never disappointed. The men, especially, had opinions on every subject.

"I understand that Malone guy has been after you to sell, Alma," I said.

She rolled her eyes. "He never gives up, that man. Never. It must be over a year now he's been pestering me."

"You're not going to sell, are you?" Hank asked doubtfully. "The first thing he'd do is raise the rent. I'm barely making a living now."

"I have no intentions of selling. Especially not to Dave Malone."

"I don't know what he'd want with this place anyway," Gil chimed in as he considered his hand. "I don't see him selling bait or slinging hash."

Alma gave him a withering look. "I don't sling hash, I'll have you know."

Gil patted her arm. "Just an expression, love. Can you open, Ryn?"

I tossed a quarter onto the pile in the middle of the table. "I'll take two." My three spades made me moderately hopeful for a flush.

"Did he ever say why he wants the place?" Gil asked.

"Nope. Just keeps asking when I'm going to give it up and go back to Denver. Know what he had the nerve to say yesterday?"

"What?"

"That the place has a bad reputation now. Because of poor Heather. Said the property values would be going down, and I should jump at his offer before anything else bad happens."

I turned up the two cards Gil had dealt. One more spade and a diamond. I tossed my cards down. "I'm out." I got up, stretching my back.

Madam Gauzie bustled in from the kitchen with a tray of sandwiches cut into dainty quarters. I grabbed one as she passed by. The hand ended with Alma winning with her three queens. She scooped the quarters up. "My deal. A few more hands and I'll have to call it a night."

We played on for a while longer, with Hank and Alma winning most of the pots. Then the group broke up and said good night.

As Hank wobbled toward the door, Gil took his arm to support him. "Steady, partner."

I watched the two men leave the café and turned to Alma. "I'll help clean up, Alma. You go to bed."

"Thanks. I think I will. Good night, Madam Gauzie."

"Good night, Alma."

I gathered the plates and glasses from the table and took them to the kitchen where Madam Gauzie was leaning over the sink. "Here's the last of them."

"Thank you, dear."

I watched her for a moment. She was quick, energetic, and thoroughly efficient in everything she did. She fascinated me. I took the dish towel and started drying the glasses. "Will you be coming to the barbeque next week?" I asked.

"I wouldn't miss it. A Trout Fork tradition for at least twenty years."

"Nice of Gil to treat everyone that way. Must be expensive."

She looked at me over the glasses perched at the end of her nose. "My dear, Gil can afford it. He is very well off." Her eyebrows went up as she emphasized the word "very."

I thought of Gil's cut-off flannel shirts and his dreary bait shop. "Really? His income from the store can't be that much."

"Oh, the bait store is just a hobby. His father was in real estate and helped develop the ski areas many years ago. He left Gil quite a legacy. And he has his army pension. Of course, he has to pay alimony to his wife, I believe. But they only had the one child, Gil Junior."

"Whatever happened to him?"

"Rode off on his Harley and never came back. I don't know what happened to him. Gil never mentions him."

"That's too bad. He must be lonely."

"The folks here have become Gil's family. He's very generous. Not only the annual barbeque, but he supports the local police league and the Wounded Warriors project. If it has to do with law and order or the military, he's for it. He has quite a reputation for his stand on that kind of thing. I must say it's a comfort having him here with his military training. I know he has weapons."

"I can see why people feel comfortable with him

here. I mean, after finding Heather's body and all. I guess it has everyone on edge."

She handed me a glass and looked out the window. "It's not only that, although that was certainly the worst thing that's ever happened here. There's been a feeling here the last few years. Even before that girl came. I can't quite put my finger on it. Something unnerving. Like an aura about the place."

"What kind of aura?"

She shook her head. "Don't get me wrong. This is a lovely little place. And yet, I can't help feeling there's something below the surface. Something that's just not right. Something that will bubble up one day and explode over all of us." She emptied the water out of the sink and picked up a towel to dry her hands. "Well, I'm off. Can you lock up, dear?"

"Sure. Good night."

She started toward the door, but turned back to me, concern increasing the lines on her face. "Do be careful on your way back to the cabin, won't you? Look around before you lock the back door."

"What am I looking for? Bears?"

"No. We won't see the bears until fall. Then they'll be in the garbage cans every night."

"What, then?"

She hesitated. "Oh, nothing, dear. Don't mind an old woman's fantasies. Good night."

CHAPTER 7

The next night, Ashley and I stood before the mirror in her room. She was using her curling iron on my short hair, trying to give it some body. She had fussed over me for an hour, almost as though she was preparing for her own date, instead of mine. I had to admit her burgundy blouse looked lovely, even paired with jeans. But she looked at my Birkenstocks and grimaced. "They look awful. Don't you have anything else?"

"Just my running shoes. I travel light."

She rummaged in her closet. "Here," she tossed a pair of gray sling-back shoes to me, "see if these fit."

I had to admit they looked a lot better than the sandals. "They're a little tight, but I think they'll work. How do I look?"

"Awesome. He doesn't stand a chance."

We giggled at the idea of Garrett being overcome by my beauty, and I felt like a teenager again. I hadn't had this much fun getting dressed in years. I'd had my share of dates in New York and at college, but there was something about being in this remote place that brought back memories of a time of innocence and simplicity.

"Ryn," Alma called from the living room. "Garrett is here."

"She's almost ready, Mom." Ashley lifted a delicate silver chain from her dresser drawer and held it up. "What do you think of this?"

"Pretty."

"It will go with the blouse. Here. Turn around." She fastened the chain at the back of my neck and admired it over my shoulder. "He's toast."

She followed me out to the living room. Alma sat on the sofa with Garrett, who stood politely when he saw us. He was wearing a light blue dress shirt open at the neck, gray slacks, and black loafers. He was clean shaven, and his thick black hair was brushed back from his forehead. His eyes assessed my outfit, and I felt myself blush. Behind his back, Ashley caught my eye and mouthed "toast."

"Ready?" he asked.

I nodded, and we said good night to Alma and Ashley. Outside, the light from the full moon was nearly as bright as day, covering the landscape like a shimmering silver mantle. We left the cabin and walked along the path around the café to the parking lot.

There were several cars still there, as well as the motorcycle group parked under the trees.

"I wonder if those guys are going to spend the night there," I said. "Is that legal?"

"It's legal as long as the property owner doesn't complain. I doubt Alma will bother about them." He held open the passenger door of his gray Mazda pickup, and I slid in.

The interior of the truck was clean and neat, not what I would expect from a bachelor. There was a paper sack on the floor that held two wine bottles. A police scanner was attached to the dashboard, its lights flickering and the metallic voice of a dispatcher crackling intermittently.

Garrett got in the driver's side and reached to switch

off the scanner. "I'm off tonight. If they really want me, they have my cell number." He nodded toward the bottles. "I picked those up from Hank's. I didn't know which you prefer, red or white, so I got both."

"Either one is fine with me. Probably the red since we're having Italian. You did say lasagna, didn't you?"

"It's in the oven. Should be done about the time we get there. It won't be much compared to what you're probably used to. I understand New York has some of the best Italian restaurants in the world."

"That's for sure. We used to eat at this place in Little Italy owned by a little old lady named Lena Corradetti. Everyone called her Mama C. She was four by four."

"Four by four?"

"Four feet tall and four feet wide. That's what happens when you eat that much pasta. She would bring a huge bowl of meatballs, sausages, and chunks of tender beef to the table. And that was before the meal came."

"I hope you're not disappointed with my concoction."

I didn't think anything could disappoint me that night. Between the moonlight, the wine, the dinner, and the handsome chef, I was beginning to think I might be the one who was toast.

We drove along the winding road toward Pineland Park until we pulled into a gravel driveway. I could see the lights of his cabin at the end of the drive, about fifty yards from the road. "Pretty remote. Do you like living here?"

"I like the peace and the distance from town. It can get lonely, though." He stopped in front of the door and turned off the engine. As he reached across to take the wine from in front of my seat, I tried not to enjoy the scent of his aftershave. I didn't wait for him to open my door. I wanted the evening to be informal and comfortable for both of us, so I got out and closed my door.

He unlocked the front door of the cabin and held it open for me. "Make yourself at home while I put these away. Can I get you a glass of cabernet?"

"I'd love one. Thanks."

He headed for the small kitchen that had a counter with two stools separating it from the large open room that served as both living room and dining room. I assumed the two closed doors at either end of the room led to bedrooms. A small dining table was set with two places and two tall candlesticks. The cabin was similar to Alma's, pine siding and a stone fireplace on one wall, with a sofa, recliner, and coffee table facing it. The other wall was shelving from floor to ceiling filled with books, CDs, and DVDs. I perused the titles, surprised to find a number of volumes of poetry, especially the Romantics. Wordsworth, Shelley, Keats, and Byron were prominent among them. A small bronze plaque hung on the wall.

"The world is too much with us."
~ William Wordsworth.

He had lit the candles on the table and turned on the stereo. Strains of *Swan Lake* wafted softly through the air. He was by my side, holding the wineglass. "Here you are."

I sipped the wine, which was delicious. I nodded at the bookshelf. "Romantic poetry and ballet."

"Not what you were expecting from a cop?"

"I don't know what I was expecting. Maybe the collected works of Robert B. Parker and Raymond Chandler?"

"With the theme from *CSI* playing in the background?"

We both laughed.

"Serves me right for prejudging."

He led me to the sofa, where we sat facing the fireplace and sipped our wine. "Dinner will be about ten minutes."

I settled into the comfortable sofa. "How long have you lived here?"

"A few years. I moved down from Denver about five years ago and lived in Pineland Park for a while. Then I bought this place."

"Do you like the police department here?"

"I like the slower pace."

"Where are you from originally?" I leaned back against the sofa cushions and regarded him, trying to remain detached and analytical as I questioned him. But the wine and the nearness of this engaging man were making that difficult.

"Texas. I studied criminal justice at UT in Austin. I got an internship with the police department there. Then I moved to Denver."

"Is your family still in Texas?"

"No. My parents moved to Florida, and my brother and his wife live in Phoenix now." He set his wineglass on the coffee table. "But I'm not answering any more questions, my journalist friend, until you tell me about you." He leaned toward me and put his arm over the back of the sofa.

"Okay, okay. I guess I do tend to give people the third degree. Occupational hazard. What would you like to know?"

"Anything. Everything."

"I was born in New York City, went to school there, studied journalism at Columbia." I decided to leave out the whole debutante scene.

"No doubt a straight-A student?"

"More like straight Cs, actually. I couldn't abide the

classroom. All during lectures, I'd be gazing out the window, longing to be somewhere else."

"Where was that?"

"Anywhere. As long as it was away from where I was. The classroom was too stifling for me. I couldn't concentrate. Oh, I did enough to pass my courses and got a pretty good education, but mostly from what I did on my own, not from listening to lectures. After graduation, I tried freelance writing, but that didn't pay enough to support myself. Then I landed the job on the travel magazine, but after a while, my editor could see I wasn't cut out for the office routine, so he offered me the column. I've been at that about a year now."

"You like the traveling? Just you and your cat?"

"I do."

"Don't you ever get lonely? For a less nomadic lifestyle?"

"Sometimes."

The timer on his oven went off, and Garrett got up. Saved by the bell. The conversation was becoming a bit too personal. I was determined to keep it on a friendly basis. Nothing more.

He brought the food to the table and held my chair out for me. We chatted as we ate the lasagna, along with the tossed salad he'd made and hot garlic bread. He kept the wineglasses filled until I leaned back. "I can't eat another bite. Everything was delicious, Garrett. Just perfect. Really."

He seemed genuinely pleased. "Let's finish the wine in the living room."

As I sat on the sofa, I noticed a folder on the coffee table. The tab at the top said, *Coroner's Report—Heather Lynn Blaine.* "Oh, you got the autopsy report. Anything interesting."

He sat down beside me. "Do you really want to ruin

a perfectly good evening with an autopsy report?"

It seemed exactly what I needed to slow this perfect evening down a little. I felt in real jeopardy from this gentle, handsome man with his poetry, wine, and candlelight.

It was all too perfect, too romantic, and I wasn't sure where the evening was heading. "It won't ruin the evening. And I'm curious. After all, I was the one who found her."

He leaned forward, set his wineglass down, and opened the folder. "Well, there are some interesting things that came out. The cause of death was a single stab wound to the heart. No sign of sexual assault. There were ligature marks on her wrists and ankles."

"Someone tied her up."

"Yes, but the marks were much deeper than we normally see. Even tying someone very tight wouldn't make marks that deep."

"What does it mean?"

"It could mean she was dragged by the rope that made the marks. Or even hung from something. And another thing. The people interviewed that day all said she had piercings in her ears, nose, and lips."

"That's right. I saw a picture of her, and she had a bunch of them."

"But no piercings were found on her. They had all been removed."

"Why would she do that?"

"Maybe she didn't. Maybe the killer removed them." He turned the page. "Remember that swimming pool smell you told me about?"

"Yes."

"It was chlorine bleach. She'd been completely washed in it."

"The killer was trying to remove the blood?"

"Probably. Or fingerprints and DNA." He pulled another paper out of the folder. "The tox screen indicated
no drugs or alcohol in her blood. But there was chloroform."

"Chloroform?"

"The Denver PD believes she was chloroformed by
the killer. Then once unconscious, she was tied up, or
hung from something, then washed with bleach and
stabbed and buried."

"How awful." I thought about how terrified that poor
girl must have been. Hopefully, she was still unconscious
from the chloroform when he killed her and wouldn't
have suffered the horror of it all.

He tossed the folder on the table and sat back. "Murder is always awful. I never want to become hardened to
it. That's why I left Denver."

We sat silently for a few minutes. "Can't the police
trace the chloroform? Who bought it and where?"

"They might be able to trace it because it's not easy
to buy, especially by an individual. But someone who
knows what they're doing can make it at home with
bleach and ammonia. We already know he had the
bleach."

"What do they think in Denver about it? Do they
have any idea who could have done this?"

"To be honest, I don't think it's a priority for them.
Jenkins is convinced it was related to her biker gang lifestyle."

I remembered Jenkins's conversation with Alma.
"Yeah, he said something about her dubious lifestyle."

"That's about it."

"Well, I think that's rotten. It shouldn't matter what
her lifestyle was. Every murder should be treated the
same."

"Do you know how many open murder cases there

are in Denver right now? Eight. That's a lot of leg work."

"That means they're not likely to spend much time on one girl in a remote mountain town like Trout Fork."

"I'm afraid so. Don't think too badly of them. It's a matter of logistics."

I shook my head. "Logistics. That's what one girl's life comes down to? Logistics?"

"It would be different if there was any evidence of danger to the community, but in this case..." He shrugged.

I sat there fuming. The more I thought about the waste of a young life, and especially the devastating effect it had on Alma, the angrier I got, and the more determined I was to do something about it. "Garrett, why can't you investigate this? Why does it have to be all done from Denver?"

"I don't decide which cases I investigate. Those assignments come from my captain, and he's not likely to assign me to one of Denver's cases. It's their jurisdiction."

"Well, can't you do it on your own time?"

He looked at me like I was a child asking for a pony.

I decided to take a different tack. "Look. I'm a journalist. I know how to ask questions, I have a sixth sense when someone is lying or hiding something. One time in college I was on a team doing a story on a small town in upstate New York. We were writing about how small town governments allocated funds to various projects. But as I dug into it, something didn't feel right. I dug a little deeper, asked a lot of questions, and uncovered a whole system of graft and corruption. It was in all the papers."

He massaged his temples with his fingertips. "Graft and corruption in a small town. Hardly the same as a murder."

I took a deep breath, trying to keep my temper under control. Wasn't anyone concerned about this girl's death? Were Heather and the people in Trout Fork to be written off as unimportant because they weren't big city dwellers? "No, it's not the same. But maybe if we work together, we can find out who did this."

He turned and stared at me with intensity. "Now listen to me. Murder investigation is not for amateurs, not even journalists. If the killer is still in the area, you could be his next victim. Have you thought of that? And even if he's not, asking questions in a little burg like Trout Fork can stir up a lot of mud, and people don't like their personal mud stirred up. Understand?"

I felt like a child again. I folded my arms. "What I understand is that you won't help find out who killed that girl."

"I'll help if I'm assigned to the case. Period."

I stood up. "It's getting late, and I have to open the café in the morning."

He hesitated a moment then stood and grabbed his keys off the coffee table. "I'll take you home."

The ride back to Trout Fork was chilly, to say the least. We hardly spoke two words to one another. He pulled up to the café, and I opened my door. "Thanks for dinner. It was great." I got out, slammed the door, and started down the path to the cabin.

As I turned the corner around the patio, I heard him say, "Wait. I'll walk you…" Then his voice faded out. The path was well lit by the moonlight through the trees. I felt slightly uneasy, remembering Madam Gauzie's warning. But nothing stirred.

I opened the cabin door with the key Alma had given me. The living room was dark and quiet. I slipped into the bedroom, hoping Ashley would be asleep, but she was sitting in bed with both cats, writing in her journal.

Something told me she would want the whole report. More like a post mortem.

Before she could ask, I said, "It was nice. He's a good cook. End of story." I went into the bathroom and turned on the shower, determined to end the conversation.

I cooled off in the shower and returned to the bedroom to find Ashley asleep with Sasha. Jack was sitting on my bed, waiting for me. I turned off the lamp and pulled the curtain aside so the moonlight could flood the room. I lay back, and Jack curled himself against my side. "I lied, Jack," I whispered. "That's not the end of the story. Not by a long shot." With or without Garrett Easterbrook's help, I was going to find out who killed Heather Blaine.

CHAPTER 8

The next morning, Sunday, the café was filled with people from the moment we opened. Ashley and I were rushed off our feet. Alma was so busy in the kitchen that Ashley had to take the orders at the counter and keep the coffeepots full, which left me taking orders in the dining room, serving by myself most of the time. About mid-morning, Garrett came in and sat at his usual table by the fireplace. I nodded to him as I passed his table on my way to the patio. His eyes told me he had been hurt by our cool parting the night before.

I came back and stood before him. "Hi. What can I get for you?" I stared at my order pad in an effort to remain aloof and professional. I took his order and went back to the kitchen.

I hung up the ticket while Ashley stood by watching me. "Are you gonna tell me what happened?" she whispered.

"Nothing happened. We had a slight disagreement, that's all."

I delivered Garrett's breakfast to his table. As I refilled his coffee cup, he said, "Maybe we can talk later?"

I looked around at the full dining room and the growing line ordering at the counter. "I don't know when we'll slow down. It's been a zoo all morning."

The disappointment in his eyes made me regret the way the evening had ended. Even if I didn't want to become involved with this man, his help in solving Heather's murder would be invaluable.

"I'd like to, though. Can you hang around for a while?"

His face brightened. "Sure. Just keep the coffee coming."

Madam Gauzie came in to join Hank and Gil who sat at their table watching Duane and his four friends quietly talking at a table nearby. Zach sat by himself at a corner table reading his Bible and writing in a notebook. He was dressed in a jacket and tie, no doubt preparing for church later that morning.

Suddenly, the door banged open, and the old man they called Sarge stormed in wearing waders and carrying a basket. He began shouting to no one in particular. "Look at this. Look! They're dead. All of them." He was holding out the basket filled with speckled trout.

They looked to me like any other fish that had been caught by a fisherman. What was he raving about?

"The creek is full of them. They're floating downstream by the dozens. Belly up. Dead. All of them. What's doing this? What's happening?" He paced around the room showing the dead fish to all the customers.

Alma came out of the kitchen. "What's all the noise? Sarge, what's going on?"

The man turned to her. "Alma, look at this. And these are only a few of the ones in the creek. There are dozens."

Alma peered into the basket. "What's happened to them?"

"Damned if I know. I was fly-fishing up at the cove and all of a sudden this dead fish floated by. You see a dead fish now and again, so I didn't think much of it. But then another one floated by, then another. I pulled some in with my net. Here they are. Look at them." He pushed the basket under Alma's nose, causing her to back away slightly.

"Calm down, Sarge. There must be a simple explanation."

His watery blue eyes were red-rimmed and wild. "Yeah? What? Something is killing the fish. Explain that."

By this time, a small crowd had gathered around the man who appeared to become increasingly agitated.

Gil picked one of the fish out of the basket and turned it over to examine it. "No marks on it, so it can't be a boat propeller. No bite marks, so it's not a bear or a predator." Then he sniffed it. "Smells fine. I don't know." He dropped the fish in the basket. "Maybe the water's contaminated."

There was an audible gasp from several people in the room.

"My God," Madam Gauzie said, drawing her shawl around her shoulders protectively. "We'll all be poisoned." Her eyes were wild with fright.

Zach stood and picked up his Bible and notebook. Clutching them to his chest, he proclaimed in a high, thin voice, "When God wanted to punish the Israelites for their sin, he brought plagues upon them."

The room became silent for a moment.

Hank turned to him angrily. "Oh, sit down, Rev. We don't need your preaching today."

Zach started toward the door then turned back. "He gave us the fish, and he can take them away from those who won't repent. Your sins will find you out. God punishes sin." He surveyed the room. "You know who you are."

He gave the crowd one final glare and left the café.

"Yeah, we know who you are, too," Hank shouted after him. "A head case."

At that point, I looked at Garrett, hoping he would restore some order to the crowd which was becoming more and more anxious. Only Duane and his group seemed unfazed by the fuss. I caught Garrett's eye. He got up, came to Sarge, and lifted one of the trout from the basket. "I can take this to our lab," he said quietly. "Maybe they can find out what killed it."

Alma looked gratefully at Garrett. "Thank God someone has some sense."

"I'll take a sample of the creek water with me, too, for the lab to analyze. If they can't find anything, we'll have to bring in the EPA."

"Oh great," Hank growled. "Just what we need. The feds hanging around getting into everyone's business."

"Maybe it won't come to that. In the meantime, I'll have the local fish and game warden print up some signs. No one should drink the creek water or eat any of the fish until we get some answers."

Duane left his table and joined Garrett. "Anything we can do, sir? My friends and I can post some signs, if that will help."

"That would definitely help. How long will you be around?"

"As long as we're needed. There's no place we have to be."

"All right. I'll be back this afternoon with the signs. Then maybe you guys can put some up. I only wish we knew how far upstream these fish came from." He took the fish and headed for the door. He looked back at me and shrugged his shoulders. I knew we wouldn't be having our talk that morning.

The café was busy throughout the morning until well past the lunch hour. I stood in front of the window, waiting for my orders. "This is brutal. Where do all these people come from?"

"Sunday is always our busiest day," Alma explained as she put several plates on a tray and wiped her forehead with her sleeve. "We get a lot of day trippers from Denver trying to escape the heat. It will be like this through August and then on the weekends through the fall. And there will be more motorcycles, too. The winding roads through here are very popular."

Almost on cue, the roar of another group of bikes resounded through the café.

Ashley was watching them out the window, and I heard her gasp. "Oh, my God. He's back."

I moved toward the window. "Who's back?"

"Mom," she called. "It's that guy, Digger."

I peered out the window. "Who's Digger?"

"He's the one Heather came here with."

Alma came out of the kitchen and hurried to the window. "Well, he's got his nerve. After leaving her here the way he did. And then to have her end up..." She shuddered slightly and returned to the kitchen, mumbling to herself.

Digger and his gang dismounted from their Harleys after revving the engines loudly, as though announcing their presence. Digger was long-haired, bearded, and stocky, with a pugnacious air about him. His group had a distinctly different look compared to Duane and his friends. They all sported drawings of hideous snakes and skulls on their vests, along with bright red patches that declared them to be the Sons of Evil. I wondered what Zach would have to say about that.

They parked their bikes in front of Hank's liquor store and went inside. After a few minutes, they came out with several six packs of beer which they proceeded to drink while lounging on the walkway, blocking access to the stores. As they drank, they became steadily more threatening, laughing crudely at the women who came by and making surly remarks about the other group of bikers who had left the café and were now relaxing under the trees. Fortunately, Duane's group ignored them. They seemed to have no interest in a turf war.

I tried to keep an eye on them as I worked, watching them out the window or across the patio when I was serving outside. Several of the older tourists sitting on the patio appeared to be uneasy. They finished eating and paid their checks quickly. Leaving the café, they skirted around the ones lolling on the walkway, got into their cars, and drove off.

The group got louder and more obnoxious as the afternoon wore on. They fired f-bombs at everyone who passed by, snickering at the discomfort they were causing, especially among the older tourists. At one point, Gil came out of his store, his face like thunder. He surveyed the scene in disgust for a moment then disappeared back inside. I had a fleeting thought about the weapons Madam Gauzie said he owned.

After several hours, Garrett's gray pickup pulled into the lot. He got out of the truck carrying the signs and sized up the scene in front of him. With an attitude of quiet authority, he asked the bikers to move off the walkway. As he spoke, he moved the signs from one arm to another, clearly revealing the detective's badge displayed on his belt.

The one called Digger gave him a sullen smile. "Anything you say, Officer."

But none of them moved.

Duane and his four friends had crossed the lot and were now standing beside Garrett. They all had the same look of peaceful nonviolence, but there was still an aura of strength among them.

The outlaw gang glared at them for a moment, then Digger said, "Let's move off, boys."

The group got up and went to sit on their bikes.

One of them said, "Let's blow this place, Dig."

"Not without I find my woman," Digger replied.

I heard a sharp intake of breath from Ashley, who stood by my side at the window.

"Oh, my God. He's looking for Heather." We watched the man slouch toward the liquor store again, the chains on his belt rattling, his leather boots scuffing on the wooden walkway.

Garrett watched him go then turned to Duane and his group. "If you fellows will put these up along the road wherever there's an access trail to the creek, I'd appreciate it. Go as far north and south as you can, as long as the signs last. That should do it." He parceled out the signs to the men, who returned to their bikes and rode off in both directions. Garrett followed Digger into the liquor store.

Ashley and I responded to Alma's call from the kitchen. "Orders up, girls!"

We hurried to pick up our orders and serve them. In a few minutes, Garrett came into the café and went through the kitchen door. I stood at the serving window, listening.

"Have you got any fish from the creek, Alma?" he asked.

"About two dozen in the freezer. Hank and Gil give me some of their catch each week."

"Well, keep them there until we find out what killed the ones in the creek. You may have to dispose of them."

"That would be a shame."

"I'll let you know what the lab finds."

"Did you speak to that man, that Digger, about Heather? Does he know what happened to her?"

"He didn't know, but I gave him the bad news. He

seemed genuinely upset. I guess he was more attached to her than we thought."

"Humph," Alma snorted. "Then why did he ride off and leave her here?"

"I asked him that. He claims it was her idea. She refused to go with him when he left. She said she was on to something here. He doesn't know what she meant. He said he came back today to see if she'd changed her mind."

He came through the dining room door and stopped. I was pretending to be busy with my order forms, but he must have known I'd been listening. "Ryn," he said. "I have to get back to the station, but we need to talk."

"Okay. I'll walk you out."

We left together and stood by his pickup.

Unlocking the door, he turned to me. "I've been thinking about what you asked last night. It's not that I don't want to get involved with this case. You have to understand my position. I can't assign myself to a Denver case. My captain would never go for it."

I nodded, wondering how big a role politics played in even small town police forces. "I get it, Garrett. There's nothing you can do. Your hands are tied."

He ran his hand through his hair. "Not entirely. There's no reason I can't look into a case on my own time."

I smiled gratefully at him. "That's all I'm asking."

"On one condition."

I regarded him skeptically. "What's that?"

"That you stay out of it."

"But—"

"No buts. If there's a killer of young women on the loose, you could be his next target, especially if he thinks you're getting nosy. If you want me to look into it, you have to stay out of it. Deal?"

I hesitated, hating to lie to him. "Okay, deal. And thank you."

ᑯᑯᑯ

That evening Alma, Ashley, and I ate dinner together in the cabin. The café wasn't open for dinner on Sundays, giving us a welcome break after the busy week. We sat at the small table in Alma's cozy kitchen, eating leftovers from the café. The air was warm, and the evening sky was streaked in gold and purple. There were a few clouds, but the late afternoon thunderstorms so prevalent in the mountains in the summer months had been rare this summer, a cause of great concern among the locals about the dry timber. The cats were prowling around our chairs looking for treats. I couldn't help comparing this warm, inviting little kitchen to the huge formal dining room in our apartment in New York.

Alma refilled my glass with iced tea. "How was your date last night, Ryn? Is Garrett as good a cook as he thinks?"

"It was lovely and, yes, he can really cook. He is a gracious host. Wine, music, candlelight. The works."

Ashley peered at me. "Then why were you so bummed when you got back?"

I sat back in my chair. "We had a disagreement. But we're okay now. I think."

"Did he try to get you to stay overnight?" Ashley asked with her mischievous grin.

"Oh hush," her mother chided. "That's none of our business." She gave me a sideways look. "Well, did he?"

I ignored the question. "We talked about Heather. Then he showed me the autopsy report. I asked if he was going to help in the investigation, and he shut me down. It's like he was annoyed that I even asked. Then I told him I thought I might want to stay here for a while and see if I could turn up something. As a journalist, I know how to ask questions, to get people to open up to me in a way they won't to a cop."

Alma's face brightened. "That makes sense."

"Not to him. He bit my head off. Told me not to stir up the mud. Police work isn't for amateurs. Blah, blah. He treated me like a child. Or an imbecile."

"Well, he's concerned for your safety," Ashley said. "What's wrong with that?"

"What did the report say?" Alma's hand went to her heart, and she stared at me with dread. "Don't tell me she was…I mean did he…?"

"Rape her?"

She nodded, her eyes wide.

"No sign of sexual assault."

"Oh, thank God."

"She was stabbed once through the heart. It was very quick. I'm sure she didn't suffer." There was no telling how much fear and horror she suffered before the final blow, but I kept that thought to myself.

"Did it say anything else?" Ashley asked.

"She was tied by the wrists and ankles. Oh, did either of you ever see her with her piercings removed?"

Alma shook her head, and Ashley said, "No. She never took them out. Why?"

"They were all removed. And there's no record of them being found near the body."

"Strange. Who would do such a thing?" Alma asked.

We ate in silence, then Ashley said, "Are you really going to stay? Even after you finish your column? That would be awesome."

"I'll have to talk to my editor about taking a short leave of absence, but yes, I would like to stay, at least for a while. There are still too many unanswered questions.

Garrett said the Denver police don't seem to think there's any danger to the community, that Heather was a one off, or that she ran afoul of one of her biker buddies. But that makes no sense, especially now that her boyfriend came back looking for her. Why would he do that? If he killed her, wouldn't he stay far away from here?"

Alma furrowed her brow. "You're saying you think someone from Trout Fork killed her? My God."

"Not necessarily someone who lives here," I assured her quickly, "but maybe someone who comes here often. Or someone who lives nearby. I don't know."

Alma got up and started clearing the table. "Well, we're glad to have you, Ryn. You can stay as long as you like." She bent down to pet Jack, who was following her around the kitchen. "And so can you, you handsome boy."

Jack closed his eyes and head-butted her hand as she stroked him. I got up from the table and put an arm around Alma's shoulders. "I'm very grateful. I feel more at home here than—You go put your feet up. Ashley and I will clean up."

"Thank you, dear." She wiped her hands on a towel. "I appreciate it. It's been a long day. I'm going to take a hot bubble bath." She yawned and turned to us at the kitchen door. "Good night, girls. Be sure the front door is locked."

"Night, Mom," Ashley said.

I tossed a towel to her. "I'll wash. You dry." I looked out the window as I washed the dishes, wondering what my first step should be. "Ashley, you know how we overhear a lot of conversations in the café?"

"Too many. I could write a book. Do you know how boring most people are when they talk? Sheesh. I try to tune them out."

I washed a plate and handed it to her to dry. "Me too,

but I'm thinking we should listen more carefully from now on."

She looked at me with interest. "Like how?"

"Like with the understanding that any one of our customers could be Heather's killer. Or someone might know something about her that we don't know. She has been the main topic of conversation around here for a week. Let's listen to what people are saying about her. Maybe we'll be able to pick up something useful, something that might lead us to Heather's killer."

"I can do that. Nobody pays any attention to a waitress." She was quiet for a moment. "I just thought of something."

"What?"

"You know that dude Malone? The one who's always trying to get Mom to sell?"

"How could I forget him? He nearly crushed my hand. What about him?"

"He was in the café this afternoon talking to Gil about the dead fish. He said something like it would hurt Gil's business. And didn't he tell Mom that Heather getting killed would lower the property values? What if…"

Could that pushy, crass salesman with the bad hair be a killer? "I don't know, Ash, but that's the kind of thing I'm talking about. Listen to what people are saying, who they're talking to. You never know what you'll hear."

Ashley's eyes were wide with excitement. "Maybe I can use a tape recorder. I could put it in my apron and—"

"Hold on, Dr. Watson. We're talking about a murderer here. You'll have to be careful and not act like you're listening. If whoever it is gets suspicious, you could be in danger. Promise me you'll be discreet."

"Okay, no tape recorder. No one will suspect a thing. I promise."

I watched her leave the kitchen, the two cats trailing after her. I hoped I wasn't putting her, or myself, in jeopardy.

CHAPTER 9

Y ou're getting fat and lazy," I whispered to Jack early the next morning. I held up his harness and leash, a gesture that usually had him up and pacing by the door. But that morning he just regarded at me with half-closed eyes.

"Come on. Let's go," I whispered again, trying not to wake Ashley. I headed for the bedroom door, shaking the leash in a futile attempt at feline motivation.

Jack yawned and curled up. It was hopeless.

I tiptoed out to the living room to sit on the sofa while I laced up my running shoes. The way the morning sunbeams through the skylight cast a golden glow on the knotty pine walls always fascinated me. It reminded me of a landscape painting I had seen once, where the artist's technique produced a slightly varying tint to the viewer's eye, depending on the time of day the painting was seen.

Pulling on my sweatshirt, I quietly opened the front door and stood there enjoying the invigorating air. It was hard to believe such an idyllic spot could possibly be home to a killer.

After a few stretches, I scrambled down the incline to the creek-side trail behind the cabin and started off at a slow jog. After a few minutes, I decided today was a good day for a long walk. Jogging could wait until tomorrow.

Moving slowly through the woods enabled me to enjoy a closer look at my surroundings without disturbing the wildlife. Squirrels, rabbits, and chipmunks were abundant along the creek. At one point, I came upon a doe standing ankle deep in the creek, drinking while her twin fawns waited for her at the water's edge. When she heard me approach, her head came up, and she froze, water dribbling from her muzzle. The fawns stared at me then scampered into the brush, their spotted coats perfectly camouflaging them in the foliage. The beauty of the scene and Nature's perfect harmony caused an ache in my heart.

Farther on, I saw a man approaching from the opposite direction. I couldn't see who it was, but he carried a fishing pole and basket. That reminded me of the signs I had passed along the trail, warning people not to fish in the creek or drink the water, by order of the fish and game warden. As the man came nearer, I recognized Zach, wearing waders and his usual long-sleeved shirt.

He beamed and waved. "Good morning," he said cheerily as we met. "Beautiful day, isn't it?" His thick glasses reflected the sun dancing on the water, almost hiding his eyes from me.

"Lovely. How's the poison oak?"

He bent down to put his pole and basket on the ground. "The what?"

I pointed to his arm. "The poison oak. Must be uncomfortable. I had poison ivy once. It drove me crazy. I don't know how you can stand having those long sleeves rubbing on it."

He pulled at his sleeve. "It's okay. Doesn't really bother me. I forget about most things when I'm out here fishing."

"But I thought the creek was unsafe to fish in. Isn't that what the signs say?"

"The fish are fine. Come see for yourself." We walked to the water's edge where the doe had stood and watched several speckled trout swimming downstream next to the bank. One of them leaped out of the water with a splash. "Whatever killed those fish yesterday is gone now. The Lord always provides."

I watched the odd little man's face as he spoke. Did he really believe all the drivel he spouted? My journalist's natural nosiness came to the fore, and I asked him if he had always been religious.

He seemed more than eager to talk about himself. "Always. I grew up in the church. My father is a pastor in Georgia. I was involved in church since I was little. I always went to Christian schools then to a Baptist university. I was supposed to go to seminary, but that didn't work out."

"What brought you to Trout Fork? Seems a long way from Georgia."

"I need to be in a quiet place away from modern culture and all it entails—technology, media, noise." He rubbed the back of his neck. "It has a negative effect on me. On all of us, if we're honest. But what about you? I understand you're a writer of some sort."

"A columnist for a New York travel magazine."

"Is that where you call home? New York?"

"I guess. When I'm there."

"Do you have family there?"

"Parents, one brother, and one sister. I had another brother, but he died when he was two."

"Oh, how sad. An accident?"

He seemed genuinely sympathetic, so I told him all about Davey's drowning in the pool and the way it had fractured the family. The more I revealed to him, the more I realized it had been a long time since I had unburdened myself to anyone about that day. All those horrible long-buried memories came flooding back and, this time, I was unable to force them back into my subconscious. It was as though I had put them in a freezer for years, only to have them thaw and come out as fresh and raw as ever. I glared at him through my tears. "Where was your God then, I'd like to know. Why did he ignore my family and the priest when we begged God to save that innocent little boy?"

Zach drew himself up in what seemed a defensive posture. "What you reap, you shall sow. There must have been some sin in your lives that brought about the tragedy."

I stared at him incredulously. Even my tears and heartbreak couldn't hold back my rage, and I unloaded on him. "So it was our fault he died? Is that what you're saying? God was punishing us for something we did by taking Davey? What could we possibly have done to deserve that?"

He bent over to pick up his basket and pole. "I wouldn't know. There are both sins of commission and omission. The bad things we do as well as the good things we neglect to do."

"If that's who God is, he's just cruel," I said through hot tears. "And I want nothing to do with him." I walked away from him, angrier and sadder than I had ever been in my life.

⁊⁊⁊

I got back to the cabin in time to change for the morning shift at the café. I passed Alma as she was going into the kitchen. She wore her long white apron over jeans and a T-shirt, and her dark hair was tied up in a scarf.

"Morning, Ryn. Coffee?"

"Love some. Thanks." I followed her into the kitchen, keeping my eyes averted in case they were swollen from crying, but as she handed me the coffee, she scrutinized my face with her motherly instinct.

She rubbed my arm. "What's wrong, dear?"

Of course, that made things worse, and I started crying all over again. I gave her an abbreviated version of Davey's death and, unlike Zach, she listened with sympathy and affection. I related meeting Zach on the trail and his assessment of the situation, as well as the anger and guilt it had brought on.

She sat down close to me at the tiny kitchen table. "That Zach. I wouldn't pay too much attention to what he says. He can be so kind and so helpful. But when he starts talking religion, he turns everyone off."

"Kind and helpful? Zach?"

"Oh, yes. Do you know what he did for Madam Gauzie? Practically rebuilt her cabin. Remodeled her bathroom, retiled her kitchen, repaired her roof. And wouldn't take a dime from her. He does things like that. He's always volunteering at his church—carpentry, plumbing, electrical work, landscaping. He teaches Sunday school for the kids, too."

I blew my nose. "He sounds too good to be true."

"He's definitely got his good points. He's helpful, pays his rent on time, and is kind to everyone. But you don't want to get him started on religion. He's got some strange ideas."

"What does he do for a living?"

"He takes on odd jobs with a builder in Pineland Park. I think he gets regular checks from someone in Georgia. He's referred to them once or twice. I don't know who they're from."

"How long has he lived here?"

"Let's see. About ten years now. Ashley was just a little girl when he first rented that cabin from me. My husband was still here then. Did you know I'm divorced?"

"I didn't know. That's too bad."

She sipped her coffee and gazed out the window. "Robert is a good man. He always treated Ashley and me well. We just weren't ready for marriage, I guess. When you're young and in love, you don't see that. Or if you do, you think you can overcome it. It's been okay, though. He sees Ashley a lot. She spends some weekends and holidays with him in Denver. And he comes down here once or twice each summer, too. We get along fine, as long as he keeps up the child support payments." She got up and put her empty cup into the sink. "Well, let's get over there and open up. See if Ashley is ready."

ⁿⁿⁿ

The café was busy all that day and the next, even with the creek closed to fishing. I didn't see Zach during those days, and I was glad of it. I had calmed down since our talk on the trail, but every time I thought of him, I got angry all over again. Maybe he was staying away to avoid me. Or maybe he had an odd job in Pineland Park. Whatever the reason for his absence, I was grateful I would have time to cool off before I encountered him again.

I hadn't seen Garrett either. I wondered if he was looking into Digger's background. I felt bad about lying to him, but I remembered my journalism professor telling the class a journalist should be willing to do pretty much anything for a story. How much more should we be willing to do to solve a murder? That sounded good to me, but my conscience still told me lying wasn't the way to forge a relationship, personal or professional.

During the lulls in the café, Alma and Gil were busily preparing for the next day's barbeque. They huddled together over the guest lists and plans for decorations, food, music, guests, and games. Ashley and I looked forward to a day off, a day to relax and enjoy our friends and neighbors. From what Alma said, both groups of motorcyclists planned to attend, although both had left several days ago, riding off in opposite directions.

As we closed the café that night, we heard the roar of the motorcycles approaching. Duane's group pulled into the empty lot under the trees and began to unpack their gear.

Duane strolled along the sidewalk to Gil's Bait Shop, looking in the window of the shuttered store. Then he came into the café with a box he had carried on the back of his bike. "Evening," he said as he saw me. "Is Alma around?"

"She and Gil are in the kitchen. What have you got there?"

A slow smile spread across his face. "Just some toys for the kids at the barbeque tomorrow." He opened the box and pulled out some toy motorcycles, complete with little plastic riders dressed in authentic-looking biker outfits. There were also kid-sized fishing rods. "Brought some sparklers, too. Since fireworks are illegal, at least the kids can have something to wave around."

"That's so nice of you, Duane. The kids will love them."

This man was a mystery to me. He had the same leathers, the same long hair and beard as all the other bikers, but he was completely different from them. What was it about him? I gazed into his eyes and compared what I saw there to what I had seen in Zach's eyes. Duane's were shining with the light of peace and joy, while Zach's were dimmed with…what? Something I couldn't identify.

Alma and Gil came out of the kitchen and greeted Duane like an old friend. They oohed over the toys, laughing at the little fishing rods.

"Thank you, Duane. This is a wonderful gesture," Alma said.

"It's from all five of us, not just me. We saw these in a store in Steamboat Springs. We thought the kids might like them."

"I have an idea," Gil said. "Let's have a drawing of some kind for the kids who get these rods. Two bucks a chance. Whoever wins will get free fishing lessons from me. The parents can chip in the dough, and it can go to some worthy cause. Maybe the local police athletic league."

"Great idea, Gil. I'll get Ashley to make signs about the drawing." She smiled at the two men, her eyes shining. "This will be our best barbeque ever."

I watched the three as I continued cleaning tables. They chatted and laughed together, all so cheerful, almost like children on Christmas Eve. Were they always this way about Independence Day? Or were they just trying to forget that a young girl had been brutally murdered weeks before?

❧❧❧

That night, I sat on my bed with my computer on my lap, trying to make at least a start on my column. The page was as blank as ever. Jack batted his toy mouse toward me, and I tossed it to the end of the bed. He chased it and brought it back to me in his mouth. Then he sat waiting for me to throw it again.

Ashley was writing in her journal, her ear buds in as

she listened to something on her iPod. Alma had gone to bed early, exhausted but happy with the preparations for tomorrow's barbeque. She seemed to have accepted Heather's death, and she may have also taken to heart what I told her about Ashley's jealousy of her affection for Heather. They appeared to have called at least a temporary truce to their mother/daughter conflict. I thought about Mother and our ongoing conflicts. But I was long past my teen years. Would the tension between us ever be over?

Ashley pulled the buds out of her ears. "Hey. I forgot to tell you what I heard today." She came over and sat on my bed, her eyes aglow. "You know how you told me to listen to conversations in the café?"

"Yeah?"

"Well, I've been doing it. Did you see Malone in there today?"

"Couldn't miss him. He keeps calling me 'Ryn as in Kathryn.' Then he always laughs at his little joke. Too bad he's the only one who thinks it's funny."

"Well, he wasn't laughing today. Not when I heard him. He was on the phone to someone named Esther, and he was giving her hell about something. I heard him say something about needing more information. He kept saying, 'When? I need to know when.'" She pulled a piece of paper out of her pocket and read from it. "I wrote it down after he left. He said time is growing short. Then he said he wasn't having any luck here, but that was going to change. Then he said he'd be home late tonight. That's all I could hear."

"Esther must be his wife or girlfriend. Do you know if he's married?"

"I don't know. He's always alone when he comes here. Mom invited him to the barbeque. God knows why. Maybe he'll bring her tomorrow."

I typed "Dave Malone" on the blank document on my laptop. Might as well use it for something. "Okay, let's see." I typed what she'd told me. "He said he needs more information about something and he needs it soon. Right? Then he said he's having no luck but that's going to change." I looked at Ashley. "Do you think he means about getting your mom to sell?"

Ashley shrugged.

I leaned back and stared out the window. "If it does, what does he think will happen that will change her mind when she's been adamant about not selling?"

Jack brought me his mouse for the umpteenth time and dropped it on my lap. "Not now, Jack," I said, irritated at the game. I brushed the mouse away, and it hit the wall, sliding down between the bed and the wall.

His amber eyes regarded me in that way he has of inducing guilt.

"Sorry, Jack. I'll get it." I scooted over and reached down, feeling around among the dust bunnies. My hand touched something hard. It was a book. I pulled it up and set it on the bed.

Ashley gasped. "That's Heather's. It's her journal."

I handed it gently to her, not wanting to intrude on something as personal as a journal.

At the same time, it might offer some clue as to what had happened to her. I watched Ashley carefully as she opened it and began to read.

"It starts over a year ago, if these dates are right. And look at the way she wrote."

I looked over her shoulder at the entries. She used no capital letters and little punctuation. "It looks like e. e. cummings, doesn't it?"

"Who's that?"

What are they teaching kids in school these days? "He's an American poet who used no capitals and little punctuation. His writing looks a lot like this."

Ashley frowned. "Do you think we should read this?"

My journalist's instincts overrode my sensibilities or privacy concerns. "Definitely. That's now your job. Read through it and find out all you can about her. Let's look at the last entry she made. What's the date?"

"June eighteen," she whispered, her eyes wide. "That's the day she went missing."

We read the entry together. "'gonna talk to gs today. its his last chance. he pays up or i tell everbody about gj.'"

"My God," Ashley said. "Whoever G.S. is, he must be the killer."

CHAPTER 10

Ashley and I had stayed up late trying to figure out who "G.S." could be. She knew of a couple of local fishermen in the area with the first names of Gary and Greg, but she didn't know their last names. After we had exhausted all possibilities and come up empty, we dropped off to sleep.

We slept later than usual and woke to the sounds of Alma banging around in the kitchen. Jack and Sasha were prowling by the door, anxious for their breakfasts. I opened the door, and they dashed into the kitchen ahead of me.

I must have looked pretty ragged because Alma handed me a cup of coffee without being asked. "Is Ashley up yet? There's a lot to do today."

I poured cat food into the bowls. "She's coming."

Ashley staggered into the kitchen, yawning, plopped down at the table, and gave her mother a bleary-eyed look.

"You two stay up late last night?"

Ashley mumbled something. Then her eyes got wide. "Mom. You won't believe what we found last night. Heather's journal."

Alma's eyes searched mine eagerly. "Really? Anything interesting in it?"

I sat at the table with my coffee. "It's pretty long and written in a kind of code. Ashley's going to read through it and see what she finds."

"Mom, you know those two guys that come here to fish, Gary and Greg?" Ashley said.

"Sure. What about them?"

"Do you know their last names?"

Alma leaned against the counter. "Let's see. Gary's is Kowalski. And Greg Blake. No, Blakely. That's it. Why?"

Ashley got up and took some orange juice out of the fridge. "The last entry in the journal was made the day she disappeared. It said she was going to talk to someone with the initials G.S. We're wondering who that is."

"Talk to him about what?"

I sipped the dark, strong coffee and exhaled slowly. "We don't know. But she said it was his last chance to pay up or she was going to tell everybody about someone with the initials G.J."

"Tell them what?"

"No idea. But whoever it is, it's pretty clear she was blackmailing him. And that someone is probably the one who killed her."

Alma sat down with a slight groan. "Good God. What was that girl up to?"

"Not what we thought she was, huh?" Ashley said with a hint of spite.

I gave her a look that told her not to go there.

She cleared her throat and looked contritely at her mother. "But who knows? Maybe it's not what it sounds like."

Alma shook her head.

"Do either of you remember what day she got here?" I asked.

"It was around the first of June," Alma replied.

"Ashley, maybe you should start reading the journal from around that time. If she was blackmailing someone, and I say 'if,' she must have met him here. That would mean sometime after the first of June. If that doesn't turn up anything, you'll have to go back to the beginning. See if you can figure out where she came from, when she hooked up with Digger, where they were heading when they stopped here, anything."

"Okay. I'll start tonight."

"It won't be easy with all those abbreviations. Maybe make a list of the code words she used. Then we can try to cross-reference them with dates and places. What do you think?"

She nodded eagerly, but Alma's expression was one of motherly concern. Seeing her face, I added, "Ash, don't mention the journal to anyone, not even in casual conversation."

Ashley mimed zipping her lips. "This is exciting. I feel like a detective."

That brought Garrett to mind, our reluctant detective. I determined to corner him at the barbeque and tell him what we had found in the journal. If he hadn't been convinced before, I was sure this would get him to concentrate on finding Heather's killer.

ero

It turned out to be perfect weather for the barbeque. The cloudless sky predicted another warm, dry day with still no afternoon storms. It was nearly noon when the three of us left the cabin, heavily laden with Alma's potato salad, the huge pot of baked beans, and a tray of condiments. Gil and Hank were already on the lawn behind the stores. Gil, sporting his Made in America barbeque apron, was cleaning his huge grill while Hank ferried coolers of beer, soda, and ice back and forth from his store. One glance at him told me he had already gotten a head start celebrating.

"Can we borrow a couple of coolers and ice, Hank?" Alma asked. "We need to keep this potato salad cold. We don't want to poison anyone, do we?"

"Sure, Alma. I'll fill a few with ice for you." He headed back toward his store, weaving slightly as he went.

Madam Gauzie fluttered over from her cabin, wearing a star-spangled Uncle Sam hat and carrying yards of red, white and blue bunting. "Here it is, Gil," she called. "I knew it was in the attic somewhere. Where should I hang it?"

"Same as last year, ma'am. And the year before."

She began draping the bunting among the trees and shrubs, standing back occasionally to admire the effect. Zach arrived shortly afterward and began helping her.

Garrett came around the corner of the building casually dressed in a T-shirt, shorts, and sandals. I couldn't help admiring his muscular physique and great legs. He looked around for a minute, as though unsure of his welcome, then smiled when he saw me. He came to where I was standing. "Hey. Am I early?"

"Not at all. People should start drifting in any minute now. We're just getting set up. Help me with this, will you? It's pretty heavy."

He lifted the large pot of baked beans as though it was weightless. "Where do you want it?"

"In the café kitchen." I held the door open for him, and as he moved past me, the slight whiff of his aftershave reminded me of our evening together.

Alma was stacking plates and silverware on trays. She looked up when we came in.

"Hello, Alma. Where do you want this?"

"Oh, Garrett. Nice to see you. Right here on the stove." She raised her eyebrows at me behind his back. "Thank you, dear. Now you two go enjoy yourselves. I'll be out in a minute."

We left the kitchen together and stood in the shade of the building's overhang. We both seemed to find the situation a bit awkward.

After a few minutes, he said, "I thought you might like to know what the lab found out about the fish."

"Oh, yeah. What killed them?"

"Ammonia. They had a high concentration of it in their bloodstreams."

"Ammonia? How did that get in the water?"

"We don't know, but it looks like someone poured a huge amount of it into the water somewhere upstream. The fish that swam through it ingested it and died. Then they floated down here. As it became more diluted in the water, other fish weren't affected."

"How bizarre." The tragedies of Love Canal and other environmental disasters went through my mind. "Do you think it was some kind of industrial pollution?"

"I don't see how. There are no industries upstream of here, not for miles and miles. No. I think it was a one-time dumping of the ammonia."

"For what reason?"

"I can only guess."

"Yes?"

"Someone wants to discourage people from coming to Trout Fork by giving the impression there's something wrong with the water. That would drive off the fishermen, and that's a big draw to this area. Probably the biggest."

"But why? Why would anyone want to keep people away from Trout Fork?"

"No idea. Maybe it's a hermit with a pathological hatred of people. Maybe it's someone trying to make an ecological statement. Anyway, the fish are healthy now, and the stream is clear. Let's hope that's the end of it."

We watched as couples and families arrived. Gil had even invited the campers and counselors from the YMCA camp across the street. My heart sank when Digger and his gang came slouching into the area, grabbed some beer from a cooler, and made themselves at home by sitting on the picnic benches and tables. Even in the heat, they were dressed in their leather vests and heavy boots. I watched Gil's expression as he eyed them. I was relieved to see him greet them with a cordiality he might not have really felt, but I had to give him an A for effort.

"Happy Independence Day, gentlemen," he said. "Welcome."

"Thank you, General," Digger said with exaggerated courtesy. "Love your apron."

His buddies snickered.

Gil ignored the remark about his apron, saying quietly, "Actually, I was a lieutenant in the army, but thanks for the promotion."

Digger casually flicked his cigarette butt away. It landed near the area where the grass ended and the dry pine needles began.

Gil glared at him. "Please pick up your cigarette butt. It's a fire hazard. There are cans with sand in them at each table."

Digger squinted at him. "Maybe you should take off your apron and pick it up yourself." The biker didn't move, and the tension rose.

People stopped talking and listened nervously to the exchange. My hand went to Garrett's arm.

He moved to the two men and spoke with his quiet authority. "We want no trouble here. All these folks are here with their families for a nice, peaceful day."

The two men glared at each other, neither one willing to back down.

Garrett got close to Digger. "Now, sir, please pick up your cigarette butt and dispose of it here." He lifted the metal can and shook it. "Fire is a real danger in this area. Especially this dry summer." He shook the can again. "I did say please."

Digger rolled his eyes at his buddies and got up with a mock salute. "Yes, sir, Officer, sir." He picked up the butt and plunked it into the can Garrett was holding. Then he sat back down.

Gil turned back to his grill and began pulling raw steaks out of a cooler.

I brought him a beer and patted his arm. "Thanks for doing this, Gil. It's very neighborly of you."

He shrugged. "It's the Fourth." He eyed Digger and his gang. "It's just too bad some people have no respect."

Alma came out the kitchen door with two bags of garbage. "Here, you two. Put these in the dumpster, will you?"

Garrett and I took the bags and headed for the large green dumpster at the far end of the building behind Madam Gauzie's Antiques. Garrett opened the top, and I started to toss my bag in when I noticed something odd. Everyone was careful to put their trash in black plastic bags, but there were four empty bleach bottles among the bags. I stared at them for a moment. Then the words from the autopsy report echoed in my mind. Heather had been completely washed in chlorine bleach. That was the smell that had reminded me of a swimming pool. "Garrett, look at this."

He opened the top wider and peered into the dumpster. Our eyes found each other's, and I knew he was thinking the same thing. He lowered the top again. "Stay here for a minute. Don't touch anything." He walked quickly toward the parking lot and came back in minutes, wearing rubber gloves and carrying a large clear plastic bag. He opened the dumpster, climbed up on the edge of it, and pulled the bleach bottles out. He carefully put them into the plastic bag. Then he sealed the bag and jumped down. He pulled out his pen and began writing on the bag. "I'm noting the date, time, and the location we found these. You are a witness to it. Correct?"

I nodded. "Do you think these are—"

"I don't think anything yet. But I'll have them checked for fingerprints anyway."

I watched him walk back to his truck and put the bag into the cab. As he was locking the door, a car with three young men in it pulled up next to him. Garrett greeted them as they got out of the car. They were all well-built and tanned, wearing shorts, T-shirts with the police athletic league logo, and baseball caps that said "Pineland Park Police." Garrett directed them to the path around the café and came back to me.

"Those are some of the cops from my station. I didn't know they were friends of Gil's. Nice guys. I'll introduce you later." He rubbed his hands together. "Let's eat. Those steaks smell great." He took my hand and led me to one of the picnic tables.

I couldn't help feeling proud to be with him.

The three cops stood at the grill with Gil, beer bottles in hand, laughing and enjoying themselves as the area filled up with local families. Digger's group had separated themselves from the rest of the crowd, sitting on the periphery and helping themselves to Hank's beer.

Then one of them said loudly, "This place is stinking with cops."

The policemen regarded them for a moment then apparently decided to ignore them and turned away.

"Yeah," Digger said, his voice slurring. "You'd think

with all the pig power around here, someone could find out who killed my girlfriend."

His buddies muttered and nodded their heads in agreement.

"I think we've had about enough of this," Garrett said quietly. He left the table, walked over to the group, and stood in front Digger. "Gentlemen, I think it's time for you to leave."

Digger stood up and faced him belligerently. "Oh, yeah? Well, it's a free country."

"True. But this is a private party. And you and your friends have outstayed your welcome."

The bikers stood up, their surly attitudes declaring they were itching for a fight, but Gil and the three young cops came and stood behind Garrett.

One of Digger's friends took his arm. "Let's go, Dig. We don't need to be at this pig roast."

Digger ripped his arm away. "Okay, we'll go. But we'll be back." He spat on the ground and stalked away, his group trailing behind him like a wolf pack shadowing the alpha male.

For the rest of the afternoon, I tried to forget about the bleach bottles, about Heather, about biker gangs, about anything except having a good time with the people I had come to have such affection for. There was a great deal of laughter and joking as everyone devoured Gil's steaks and Alma's delicious side dishes.

"This is the best potato salad I've ever had, Alma," Garrett said, spooning a second helping on his plate.

"Oh, go on," she said, clearly pleased at the compliment.

The kids played several games orchestrated by Madam Gauzie and Zach. When the kids were exhausted from the games, Duane and his friends started handing out the toys. They squealed with delight at the little motorcycles and fishing rods. Ashley went around selling chances on the fishing lessons, and the drawing was held, with a shy little girl holding the winning ticket. Gil made arrangements with her parents for lessons the following week while the little girl looked at him adoringly.

Gil made an announcement about how much money had been raised. Then he made something of a show of giving the money from the tickets to the cops for the police athletic league. The crowd applauded their approval of the charity and of Gil. I heard several comments about his patriotism and his stand for law and order.

When the sun disappeared behind the pines, Duane's buddies handed out the sparklers and helped the kids light them while the parents made sure they stayed on the grass, away from the pine needles. I marveled at the genuine joy on Duanc's face as he ran around with the kids waving the sparklers in the air.

Ashley came over and sat at the table with Garrett and me. "Look who's here." She nodded her head toward Dave Malone, who seemed to be inspecting the back of the building. "Malone. And I guess that's his wife, the one he was talking to on the phone that day, asking for more information. I don't know why Mom invited them."

The old quotation about keeping your friends close and your enemies closer came to mind. What were they doing looking at the back of the building? We watched them until they noticed us. Then Malone plastered that same phony smile on his face and led the woman over to us. Ashley got up and went into the café.

"Well, hello, Ryn as in Kathryn."

I tried not to grimace at the tired old joke. "Hello, Dave."

"This is my wife, Esther. Ryn and...Garrett, isn't it?"

Garrett stood up. "Yes, sir. Nice to meet you, Esther. Having a good time?"

"Oh, yes. Very nice," she said, her hooded eyes betraying her true feelings. "We'd better be going, Dave. We have a ways to go to get home. You know what the traffic's like."

"Where do you folks live?" Garrett asked.

"North of here. About halfway between here and Denver," she replied.

Malone touched his wife's arm. "We'll be heading out now. See you soon." They stopped to say something to Alma as they left.

Garrett watched them with a pensive look. "North of here," he mumbled almost to himself. "That would be upstream."

Alma came over and plopped down next to me. "Whew. I'm all in."

At the same time, Ashley hurried out the back door of the café and came to our table. Her eyes were downcast, and she sat fidgeting with her ring.

"What's wrong?" Alma asked.

"Nothing."

"It must be something. You look all upset."

"Mom. It's nothing. Give it a rest."

Alma got up from the table. "I'm going to start cleaning up." She walked away, clearly hurt by another painful mother/daughter exchange.

I gave Ashley a few minutes to compose herself, then said, "Where've you been?"

"I went to use the bathroom in the café." Her eyes remained on the table for a minute, then she looked up at me. "Do you think Sarge could be…"

"Could be what? A pothead? Yeah, I do." Garrett chuckled, but Ashley didn't appear amused.

"No. I mean the one who killed Heather."

"Why do you ask?"

She glanced at the back door. "I was coming out of

the bathroom just now, and he was there. Going into the men's room, I guess."

Garrett studied her closely. "Did he do anything?"

"No. He just said hello. But...I don't know. Maybe I imagined it."

"Go on."

"It was almost like he was waiting there for me. Something about it freaked me out." She got up quickly. "I'm going to help Mom."

We watched her walk away. Sarge? A killer? Aside from his marijuana habit, he seemed harmless. But didn't Madame Gauzie say something about him coming back from Vietnam with a drug problem? Could he also have PTSD? Post-combat stress was known to produce flash-backs and psychotic behavior, sometimes for decades. Could he have killed Heather in some kind of hallucination?

We chatted for a while, and I gazed at Hank, who was helping Gil clean the grill. "You know, Hank is known for his quick temper. I've seen it myself. Could he have killed that girl in anger over something?"

"But the scene indicates a methodical killer, not one who kills in a fit of rage."

I shook my head. "This is driving me crazy. I'm starting to suspect everyone. It's so unfair to these people."

Garrett put his arm around my shoulders. "Welcome to my world."

The festivities were winding down as the moon rose over the pines. People started drifting toward their cabins, after thanking Gil for another wonderful celebration. Zach was clearing the paper plates and cups into a large garbage bag. He chatted amiably with Alma and teased several of the kids by feigning to dump the trash on them. They squealed and giggled as he pretended to chase them.

"What do you know about Zach?" Garrett asked.

"Not much. Since I've been here, I've only talked to him once. His views on God are offensive, but otherwise, he seems benign. Alma's known him a long time. Ask her."

Madam Gauzie came over to say good night and thank Garrett for handling those ruffians, as she put it. "Gil and Hank and motorcycle gangs don't mix," she said confidentially, "what with Hank's wife going off with them and Gil's son."

Garrett looked up at her. "What about his son?"

"Well," she said, pulling her shawl around her shoulders, "I'm not one to gossip, but there are rumors about him being involved with the drug trade in Canada. But who knows if that's true? You can't believe everything you hear these days. Well, good night, you two."

CHAPTER 11

My vibrating cell phone worked its way into my dream when it went off next to my head. The open road I was cruising in my dream turned into a jarring bed of rocks that shook my old car until it fell in pieces around me on the blacktop. I reached for the phone, its display telling me, incredibly, that it was just after five a.m. "Hello," I whispered, clearing my throat to get the sleep gunk out.

The jarring voice of my editor exploded in my ear. "Kathryn?"

"Mr. Crenshaw. Good morning." I tried to sound as cheerful as possible, although I knew exactly why he was calling.

"Oh, I'm sorry. Did I wake you?" The sarcasm in his voice was unmistakable.

I raised myself up on one elbow. "Well, I—"

"Oh, I forgot you're a couple hours earlier there, aren't you? I've been here since six. You do know the files have to go to the printers tomorrow, right? They've given us an extra day because of the Fourth."

"Uh, yeah. That's nice of them."

"Nice, my ass!" he exploded. "Where the hell's your column? It was supposed to be in my inbox Friday."

I could hear him breathing heavily into the phone.

"To tell the truth, sir—"

"Let me guess. You haven't even started it."

"Well, I—"

"My God, girl, what's gotten into you? I give you that travel column, an expense account, flexibility to choose your own stories. What more can I do?"

I imagined his blood pressure monitor rocketing into the critical zone. "Nothing, sir. You've been more—"

"Are you sending me a column, or aren't you? 'Cause if not, you know what I have to do, don't you?" He didn't wait for an answer. "Use that nitwit Quigley's column in its place. That's what. And his writing has all the charm of a baboon with hiccups. Is that what you want to force me to do?"

"No, sir, I don't want—"

I could have sworn I heard his spittle landing on the receiver as he shouted into the phone. "Then send me the goddam column! Today! Got it?"

Before I could answer, he slammed the receiver down on his desk phone. I visualized him digging into his desk drawer for his Rolaids, and I actually felt guilty for letting him down. I lay back down and stared at the ceiling. How could I explain to him that my interest in Trout Fork as a travel destination was nil? That my concern was for the people here and the murder that had shaken them? That there was a certain detective whose steel blue eyes and quiet voice were invading my every thought? Jack padded up from the end of the bed and sat down by my pillow, his amber eyes staring at me reproachfully.

"Don't give me that look," I hissed at him.

He responded with one of the long, slow blinks that indicated he was being tolerant of my failures. *All right*, I determined, *if Crenshaw wants a column, he'll get a column*. Never mind that my mind was rebelling at the thought of appealing to fishing enthusiasts or describing nearby attractions, it had to be done.

I pulled my sweatshirt over my pajamas, took my laptop, and tiptoed out of the room. I glanced over at Ashley as I left, confident she was deep in the sleep of the typical teenager, and nothing short of a terrorist attack would disturb her. I settled myself on the living room sofa and opened the laptop, hoping Alma would be up soon to make coffee. But with caffeine or without it, I couldn't put it off any longer. Almost zombie-like, I started typing the trite phrases I had used before, trying to be brilliant when totally uninspired. Phrases like "Do you go for..." "Are you looking for..." and "Get away and refresh your spirit..." flowed through my fingers onto the page.

The column was finished in less than an hour and, although I wasn't proud of it, it would have to do. Then I remembered there was no Wi-Fi here and I couldn't just hit "Send" as I usually did. I saved the document and went back to the bedroom to get dressed. I would hunt down a Starbucks in Pineland Park and use their Wi-Fi to send the column. A double espresso wouldn't go amiss either.

I showered and dressed quickly, packed up my laptop, and started for the front door just as Alma emerged from her bedroom. I explained my mission and assured her I would be back as soon as possible for the breakfast shift at the café. She began to protest. Her motherly concern about my going out without my own breakfast was to be expected, but I was out the door before she could finish her sentence.

Driving along the road south with the burden of the deadline lifted, I was free to reminisce about the events of the previous day, and especially those of last evening. The memory of the way Garrett looked at me when he thought I didn't notice came back to me in a rush and made me feel uneasy. Where was this relationship headed? More specifically, where was I headed? The column was finished, meaning I had no legitimate reason to remain here. But I knew I couldn't leave. I was committed to finding Heather's killer. I cringed at the idea of explaining that to Crenshaw. He'd probably tell me to find a job writing for a crime magazine.

The top rim of the red sun was clearing the mountain range to the East, reminding me of the way I had watched it peek above the ocean's horizon during my early morning walks on the beach at South Hampton when I was young. I would sit on the beach before sunrise, my arms wrapped around my knees, and stare at the horizon, waiting for the exact moment the sun came up. I had read somewhere that there was an elusive magic involved with seeing the exact second the sun rose. I dared not blink for fear I would miss the enchanted moment. The sky would turn from dark gray to purple to light blue. Crimson and gold streaks would appear. Then suddenly the sun would pop up like a huge yellow beach ball held underwater. Gulls would soar overhead, screeching with the sheer joy of another morning, and I would sit mesmerized at the wonder of it all. I hoped I would never lose my delight at seeing the sunrise.

Sailing into town in search of a Starbucks, the first building I passed was the police station. I glanced at the parking lot, wondering if Garrett was there yet with the bleach bottles he had taken for fingerprinting. That the killer had thrown them in the dumpster after ending that poor girl's life was obvious. But who was he? Hopefully, those bottles would provide a clue.

My car almost guided itself to the green awning of the coffee shop at the first intersection. I dashed in, ordered a double espresso and a slice of coffee cake and wolfed them down while emailing my column to Crenshaw. As soon as I'd hit "Send," I logged off my email account before he could respond with a question about my next destination. The last thing I said in the email was I had no Wi-Fi and only spotty phone service where I was staying. Hopefully, that would keep him at bay for a few days.

I completed the twenty-mile trip back to Trout Fork in record time, slowing down a little as I passed Garrett's driveway. His gray pickup wasn't in front of his cabin. I pulled into Trout Fork, surprised to see his truck parked in front of Alma's. He couldn't have gotten the results of the fingerprinting already. What was he doing here? I parked next to his truck and peered into the front of the cab. The plastic bag with the four bottles in it was still on the seat. Why wasn't he taking those bottles to his lab?

The café was nearly empty. Garrett was seated at his usual table near the fireplace, sipping his coffee and reading the paper. He glanced up as I came in, and his smile was warm and genuine, but it disappeared when he saw the anger in my eyes. I went right to his table and plopped into a chair opposite him. I don't know if it was Crenshaw's call, the espresso, or the dash back from town, but I was wired, and I lit into him with no holds barred. "What are you doing here?" I hissed at him. "Why haven't you taken those bottles to the lab?"

His expression was one of hurt, only slightly concealed by annoyance. "Are you telling me how to do my job now? If you must know, I'm taking them to Denver. Their lab is more extensive, and besides, this is their case."

"But you said you were going to have your lab do it."

"I thought better of it. Like I said—"

"I know, I know. It's Denver's case. Convenient for you." I folded my arms and glared at him.

"What's that supposed to mean?"

"It means you don't want to get involved with this case any more than you want to get involved in any big case. Let's face it, Garrett. You left Denver to hide out in that small town police force. To do what? Give out parking tickets? You're wasting your talents here."

"That's hardly fair."

"No?"

"No. And while we're on the subject of hiding, what about you? Aren't you doing the same thing?"

I gave him one of Ashley's eye rolls. "I'm not hiding from anything."

"Then what do you call constantly going from one place to another? You have to keep moving, don't you? Doesn't matter where, as long as it's somewhere else. Just you and your cat. That way there's no danger of anything tying you down. No danger of becoming involved."

I wasn't about to let him see how much his diagnosis hurt me. "You're wrong. I'm staying here to find out who killed Heather. And I'm doing it because I *am* involved with the people here."

"Suppose you do find him. What then? You'll be off on your next adventure. What was it the poet said? 'Nothing behind me, everything ahead of me, as is ever so on the road.' That about it?"

Quoting Kerouac to me seemed an especially low blow. Once again, I had the sensation of being treated like a child, which I bitterly resented. I got up and pushed the chair in with a bang that drew the attention of the few customers seated nearby. "I have to get to work." I stormed into the kitchen and could feel my face flaming. I wasn't sure whether it was from disappointment that we wouldn't be working together to find Heather's killer or from the nagging feeling that he was right about my reasons for not staying too long in any one place.

❦

The café was busy enough through breakfast to keep me from dwelling on Garrett, and I did my best to avoid looking in his direction. When I did finally steal a glance at his table, he was gone. Ashley had been giving me inquiring looks which I studiously ignored. At around midmorning, I told Alma I was taking a break.

"Take off 'til noon," she said. "Ashley and I can handle it."

Grateful for the chance to clear my head, I strolled along the boardwalk, hoping the cool morning air would help clear the jumble of thoughts plaguing me. I sat on the bench in front of Gil's and leaned back, allowing the sun to warm my face. I watched Duane tinkering with his machine in the grassy area he and his friends were calling their temporary home. He saw me and waved, that ever-present expression of peace on his face. If there was ever a time I needed a little peace, this was it. I got up and headed toward him. He stood up as I approached, wiping his hands on a rag.

"Having a problem with your bike?"

"No. Just giving it a little tune-up." He turned the ignition switch, and the bike hummed to life.

I ran my hand along the black leather seats, the one in the back the higher of the two. I had seen so many women perched up on those seats riding behind their men. What must that be like? Cruising along in the open air, nothing between them and the sky. The sensation of freedom must be amazing.

"Ever ridden one of these?" Duane asked.

"No. Never."

He must have sensed the regret in my voice because he straddled the bike and said, "It's time you did. Hop on." He handed me a helmet.

I didn't need urging. I pulled the helmet over my head and settled myself onto the seat behind him.

He put the bike in gear and slowly guided it through the parking lot. Once on the road, the bike accelerated smoothly. The trees flashed by, the wind whipping my shirt and jeans. The feeling of freedom was overwhelming and thrilling. My only regret was that the helmet prevented me from feeling the wind in my hair.

Duane maneuvered the bike expertly, leaning it over as we moved through the twists and bends in the road. The sensation of falling over was unnerving at first, causing me to grab Duane to hold on, but leaning into the turns with the bike soon became second nature, and I let go and relaxed, propped comfortably against the leather backrest.

We wheeled north along the same road I had driven on my way into Trout Creek, but this time it was as though I wasn't merely seeing the scenery. I was part of it. The sensation was amazing, and I understood the attraction of the bikers' lifestyle and why men, and women like Heather, were drawn to it.

After about an hour, we returned to Trout Fork and pulled into the lot. We dismounted, and I handed him the helmet. "That was amazing. I had no idea." I ran my hand along the handlebars. "Are they hard to learn to drive?"

"Not at all. Lots of women ride their own motorcycles. All it takes is a little practice. Thinking about getting one?"

I had a fleeting impression of free-wheeling down the highway with Jack strapped in a basket in front of me wearing a little helmet and goggles. "You never know." I noticed Duane's friends loading up their bikes for what appeared to be their departure. "Are you guys leaving?"

"Yeah, there's a bike rally in Fort Collins starting tomorrow. We go every year."

"Maybe you'll see Digger and his buddies up there," I said.

He looked at me with a furrowed brow. "I doubt it. Those guys are the one-percenters. They don't hang with the rest of us."

"One-percenters?"

"Also known as outlaw gangs. They like to call themselves names that include Satan, Devils, Hell, Sin, Rebels, Pagans. It's the image they want to project. They're some bad dudes. Into all kinds of drug dealing, extortion, smuggling. It's how they support themselves."

"But why are they called one-percenters?"

"That comes from a quote by some guy from the National Motorcycle Association. He said once that ninety-nine percent of bikers are law-abiding citizens. The outlaw gangs take pride in being the other one percent."

I thought about Heather and her life with Digger's gang. "Where do the women fit in with those gangs?"

"It's not much of a life for them. They're often turned into slaves, sometimes prostitutes. A woman has to be pretty desperate to get in with one of them."

How desperate must Heather have been to get herself involved with Digger? And why did she leave him? Duane began loading his gear onto his bike.

"Will you be coming back this way?" I asked, suddenly sorry to see him leave.

"Maybe."

I thanked him for the ride, and he mounted his bike. His friends joined him, and the five of them roared off. As I headed back toward the café, I saw Garrett standing next to his truck watching me. What would he say if he could read my mind? That I was thinking of running away again?

I approached him, determined not to argue. "On your way to Denver?"

"Yeah. Where did you go?"

"Duane gave me a ride on his bike. It was fun."

"Motorcycles are dangerous. I hope you wore a helmet."

There was that irritating parental attitude of his again. "Yes, Daddy. I was a good girl."

His brow furrowed. "You know what they call those things in the emergency rooms? Donor-cycles. Those who ride them are perfect candidates for organ donation after they splatter their brains on the highway."

"Charming. I'll have to use that in my next column," I said, unable to control my sarcasm. I brushed past him and went into the café.

Ashley had been watching us out the window and gave me that raised-eyebrows look again. "Have you two had a fight?"

"Several, actually. He disapproves of my lifestyle."

"Oh. That's too bad." She seemed genuinely disappointed.

"The fairy tale romance thing is just that, you know. A fairy tale. Real relationships are a lot more complicated."

She swiped a cloth across the table. "At least you have a relationship. All I ever see around here are hairy bikers and old guys that smell like fish. I'll be glad when school starts, and I can see my friends. I'm actually looking forward to school again."

We cleaned the table together for a few moments then I said, "Ash, did Heather ever talk to you about Digger? About why she left the gang?"

"Never. We always thought he left her here and took off without her. Maybe he's lying about it being her idea."

"There have to be more clues in that journal. Keep reading. Be sure to take notes, especially of the code words and initials. I'm going back into town tomorrow to do some internet research. Maybe I can dig up something on Dave Malone."

"Good idea. I don't trust that dude."

CHAPTER 12

It was Jack's yowling that woke me up that night. He was standing next to my pillow, his eyes wide, his tail bushed out. I would have pushed him away as I usually did when he disturbed me in the middle of the night, but he had never before made that other-worldly sound of terror. I sniffed once and sat bolt upright. Choking black smoke had filled the room, causing Ashley to cough in her sleep. I pulled the window curtain aside, and my heart leaped into my throat. There was an eerie red glow on the hillside behind the cabin. Flames had consumed some of the pines and were working their way quickly up the hill toward us. Thick smoke was creeping from the trees to the cabin like sinister fingers of silent death.

"Ashley!" I screamed as I bundled Jack in my arms and dashed to her bed. "Wake up. Fire!"

She sat up and stared at me uncomprehendingly.

I grabbed her arm. "Get up! There's a fire behind the cabin."

Ashley jumped out of bed and began frantically searching for her cat. "Sasha! Where are you?"

"Look under the bed. Hurry!" The smoke was getting thicker, and it was becoming harder to breathe. Ashley bent down to find Sasha cowering in the corner. She called to her gently, not wanting to scare her.

"Just grab her," I shouted. "We have to wake your mom."

She reached under the bed and hauled Sasha out by her front legs. The terrified cat scratched her as Ashley held her to her chest.

"Here," I yelled as I tossed a towel to her. "Wrap her in this. Come on!"

I put Jack over my shoulder, grabbed my purse and laptop, and raced out of the bedroom.

Ashley started after me. "Wait!" She ran back to her bed to retrieve the two journals from under her pillow. We dashed across the living room and banged on Alma's door. I could hear her coughing and opened the door. She was crawling along the floor toward the door, avoiding the smoke hovering more than halfway down from the ceiling. "I'm coming," she gasped. "Where's Ashley?"

"I'm here, Mom. Hurry!"

Alma stood up, and the three of us raced for the front door. Outside, the whole scene was bathed in the angry red glow from the fire. Ashes were falling all around us like snowflakes. I looked back as we hurried along the path next to the café. The dry pine trees along the hillside behind the cabins were aflame, making popping noises as the sap within them boiled and burst through the bark. Flames hungrily devoured the dry pine needles that covered the ground a foot thick in some places.

In the parking lot, we saw Gil running toward us shouting, "Get in your cars! Head south. I called the fire department."

People were streaming down the hill from the cabins and dashing toward their cars. Zach raced by, his thick glasses reflecting the red glow. He jumped into this Ford and gunned it out of the parking lot without a backward glance. Alma and Ashley ran to their car and tossed

Sasha into the backseat. Jack remained over my shoulder, fairly calm, considering the circumstances, although I could feel his claws gripping me through my thin pajamas. The smoke was getting thicker, making it difficult to take a deep breath. Red embers swirled around us propelled by the fire-generated wind. Several of them landed on the dry pine needles and immediately began smoldering. Others landed on the roof of the building.

Alma stood next to her car looking around frantically. "Where's Madam Gauzie?" she shouted over the roar of the approaching flames. "Did you see her leave?"

"No! Her car's still here," Ashley yelled.

"Oh, my God! She'll die!"

We stood immobilized in fear, not knowing what to do, when Hank suddenly appeared around the other end of the building, running with, and half carrying, Madam Gauzie. He had a handkerchief clamped to her face as he propelled her toward her car. He urged her to get in, but she seemed nearly catatonic, mumbling to herself and clutching her flimsy nightgown to herself.

"She can't drive," I yelled to Hank. "I'll take her with me."

Hank dragged her to my car, and together we bundled her into the front seat of my Corolla. Jack jumped into the back to hide under some clothes I had left there. I tossed my purse and laptop in after him, ran around to the driver's side and got in. I tried to talk soothingly to the old woman, but I doubt she heard anything except the crackling and roaring of the fire as it came closer and closer. She stared at the flames and swirling embers, her eyes wide with terror, and began mumbling something I couldn't understand.

Gil and Hank jumped into Gil's SUV and took off. I floored the car out of the parking lot, the tires sending the gravel in all directions, following Gil south on the road to

Pineland Park with Alma close behind. I could hear the sirens of the fire engines wailing in the distance. A car's headlights approached, and I wondered who would be heading toward the fire instead of away from it. I slowed and put my hand out the window.

Garrett's gray pickup screeched to a halt next to me, the back end fishtailing across the lane. "Is everyone out?" he yelled.

"I think so."

"Go to my place. Here's the key." He handed it to me through the window. "I'll be back as soon as I can." The sirens were getting louder, and I could see the lights of the oncoming fire trucks and police cars. Garrett glanced at his rearview mirror and tromped on the gas, causing his tires to squeal.

I pulled off to the right to let the vehicles go by, their sirens screaming and red lights flashing.

Madam Gauzie clamped her hands to her ears, moaning in terror.

I reached over and patted her shoulder. "You're okay. It will all be fine." I wished I felt as confident as I sounded. What would we find in Trout Fork when we returned? Would there even be a Trout Fork to return to? Or would there be nothing but gray ashes and the blackened frames of all those destroyed homes and businesses standing stark and lonely? I felt a little sick at the thought that I could simply drive away to write another column in another destination, while the people of Trout Fork tried to pick up the pieces of what was left of their lives.

My heart was still pounding when I pulled into Garrett's driveway and parked in front of the cabin. Alma pulled in next to me, got out, and hurried to my car. She opened the door to begin helping Madam Gauzie.

The old woman looked around frantically. "Where are we?"

"We're at Garrett's house," Alma soothed. "We'll be safe here. Come with me."

She led her to the door where I stood fumbling with the key. Ashley followed with Sasha, still wrapped in the towel, her little black and white nose protruding from the folds. Jack was watching us through the windshield of my car, standing in the driver's seat with his paws on the steering wheel. He was the calmest of us all.

Once inside, I switched on the lights, led Madam Gauzie to the sofa, and sat her down. She was shivering in her thin nightgown, so I went back to the car and got my jacket to wrap around her. I carried Jack into the house and put him down. He joined Sasha who had hidden under a chair, and the two of them huddled together, staring at us with wide, fear-filled eyes.

Ashley sat on the sofa with Madam Gauzie, who still had that bewildered expression common to the elderly when they become disoriented.

Alma had apparently decided to take the situation in hand. "Ryn, see if you can find some clothes or blankets. I'm going to see if I can find us some coffee or tea." Then she went off to the kitchen, where I heard her rooting through the cabinets as I opened the door to Garrett's bedroom. The bedclothes were thrown aside as though he had gotten up quickly. The low hum from the police scanner on his night table told me that was how he knew about the fire.

I opened a few dresser drawers and found some sweats which I brought out to the living room, along with a blanket from the bed. Ashley, Alma, and I put on the sweats and wrapped the blanket around Madam Gauzie. Sitting in that room, with the smell of Garrett's aftershave on his sweatshirt, made me long for his strong, comforting presence. After a few minutes, Alma brought cups of steaming tea out to us, and the four of us sat there sipping it and staring into space, each of us still reeling from to-night's experience.

Ashley broke the silence. "I wonder if there will be anything left to go back to."

"Don't talk like that," her mother admonished. "The firemen will put it out."

"How did it start? That's what I'd like to know," I said. "It couldn't be lightning. There hasn't been a storm in weeks."

"It must have been caused by someone, either by accident or…"

Our eyes met, and I knew we were thinking the same thing. How could it have been an accident? Who would be in those trees in the middle of the night? There were no campgrounds up there. But the thought that the fire could have been intentionally set was too frightening to contemplate. And for what possible motive? It didn't make sense.

We sat quietly together while Madam Gauzie dozed off sitting up. Alma tucked the blanket more closely around her. The cats were still crouching together under the chair, so Ashley went to sit by them, stroking them and whispering endearments.

After several hours, we heard Garrett's truck pull up outside. He opened the door, bringing the smell of smoke into the room with him. "It's under control," he said wearily. "They stopped it before it reached the stores."

"Oh, thank God," Alma said. "Was anyone hurt?"

"No. Everyone got out safely. But two of the cabins were destroyed. Not yours, Alma. I don't know who lives in them."

I thought of Hank and Gil, and especially of Madam Gauzie, who was still asleep. Would they have homes to go back to?

"Hopefully it was two of the empty ones. I'll have to

call the insurance company in the morning," Alma said. "Do they have any idea how it started?"

"It's too early for that. The investigators will begin tomorrow. In the meantime, no one will be allowed back there for a while." He glanced at the four of us wearing his clothes. "Did you bring anything with you?"

"Just the cats," Ashley said. "We don't even have clothes. What are we going to do, Mom?"

Alma got up and began to gather up the teacups. "The first thing we'll do is go to your father's house. He'll be glad to put us up for a few days. We can take Madam Gauzie with us. Then we'll wait to hear from the fire department. They will contact us, won't they, Garrett?"

"Yes, ma'am. As soon as they're finished. I'll try to keep you updated on what they find out."

"You're a blessing." She turned to me. "Ryn, you're welcome to come and stay with us in Denver."

"Thanks, but I think I'll stay here." I saw Garrett's eyebrows raised slightly.

"I can get a motel in Pineland Park."

"You can pick up some clothes at Goodwill to tide you over until we can get back into the cabin," Alma said.

Garrett ran his hands through his hair. "I wish I had room for you all here, but I only have the two bedrooms."

"Nonsense, Garrett. You've done plenty already." Alma woke Madam Gauzie. "Come on, Madam G."

The old woman looked up at me and Garrett. "Where are we going?"

Alma helped her up and led her toward the door, and Ashley followed with Sasha.

"We're taking you to Denver," Alma said a little louder. "We're going to stay with Robert for a few days. You'll be safe there."

The old woman nodded but still seemed disoriented and confused.

Garrett and I stood at the door, waving to them as they drove off. We turned back into the room, and Garrett touched my shoulder. "There's no reason to go to a motel, you know. You and Jack are welcome here. I have everything you need. I see you already found some clothes."

I looked around at the warm, comfortable cabin, at Jack who was now sitting on the chair, and at Garrett's sincere eyes, and I realized there was no point in resisting. "That's very kind of you."

"Nonsense. Let me show you to your room."

I gathered Jack in my arms and followed Garrett to the second bedroom, which was small but nicely furnished with a double bed, night table, and lamp. He must have seen how tired I was because he closed the door and left me alone. I lay down on the bed and pulled the comforter over me. It didn't take long for me to fall into a deep sleep with Jack cuddled next to me.

෧ඏ෧

The two days I spent at Garrett's were a delightful experience. I'd had roommates before, but never one of the opposite sex. After tiptoeing around each other for a while with exaggerated politeness, we settled into a surprisingly comfortable existence. Garrett went to work while I stayed in the cabin most of the day, lounging around in his oversized clothes and using his Wi-Fi to surf the internet for information on motorcycle gangs and anything I could find about Dave Malone, which wasn't much. He was a real estate developer, apparently not a very successful one.

I took several walks through the wooded area around

his house, which was peaceful and lovely, although I could still smell smoke from the fire. At night, we enjoyed Garrett's cooking and listened to his eclectic music collection while Jack sat purring between us on the sofa. We spent hours talking, never once mentioning murder, the fire, or anything else unpleasant. It was like an idyllic vacation on a remote island.

The third day, Sunday, we were having breakfast when Alma called me to say she had been given permission to return to Trout Fork and was at the cabin. If possible, she would be opening the café the next day. "Did you find a decent motel?" she asked.

"I've been very comfortable," I said, avoiding the question. "I'll be there as soon as I can."

After I hung up, I stood there a moment and suddenly felt desolate at having to leave.

Garrett gave me a sideways glance. "Did you tell her you're staying with me?"

"I don't want rumors getting started. I'd better get back there. She wants to open the café tomorrow, and she'll need help." I went to the bedroom to pack up my laptop. I looked around and felt like I did the first time I left home. "Stop it," I whispered to myself. "Just stop it."

When I came back, Garrett was on the sofa with Jack, who had become quite attached to this new tall person in his life.

"I can't thank you enough for letting us stay, Garrett. And for the clothes and the meals. It's been a lifesaver."

He stood up and handed Jack to me. "I've enjoyed having the company. It can get lonely out here."

Jack and I got into the car while Garrett stood on the doorstep, his coffee cup in hand. As I drove away, I glanced in the rearview mirror to see Jack standing with his paws on the back of the seat watching out the back window. "It was temporary, Jack."

He came into the front and sat on the console between the seats, staring at me.

I stroked his head. "Just temporary." *Like everything in my life*, I thought. *Temporary.*

As I approached Trout Fork, I saw the blackened stumps of some of the trees on the hillside behind the cabins. Several cars were already in the parking lot, Alma's among them. The two burnt-out cabins to the north of the café sat stark and desolate, their blown-out windows staring like sightless eyes from their black frames. I carried Jack and my laptop around the corner of the café and breathed a prayer of thanks that Alma's cabin was still intact.

Ashley burst out the front door and hurried to me. "I'm so glad to see you. How are you? Where did you stay? How is Jack doing? Was he scared?" She took my laptop from me without waiting for answers. "Sasha will be so glad to see Jack. Mom is over at the café with the insurance guy. She wants to open tomorrow. Wait 'til you see the back of the cabin. The fire came so close."

I smiled at her exuberance and sense of adventure. "Let me change out of these clothes, and we'll go over and help."

"Have you been wearing Garrett's clothes all this time?"

"Yeah. They're quite comfortable, actually."

The smell of ashes and burnt wood was still quite strong, which caused Jack to wrinkle his nose and sneeze. Sasha stood on Ashley's bed and meowed as we came into the room. I put Jack down next to her, and the two of them touched noses. Then Sasha began to lick Jack's head.

Ashley opened the window. "Check this out."

The entire area behind the cabin was blackened, the trees and bushes reduced to forlorn-looking sticks. The fire had come right up to the cabin's back wall. The ground behind the cabin was soggy, puddles of black water everywhere. The firemen must have made a stand at the cabins.

"Let's keep the window closed until that smell goes away." I sat on the bed. "Did you hear anything about how it started?"

"Mom talked to the fire chief. He said it was definitely arson. They found some kind of stuff that was used to start it…oh, what's the word?"

"Accelerant?"

"Yeah, that's it. Who would do that?"

"What about the two cabins that burned? Was anyone in them?"

"No. Both were empty."

I shook my head. "How is Madam Gauzie holding up? Did you get her home okay?"

Ashley chuckled. "She's back to normal. She's already at the café helping Mom. We better get over there."

I reluctantly shed Garrett's sweats, inhaling the scent of his aftershave one last time. I changed quickly, and we entered the back door of the café. We passed Madame Gauzie, who was in the kitchen cleaning everything to try to get rid of the smell of smoke. "Oh, Ryn. There you are. Did you find a place to stay?"

"Yes, ma'am. I did."

"Tsk, tsk. Isn't this a mess?" she said when she saw us looking around the kitchen. But she was clearly enjoying her newfound responsibility.

We left her humming to herself and went into the dining room.

Even though the café was closed, the locals had gathered on the patio, all chattering about their experiences. Alma sat at a table in the dining room with a man in a suit who was holding a fistful of papers. She smiled when she saw me. "Oh, Ryn, I'm glad you're here. Make some coffee for those folks. If we can't feed them, we can still give them a cup of coffee. On the house."

I fired up the coffee machines. Once it was brewed, we took a tray of cups and the coffeepots to the patio. Hank and Gil greeted us, offering to help to pass the cups around.

The entire group exhibited that special camaraderie common to those who have shared a tragedy.

Zach was sitting with a couple of the local fishermen. He looked up at us as we passed. As our gazes met, he nodded slightly.

"Oh, no," Ashley said. "Look who's here." She nodded toward Dave Malone who came around the corner of the patio wearing a gaudy Hawaiian shirt and that pasted-on smile.

He came right to us and asked for Alma.

"She's with the insurance agent," I told him. "Coffee?"

"Sure, Ryn as in—" He must have seen my sour expression and stopped in mid-sentence. "Sure. Thanks." He took the coffee from me. "Insurance agent, huh? I wonder how much her loss will be."

"I wouldn't know."

"I can tell you this. There won't be another offer for this place coming anytime soon. See if you can talk some sense into her, will you?"

I ignored him and returned to the kitchen for another pot of coffee. I stood for a moment, watching Malone through the window.

"Anything wrong?" Ashley asked.

"Just thinking. When was the last time Malone was here? Other than the barbeque?"

"The day they found the dead fish."

"What about the time before that?"

"I'm not sure."

"It was the day they found Heather's body. Every time something goes wrong in Trout Fork, he shows up with another offer to buy the place."

"He's a grungy little opportunist."

"Maybe he's more than an opportunist. Maybe he's creating his own opportunities."

Ashley regarded him through the window. "You mean you think he started the fire and killed the fish? Then that would mean—"

"Exactly. Maybe it was Malone who killed Heather."

CHAPTER 13

It took hours of cleaning and disinfecting to get the café ready to open. The windows were filthy with smoke, the patio was covered in ash, and the acrid smell seemed to linger in the air, no matter how hard we tried to clear it. Madam Gauzie was a great help, and the four of us worked until late into the night. By the time we staggered back to the cabin, Alma was confident the café was ready to open for breakfast the next day. She tottered wearily off to bed.

I came out of the shower to find Ashley sound sleep with Sasha by her side and Heather's journal open next to her. Glancing at the page she was reading, I saw a few entries in Heather's cryptic style. The one for June eighth, a week after she arrived, read:

al and ash are good peeple. there putting me up at there place. they want to know why i stayed here when d left. told them he dumped me. they dont need to know the truth. talked to gs about gj today. shoulda seen his face!

Ashley had underlined the last two sentences. Here were references to G.S. and G.J. again. Whoever G.S. was, what Heather told him about G.J. came as a shock to him. If only we could identify G.S, we could very well have the killer. Whoever he was, what could she have told him? Someone in Trout Fork had a secret he wanted kept quiet, but badly enough to kill?

I gently removed the journal and covered Ashley with her blanket. I took the book to my bed and thumbed through it. It appeared to be a one-year journal going back to the previous summer. Ashley had her work cut out for her trying to decipher the text, but she seemed to be enjoying the task. Hopefully, she would find something we could take to Garrett.

I sat back and stroked Jack's silky fur as he lay contentedly by my side. *If only I could be like this cat*, I thought. He was content to be wherever he was, while I felt like I was always being driven on to somewhere else. What was the secret to being contented in any circumstance? Jack seemed to be comfortable and relaxed anywhere, as long as he was with me. Would I ever find that? I chided myself for thinking there might be someone out there who could make me feel at home anywhere, as long as we were together. I had seen too many ideal romances turn into ugly marriages, too many bad marriages in my family, and too much disappointment among those who believed in happily ever after. I turned over. I was relieved I would be leaving here soon. If only I could find Heather's killer in the few days I had left.

೧೨೯

The café was busy the next day, but it was mostly the locals. There was plenty of tourist traffic going past the stores as the news of the fire got around, bringing the sightseers by for a look.

But only a few of them stopped. Madam Gauzie sat with Hank and Gil eating breakfast, and as I refilled their coffee cups, I overheard her holding forth her opinions on the recent tragedies. "I'm telling you, someone wants to kill us all. After killing that girl and we're all still here? Burn us in our beds, that's what he tried to do. He wants us out and will stop at nothing."

"But why?" Gil asked. "What does he stand to gain? Suppose he did burn down the whole building and all the surrounding land. What then? What's the point?"

Hank's eyes blazed. He spoke with his mouth full, bits of egg landing on the table. "I'm telling you, it was that Digger and his gang. They were pissed at us for running them off at the barbeque, so they came back to get even. Remember how he tossed his cigarette butt into the pine needles? You told him it was a fire hazard, Gil. That's when he got the idea to come back and start the fire."

"You may be right. Damn biker scum. Can't trust any of them."

I wiped up some coffee I had spilled on their table. "Wait a minute. What about Duane and his friends? They helped out at the barbeque and stood up to Digger's gang. They even brought presents for the kids. So they're not all bad."

"No, just most of them," Hank growled.

I walked back to the counter with the coffeepot, and Madam Gauzie followed me. "Don't mind those two, honey. They've got it in for the biker crowd. I guess you know about Hank's wife going off with one of them and sending divorce papers back to him. He's never gotten over it. Blames every biker he sees when it's himself he should be blaming, the way he treated her. I don't think he can handle the guilt, so he pours out his hate on the bikers."

I started wiping the counter. "I can see that, but why is Gil so dead set against them?"

She leaned against the counter, gazing at Gil. "Gil is a man without a country. At least that's how he sees himself. Ex-military, true blue American type. He sees the younger generation as ruining the country he once defended with his life. The motorcycle crowd lives outside the rule of law, and he hates that. Don't get me wrong. Gil is a good man. But there's something about those people that makes him see red. And when his only son rode off and joined them? Well, that about sent him over the edge."

"Whatever happened to the son?"

"Nobody knows. Gil never heard from him again. At least as far as I know. Sad really, what kids can do to their parents."

I thought about Ashley and the hurt she thoughtlessly caused Alma at times. I had no doubt that was part of Alma's reasons for taking Heather in. I also had a brief memory of Mother asking me why I couldn't be like my sister, reminding me once again of my failure to live up to her standards. Did parents ever wonder if they were a disappointment to their kids? "Do you know anything about Dave Malone? Has he been coming around long?"

"He first showed up last summer. All I know about him is he's always trying to get Alma to sell the Trout Fork property to him. Although what he wants with it, I couldn't tell you. Well, honey, I'd better be off to my own store."

I watched her go, her necklaces jangling and her heels tapping on the floor. She passed Zach on his way into the café, and he greeted her with exaggerated courtesy. Then he sat at his usual table, his eyes boring into mine before he looked away.

I made my way to his table. "Morning, Zach. How are things at your cabin? Did you lose anything?"

He gave me that saintly smile. "No, the Lord was

good to me. Good to all of us. Even to those who don't deserve it. But you don't want to hear about God, do you? Are you still mad at him?"

I ignored the question. "What can I get for you today?"

"The usual. Pancakes and bacon. With one of Alma's cinnamon rolls." He spoke quietly, but his eyes were averted from mine.

I left his table feeling irritated at him as I hung his order on the wheel. Was he right that I was mad at God? Who was responsible for all the death and misery I was seeing everywhere? If it was God, then, of course, I'd be mad at him. If it wasn't, then why didn't he stop it? It couldn't all be our fault, could it? Can every rotten thing in life really be traced back to something someone did or didn't do, as Zach had said? If that was the case, what did those fish do to deserve being killed by ammonia? I shook my head. The longer I thought about it, the less I understood it, and the more the idea of flying down the road on a motorcycle appealed to me.

The Kerouac quote came back to me, "Nothing behind me, everything ahead of me, as is ever so on the road." But how do we leave everything behind us when our memories plague us constantly?

"Everything okay, Ryn?" Alma asked as I stood next to the ordering window staring into space.

"What? Oh, yeah. Sorry. Alma, could I take off for a couple of hours? I want to go into Pineland Park and do some internet research."

"Sure, honey. Why don't you go now and be back for lunch? Things are pretty quiet. Ashley can handle it."

I watched Ashley deftly taking orders, pouring coffee refills, and chatting with the customers. "I hope you know what a gem you have in Ashley," I said.

"Of course I do."

"I think she'd like to hear it from you now and then. I know I'd like to hear it from my mother."

She smiled her sad little half-smile. "It's not easy being a mother. You girls have no idea."

ᥱↄᥱↄ

Driving into Pineland Park, I hoped I could find enough information about Dave Malone to get Garrett interested in doing a criminal background check on him. I knew if I suggested it, Garrett would get huffy with me and accuse me of trying to do his job for him. One had to tread lightly around the male ego.

I settled into a corner booth at the same Starbucks I had visited days before. Just as I expected, when I brought up my email account, there was a message from Crenshaw asking about my next destination. "I hope wherever you will be going, it will be more inspiring than the one you're in now. The column you sent me was less than your best."

Normally, I would bristle at journalistic criticism, but I knew he had a point. The column was the last thing on my mind right now. I was dedicated to finding Heather's killer, so he and the column would have to wait.

I pulled up a couple of websites that might lead me to information about Dave Malone. Unfortunately, that name was all too common, but when I searched with "Denver" and "real estate," I found his profile, along with his picture. I couldn't mistake that phony smile and dead eyes. Nothing in his profile or the website of his real estate agency gave me a clue as to his motive for wanting to buy Trout Fork. One of the sites linked him to his wife, Esther, and her profile told me she worked for CDOT, the Colorado Department of Transportation. I remembered Ashley overhearing him on the phone asking Esther for more information and being agitated about it. Could she be the link I was looking for?

I searched CDOT's website, and after wading through numerous pages of governmental gobbledygook, I landed on the Programs and Projects page where there was a map of every planned road project in the state. I zeroed in on the Trout Fork area and bingo. There it was. A four-lane road was planned connecting Denver with the ski resorts. The rationale for the plan was explained in detail. The interstate linking the metropolitan area to the ski areas was becoming overcrowded in the winter months, so a new highway that followed the river south through Trout Fork and then turned west was the planned solution.

I thought about Malone's passion to buy the whole area around Trout Fork. Obviously, he knew about the road from his wife, even before it was announced to the general public. But what did he have in mind? I ordered another latte and went back to researching him. After two hours, I found that he had once been a general partner in a real estate consortium in Pennsylvania. A new road from Philadelphia to the ski resorts in the Pocono Mountains had been built, and Malone's consortium bought up thousands of acres of farmland in the area. Then they developed a resort complex along the new road, complete with million-dollar homes, two golf courses, townhouses, clubhouses, and restaurants.

I sat back in my chair. So that was it. The similarities were too glaring to be a coincidence. Malone wanted to buy the land around Trout Fork to develop it like he did in Pennsylvania. Trout Fork was halfway between Denver and the ski areas in an idyllic setting, perfect for a bedroom community away, but not too far away, from the crowded city, with easy access to Aspen, Vail, and the other ski resorts. All he had to do was get title to the land, develop it, and make a fortune. And to get that title, he would have to convince Alma to sell. What better way to do that than to give Trout Fork a bad reputation and drive away business? Dead fish in the creek and a fire would certainly discourage people from going there. It already had. What about a murder? Was Malone that desperate? Desperate enough to kill a nobody like Heather? People had killed for money before and for far less money than was involved here.

I packed up my laptop and the several pages of notes I had taken and headed for the police station, hoping Garrett was there and in a receptive mood. His gray pickup was in the parking lot. I pulled up next to it, took my notes, and went in.

The middle-aged desk sergeant sitting by the door looked up at me wearily. "What can I do for you, miss?" He spoke in a voice that told me he had seen and heard it all.

"I'd like to see Detective Easterbrook. Please."

"Is he expecting you?"

"No, but—"

"Name?"

"Kathryn Lowell."

"Wait here." He hauled his bulk out of the chair, pulled his belt up over his ample stomach, and headed to a back office. The standard joke about cops and donuts came to mind, and I stifled a snicker.

He returned in a minute with Garrett, who smiled at me. "Ryn. Nice to see you. Come in." Garrett held open the gate for me, and I caught a whiff of his familiar aftershave as I passed him.

Damn him. Why does he have to be so attractive?

He led me into his tiny office, a bleak, sparsely-furnished space with none of the homey touches I would have expected.

"Charming," I said, looking at the bare walls and curtain-less window.

"I don't live here. All I do here is work." He motioned me to the chair in front of his desk and sat in his chair. "To what do I owe the pleasure?"

I spread my notes on his desk and began describing Malone's past dealings with real estate development and the similarities between the Pennsylvania project and the Trout Fork area.

When I told him about Malone's wife working for CDOT, his eyebrows raised, but only slightly. "That doesn't prove anything, but there could be a connection, at least as far as motive is—" He glanced up, his eyes focusing on the door behind me. "Yes, Captain?"

I turned to see a tall, impeccably-dressed black man with a clipped moustache standing in the doorway. "Am I interrupting, Detective?"

Garrett stood up. "No, sir. This is a friend who stopped in to take me to lunch. Captain Williams, this is Kathryn Lowell."

The man gave a slight bow. "Miss Lowell. Nice to meet you." He looked back to Garrett. "Come and see me when you get back from lunch."

"Yes, sir." Garrett came around the desk and took my elbow. I had barely enough time to gather up my notes before he ushered me out of the station to his truck. "Get in."

"I didn't know I was taking you to lunch," I teased.

"Sorry about that. He's a stickler for not getting involved in cases out of our jurisdiction. I've already taken a chance using work time to do background checks on the Trout Fork crowd."

"So you *have* been investigating," I said, somewhat surprised.

He flashed that boyish grin at me. "Of course. I can't have you thinking badly of me."

I wondered if he could do anything to make me think badly of him and decided it probably wasn't possible. "What have you found?"

"Let's find a place to eat. Then I'll tell you."

I felt guilty about leaving Alma and Ashley to handle the lunch rush at the café by themselves, but this was too important. Besides, I hadn't been alone with Garrett since I stayed with him after the fire, and I missed his company. We settled into a corner booth in a small Mexican restaurant and ordered a fajita plate for two.

Garrett took out his cell phone and scrolled through his notes. "I did checks on some of the residents. Hank and Gil have more in common than owning Trout Fork stores. They seem to have a shared hatred of all things biker related. They were arrested a couple of years back for brawling with some of the outlaw gang members in a bar here in Pineland Park. Hank and Gil managed to put two of them in the hospital with stab wounds."

"Stab wounds? What were they fighting about?"

"All it said was the argument was over a woman. It didn't say who the woman was or why they were fighting. But then again, those gangs aren't usually all that cooperative with the police. When it comes to cops, they have a code of silence the mafia would envy."

I thought about Heather, her connection with the bikers, and her death from a single stab wound. "What happened to Gil and Hank?"

"They got a good lawyer who convinced the judge it was self-defense, which it may very well have been. The two victims were out of the hospital by then, and the gang didn't stick around to testify, so the charges were dropped." He scrolled through his notes again. "Did you know Gil has a son?"

"Yeah. Was he in the fight?"

"Not that I know of, but it's possible he has connections with that gang Hank and Gil got in the row with. All I know for sure is the gang headed for Canada after that. I have a request in with the RCMP for info on them and on Gil's son. If he has a record up there, they'll tell me. But it could take a few days."

It seemed a little unnerving that the two men were being investigated as possible suspects in a murder. Visions of Gil treating his neighbors to a barbeque and Hank rushing Madam Gauzie out of harm's way during the fire came to mind. "I just don't believe they had anything to do with Heather's death. Do you?"

Garrett cleared his throat and seemed reluctant to speak. "I've thought of one possibility. We know how they feel about bikers. Maybe they wanted to get her to leave Trout Fork. Maybe they only wanted to rough her up a bit, but things got out of hand. We know they used knives in that fight at the bar. According to Madam Gauzie's interview, she saw Heather leaving Gil's store the evening she disappeared. Maybe they followed her to the trail."

"But what about the bleach? And the rope marks?"

"Maybe they killed her in back of the stores, dragged her to the trail, then went back and got the bleach to clean off any prints and DNA. That could also be why they got rid of her clothes."

"You're forgetting one thing. The piercings. Why take the time to remove all her studs and piercings?"

He shrugged. "That's the one thing that doesn't fit. But I've known killers to do all kinds of inexplicable things, especially when they're in a panic."

The waitress brought the sizzling fajitas to the table, and we dug in.

"I don't care," I said, chewing a mouthful. "My

money's still on Malone. I'll bet he made millions on that deal in Pennsylvania. People will do anything for that kind of money." I was getting excited the more I talked about him. "And remember when his wife said they lived north of here? Isn't that where the fish were poisoned? Somewhere upstream?"

Garrett watched me while he ate. Then he set down his fork. "Okay."

"Okay, what?"

His deep blue eyes gazed at me with unmistakable affection. "Okay, you've convinced me. I'll look into Malone. If he's done anything shady or if he has a record, I'll find out. Now, can we talk about something else?"

I could have kissed him. "Anything you say, Detective."

We ate in silence for a while, then he said, "Why don't we talk about what's going to happen now that you've finished your column? How do I convince you to stay here?"

He caught me off guard with that one. I wanted to ask him how long he wanted me to stay, but I was afraid of the answer. I felt drawn to the idea of staying near him and, at the same time, wary of it. "I know I want to stay until Heather's killer is found," I said evasively. "After that, I really don't know. For right now, I think I should get back to the café. Alma will be wondering what happened to her waitress."

"Maybe we could continue this discussion over dinner tonight. My place?"

"Sure. I'll come over as soon as I'm finished with the dinner rush. About eight?"

❧❧❧

As it turned out, Garrett and I settled nothing that

night regarding the future. Fortunately, he never mentioned it, and I wasn't about to bring it up. Maybe he decided that pressuring me about it was a bad strategy. That made the evening of wine, music, and good food especially pleasant and nonthreatening.

Once back at Alma's, I lay awake reliving my evening with Garrett. I thought through numerous possibilities for the future in a relationship with him, each one scarier than the last. I finally decided that leaving Trout Fork was the only really safe plan, and I fell asleep listening to the wind in the pines while Jack lay by my side, purring.

CHAPTER 14

Waking groggily after only a few hours of sleep, I opened one eye to find Ashley hovering over me with a grin. "Hey. Late night?"

I sat up. My head was pounding from the wine, and my tongue felt like it was coated with something the consistency of guano. "What time is it?"

"Almost seven. Mom sent me to find you. Are you okay?"

Poor Alma. First, I ditch the lunch shift yesterday, then I dash out right after dinner, and now I miss the breakfast shift. I was beginning to feel like a slug. "Yeah, I'm fine. I'll be over in a few minutes."

"Better hurry. You don't want to miss this."

"Miss what?"

She plopped down next to me on the bed, one long leg folded under her. Jack rubbed on her hand as she stroked him. "The Rev's parents are in town. They're over there now eating breakfast with him. I gotta tell you. They're even creepier than he is."

"Oh?" I squinted against the morning sunlight streaming in the window. I'd never thought of Zach as particularly creepy, just a bit odd.

"I gotta get back," she said, getting up. She stopped

at the door and turned to me. "Ryn. Do we need to put up a notice? I mean, for a new waitress? Are you leaving soon?"

It seemed I was getting that question from more than one person lately. "I have no plans to leave. At least not for a while."

"Good. I'd hate to have to break in another roomie."

I stumbled into the shower and turned on the hot water, nearly falling asleep under its soothing massage. *This is ridiculous*, I thought, and turned the cold water on full blast. I gasped as the shock woke me out of my stupor. I stepped out of the shower, tingling all over, at least partially ready to meet the day. Jack had disappeared into the kitchen, where I found him with Sasha at the bowls that Alma must have filled. Thank God for her mothering instincts. No creature under her roof would ever go hungry. If only Ashley could see through her hormonal teenage haze, she might begin to appreciate her mother.

I slipped in the back door of the café to find Alma standing over the grill attending to fried eggs, sausages, bacon, and pancakes. She turned each one over and then flipped them expertly onto the waiting plates. From the number of items on the grill, I knew the dining room must be full. "I'm so sorry I'm late, Alma," I said.

Her face was red from the heat of the grill, and she pulled up the end of her apron to wipe her sweaty forehead. "It's all right, dear. But I'll have to talk to Garrett about keeping you out so late," she teased.

"It won't happen again. I promise." It seemed I was apologizing to a lot of people lately for not doing what I had promised, and I didn't like the feeling. I grabbed a ticket off the wheel, read it, and started loading three of the plates on a tray. "I'll take these out. Where do they go?"

"Table four."

I pushed open the swinging door to the dining room with my hip and carried the tray toward table four where Zach was sitting with an older couple. I set the tray down on a nearby table and picked up two of the plates. "Morning, Zach. Here's your usual. Pancakes and bacon. Who gets the garden omelet?"

The older man said, "That would be mine, young lady." He sat up ramrod straight. He had iron gray hair with eyes to match, the kind of eyes that bore into you, seeking every secret thought or longing you ever dared to entertain. "My wife has the scrambled eggs."

A frail, birdlike woman gave me a small apologetic smile from behind glasses nearly as thick as Zach's. She sat with her hands folded in her lap and stared at her husband tentatively when I put the plate down.

The man bowed his head piously and said a prayer of thanksgiving. Then he looked at his wife. "Well, go on, Margaret. Before it gets cold."

She took her fork and began to pick at the eggs.

"Are these your parents, Zach?"

Rev sat hunched over his plate, his arms wrapped around himself, not touching his breakfast. "Yes." He cleared his throat. "Pastor and Mrs. Wayland, this is Ryn...I'm sorry. I don't know your last name."

"Lowell. Ryn Lowell." I held out my hand to the father.

He eyed it disdainfully for a moment then carefully folded his napkin and stood to shake my hand. His grip was firm, but his hand felt like an ice block.

"Ryn is a writer," Zach said. "For a New York magazine."

Pastor Wayland sniffed as he sat down. "New York. We're from Georgia." His Southern accent was very slight, as though he had worked hard to lose it. "Zachary, you're not eating. Is there anything wrong?"

Zach shook his head and reached for the syrup.

"I see you're still eating unhealthy food, Zachary. It's no wonder you look so pale. Wouldn't you think," his father said to no one in particular, "that someone who majored in chemistry in college would have a better idea of nutrition? Even if he couldn't manage to graduate."

Zach looked like he'd been struck in the face. His mother kept her eyes on her plate and said nothing. When she did steal a glimpse at her son, I detected pity behind those thick lenses.

I could see it was time to leave these people to themselves. "Enjoy your breakfast. Let me know if I can get anything else for you."

When I came back later to clear their plates, the father surveyed me with a critical eye. "Do you attend a church, Miss Lowell? Perhaps the same one as my son?" Zach stammered something unintelligible, but his father interrupted. "Let her speak, Zachary."

The man's steely gaze rested on me, and I felt like a truant child in the principal's office, ashamed and intimidated. Then I got angry at myself for those feelings.

"No. I don't attend any church. I've been feuding with God lately. I doubt he would want to see me in church."

He wiped his lips meticulously with his napkin and eyed me doubtfully. "It's rather pointless being mad at God, wouldn't you say?" I ignored the question. "He holds all the cards," he said condescendingly.

I loaded the empty dishes on my tray. "Maybe I don't like the way he deals them. Seems like a stacked deck to me." I continued clearing the table, refusing to look at him.

"He deals them according to our merit. What we reap, we sow."

Now I knew where Zach got his ideas. I left the

check on the table and said, "Pay at the counter."

As I walked away, I could hear the man asking his son if he had "made any headway with these people." Who the people were, I could guess. But what was the headway he was trying to make? Whatever it was, no doubt he had failed with me.

ↂↄↂↄ

About mid-morning, I heard the roar of motorcycles in the parking lot. The café had cleared out, and Ashley and I sat with Alma in the dining room. Alma rubbed her feet while Ashley shared texts with some of her friends in Pineland Park.

My eyes were drawn to the parking lot where Duane and his friends were dismounting and unpacking their gear. I hoped that meant they were staying for a while.

"I'm going to take a walk, Alma. I won't be long."

She nodded wearily and continued rubbing her sore feet. I left the café and crossed the parking lot to Duane, who grinned and waved as I approached.

He stood by his bike gazing at the burned-out hillside. "We heard you had a fire, so we came back to see if everyone was okay."

"No one was injured, but those two cabins burned down."

"What a shame. All those beautiful trees."

"How was the rally?" I asked.

"Great. We met some of the brothers we haven't seen in a while."

I wondered why the bikers referred to each other as brothers. Clearly, there was a unique bond among those who spent their lives on the road.

My journalist's nosiness got the best of me. "Duane, tell me to mind my own business, but how do you guys make a living? I mean, traveling all the time like you do."

He took off his denim vest and draped it over the seat. "We don't travel all year round, only in the summer when we're all off. We're teachers. At the same college." He nodded to his buddies who were standing by their bikes laughing and talking. "Alan there is a professor of economics. Geoff is in the English department. So is Ron. Morrie teaches math."

If it was anyone but Duane, I would have thought he was pulling my leg.

He must have seen the shock on my face and laughed. "Don't feel bad. Everyone has that reaction."

"What about you? What do you teach?"

"Philosophy and World Religions."

I shook my head. I could add these guys and their stories to my novel, but it would probably seem too far-fetched to be believed. "You teach for eight months and ride the bikes the rest of the time. Aren't any of you married? Or have families?"

"Two of the guys have very understanding wives. But they don't spend the whole summer on the road, just a couple of weeks. Morrie is divorced. Geoff and I are single."

"I envy you." I ran my hand along the black leather seat. "The freedom, the ability to pick up and go whenever and wherever." The desire to be back on that bike welled up in me. "Would you..."

"Take you for another ride?"

I nodded, feeling like a child asking for a Christmas present.

"I'll do better than that. I'll teach you to drive. Get in front."

He didn't have to offer twice. I took the extra helmet he handed me and strapped it on. Then I straddled the bike and grasped the handlebars, my heart pounding with excitement. He sat behind me and reached around me, placing his hands over mine. He gave me a brief explanation of the throttle, the clutch, the brakes, and the gearshift operated with the foot. Then he showed me how to turn on the ignition, and the engine purred. We rode around the parking lot while he told me what to do and, in minutes, I was driving it myself. The gears were a little tricky to master at first, but Duane assured me I was doing fine.

"Okay," he said, "head south on the road."

The bike accelerated smoothly out of the lot, and soon we were cruising toward Pineland Park. Riding on the back of one of these was thrilling, but it was nothing compared to driving it. We flew through the bends in the road, leaning into them and accelerating out of them as he instructed me.

We drove for several miles, then as we approached a rest area turnout, he said, "Pull in here where you can practice stopping and starting." The area was empty except for a picnic table and signs for the trailhead. I stopped the bike, putting my feet down to steady it. Then he got off and had me start again, circling the parking lot alone, gearing up and down until I could do it smoothly.

"You're a natural," he said as I stopped in front of him.

"I had no idea it was this easy."

"Park it."

I pulled up next to the sign, turned off the engine and put the kickstand down. The silence was broken only by birdsong from the treetops.

"Where does that trail go?" he asked.

"To the creek, I guess. I've never been here before."

"Let's take a walk. I need to stretch my legs."

We strolled along the trail for several minutes until we came to the Trout Creek. The sun filtering through the pines cast shimmering light on the clear water. A furry beaver slid off the bank and swam upstream with an aspen branch in its mouth. It slapped the water with its broad tail when it saw us. A speckled trout leaped out of the water, almost daring the birds in the trees to try their fishing skills.

"Let the waters abound with an abundance of living creatures," Duane said softly to himself. I looked at him, and he smiled. "It's from Genesis."

Oh, no, I thought. *Not another one*. "You don't strike me as the religious type."

"What type is that?"

I thought of Zach and his parents. "You know. The type who tells you everything bad in life is because of something you did. Or didn't do. That God is up there keeping score, just waiting for you to screw up so he can zap you."

"Well, there are plenty of people who think that way." He broke off a small pine branch and held it under his nose, inhaling its fragrance. "Have you had experience with some of them?"

It seemed the most natural thing in the world to relate my experience with Davey's death and the way Zach had explained it to me. Duane listened closely, his sympathetic gaze resting easily on me as I talked.

"I told him if God was like that, I wanted nothing to do with him."

He shook his head. "That's not God. That's what I call do-do religion. You know, do this, do that. All religion is that way, and it has nothing to do with God."

I squinted at him skeptically.

"All religion," he continued, "is essentially the same—a system that tells people they have to do something to earn God's favor, or eternal life, or the good life here and now, or rewards in heaven. Whether it's obeying the Ten Commandments, or the Torah, or the Koran, or the Vedas, it's the same thing. It's what motivates some people to fly planes into buildings."

"Wait. You're talking about different religions."

"I'm talking about religion in general. It's all alike." He watched a red-tailed hawk swoop down from a tree and skim along just above the water looking for a meal. "Tell me. Would the God who has the power to create all this really need our puny efforts? To do anything? Anything at all?"

I gazed around, taking in the serenity of the scene. "I never thought about it."

"As for Zach and his parents, do you think their religion brings them any joy?"

I thought of Zach's hunted look, his mother's fearful presence, and his father's overbearing manner. "Hardly. I've never met more miserable people."

"That's what religion does to people. Oppresses them, convinces them they have to do impossible things, then lays guilt on them when they fail. No one is ever good enough. Nothing they do is sufficient. They're caught up in a no-win system."

My Sunday school lessons came flooding back in a rush. "But surely we have to do something for God, don't we?"

"Do we?" That peaceful aura glowed from his eyes. "A Man once hung on a cross and said, 'It is finished.' I think he meant it. If you can't believe in that, look around you and believe in what the poet called the 'holy contour of life.'"

I wasn't sure what was meant by the holy contour of life. All I knew was that this rough-looking biker-philosopher had a contentment missing from people like Zach, a contentment I was still searching for.

We left the trail and walked back to the bike in silence. The clean, pine-scented air was a welcome relief from the acrid burnt smell that still hovered around Trout Fork. We put on our helmets and mounted the bike. I started the machine and maneuvered it expertly to the entrance to the parking lot, slowing long enough to allow an oncoming car go by. As it zipped past us, I recognized Garrett's gray pickup heading toward Trout Fork. His startled expression as he saw us was priceless. I pulled the bike smoothly onto the road behind him and smiled as I saw him glance at us numerous times in the rearview mirror all the way back to Trout Fork.

Ashley was sitting on the bench in front of Gil's store when we entered the café parking lot and pulled up next to Garrett's truck. She bounced up and hurried toward us, her face alight. "Wow! You're driving. That's awesome."

I took off the helmet. "Duane has been giving me lessons. It's a blast." I dismounted and thanked him.

"Anytime. A little more practice and you'll be an expert. Then you can think about buying one of your own."

I laughed. "Right."

He scooted forward on the seat, backed the bike up, and drove slowly toward the area under the trees where his buddies were resting.

Garrett approached in time to overhear Duane, his expression indicating he was less than thrilled at the idea of my buying a motorcycle.

I steeled myself for another lecture about the danger. "Hi," I said. "Did you know those guys are all college professors? Can you believe it?"

"Really?" He watched the group for a moment. "I have some information. Can we sit a minute?"

Ashley raised one eyebrow at me. "I have to get back to the café anyway. Take your time."

We sat on the bench in front of Gil's, and he pulled

out a piece of official-looking paper. "I got the report from the Denver lab on those bleach bottles. They're clean. No prints. Nothing. Whoever they belonged to was very careful to wipe them clean. In fact, when you consider the way he cleaned Heather's body, I think we're dealing with someone who is meticulous and thorough. At least I think that's what a profiler would say about him."

"That's too bad. I was hoping…"

"What? That the prints would lead us to the killer? Murder investigation is never that simple. Even if there were prints on the bottles, unless the killer's prints are on file somewhere, they would only be of use after we caught him. They wouldn't tell us who it is."

I felt as Garrett often made me feel, foolish and amateur. At least he wasn't telling me it was Denver's case. "Where does that leave us? Back at square one?"

"Not entirely. I've found something interesting about our friend, Dave Malone. Remember that information you dug up about his real estate consortium in Pennsylvania?"

"Yeah. The one that bought up all that farmland where the new road was planned."

"Right. But there's more. It seems one of the farmers was unwilling to sell. He turned down numerous offers from the consortium for the farm that had been in his family for generations."

"Then how did they build the road?"

"Oh, they got him to sell all right. But only after his house and two huge barns were destroyed in a mysterious fire."

"Oh, my God."

"That's not the worst part. One of the farmer's kids, a teenage girl, died in the fire. After that, I guess he didn't have the heart to stay there. He sold to Malone's consortium for half what they had originally offered."

My mind was reeling. It was monstrous. "That means it was Malone who set the fire that could have killed us all? Just to get Alma to sell and make more money."

"We don't know that for sure, but the similarity is striking."

"How can people do things like that?" I asked, my voice shaking with anger.

"I've heard worse than that. Much worse. And you wonder why I left the Denver PD." He got up. "Anyway, I'm going to bring Malone in for questioning. I'll let you know what I find out."

I watched him walked slowly back to his pickup, his hands in his pockets.

CHAPTER 15

After we served lunch that afternoon, Alma closed the café, and we went back to the cabin to rest for a couple of hours. Ashley and I sat on our beds with the cats, and I told her what Garrett had found out about Dave Malone.

"I knew it," she said. "He showed up the day after the fire and tried to get Mom to sell. Remember? He did the same thing after Heather was killed."

"Garrett is going to bring him in for questioning."

"Geez. Don't tell Mom. She'll freak out." She pulled Heather's journal out from under her pillow and opened it.

"Making any headway with that thing?"

She thumbed through the pages at the back of the journal. "A little. I know 'ash' and 'al' are me and Mom, 'd' is Digger, and 'fish dude' is Gil. She talks about a party in the parking lot one night when the fish dude called the cops on them. Then she says he looks familiar, like someone she's seen before."

"Gil? Where would she have met him?"

"Dunno. That's all she says. If only we could figure out who G.S. is. And why she was blackmailing him." She looked out the window at the burnt trees. "But if

Malone is the killer, then it doesn't matter who G.S. is, does it? Or maybe it's some kind of code word for Malone."

"We don't know anything yet, so keep an open mind. A good journalist gathers all the facts before coming to a conclusion."

Jack head-butted my arm and rolled over for a belly rub.

"Jack, you're getting fat. You need some exercise. We're going jogging."

I changed my clothes and picked up Jack's leash and harness. This time he seemed eager to accompany me. He hopped off the bed and led me to the front door where he stood quietly while I strapped him into his harness. Once outside, he led me toward the trail as though he knew the way. We jogged along the trail, heading south along the creek. The trail in this direction wound through stands of tall pines and heavy underbrush, much of which was black from the fire. As we trotted along, we passed the two burnt cabins standing stark and lonely. Jack wrinkled his nose at the smell, slowed his pace, and looked up at me curiously.

"You're right, Jack. This is depressing." We turned around and headed north along the creek to the area where the surviving cabins sat among the trees near the trail.

I heard the sound of hammering and sawing coming from one of the cabins. Zach was outside his cabin work-ing on a large, narrow piece of wood laid out between two sawhorses. What he was building? He didn't look like the carpenter type, but then again, Alma did say he had fixed up Madam Gauzie's cabin. Maybe he was building something for his church. I thought about his parents and what Duane had said about their oppressive religion and how all religions were the same in that they all required something. Was that what motivated Zach to do all his good deeds?

I shook my head to clear it of unpleasant thoughts, determined to try to obtain that elusive peace Duane seemed to exude. Maybe it had to do with his lifestyle. Memories of the thrill of driving his motorcycle came back to me. If only I could capture that feeling again. Maybe he was right about buying my own bike. But how would that work? I had been perusing maps and knew I wanted to stay in Colorado and write more about the out-of-the-way places I knew were abundant here. But winter was coming with its snow and freezing temperatures, hardly conducive to year-round motorcycle riding. How would I survive without my car?

Then there was Garrett. Those few days we spent together after the fire were incredibly sweet. So sweet, in fact, that I had allowed myself to wonder what it would be like to make that a permanent arrangement. But I couldn't continue to write my column if I stayed here, so that would mean giving up my job. To do what? Wash dishes, iron shirts, and make trips to the grocery store? That wasn't for me. As much as I might be able to care for this man if I let myself, I simply couldn't see how it was going to work out for us.

I slowed down and let Jack catch his breath. He was panting a little, so I picked him up and carried him on my shoulder the rest of the way. He nestled against my neck and sighed. I wished again I could be like him, content to be wherever he was at that moment.

෴

When we entered the cabin, I heard Ashley in the bedroom talking on her cell phone. She sounded agitated, her voice raised and shrill. It was impossible not to overhear her. "No, Dad. It's no big deal. I'm fine. We're all fine. The fire was...No, they don't know who it was...No, they haven't caught him yet either. I guess it could be the same person, but..." I moved closer to the bedroom door which was slightly ajar. Ashley was becoming more upset. "No. I can't leave now. I'm trying to find...well, I can't leave Mom alone in the café. Yeah, we do have a waitress, but she's not going to stay here all summer." She listened again and exhaled. "Okay, Dad, I'll see you when you get here. Love you, too. Bye."

I opened the door, and Jack scooted in to jump up on Ashley's bed, where Sasha greeted him with a playful swat. "Talking to your father?"

"Yeah. He just found out about the fire being arson, and he freaked." She looked up at me with plaintive eyes. "He wants me to come and live with him until school starts. He says it's not safe here anymore." She tossed her phone on the bed in disgust. "I can't even."

I sat on her bed with her. "Well, you can't really blame him. First a murder and then a fire. He's only trying to protect you."

"But how can I leave now? Mom needs me in the café. He's coming down tonight to talk to her. I don't think he can make me go with him unless she agrees to it. Anyway, look what I found." She was holding Heather's journal, and her eyes flashed with excitement. She opened it to the last page. "Remember this entry? The one where she says she was going to tell everyone about G.J. if G.S. didn't pay up?"

"Yeah?"

"Remember she said there was something about Gil that looked familiar? Well, I've been thinking. What if G.S. and G.J. weren't initials at all? What if they really mean Gil Senior and Gil Junior? What if she was blackmailing Gil about his son?"

I bent over the page. "Blackmailing him about what? And how would she even know Gil's son? He left here years ago."

"He left on a motorcycle, right? What if she met him on the road while she was with Digger's gang? What if she knew about something illegal he was up to? What if she met Gil here and he looked familiar because she had seen his son? What if Madam Gauzie or someone told her about his son and she put two and two together? What if she was blackmailing Gil to keep her quiet about Gil, Junior? She told me she was going to make a lot of money on meth, but not by using or selling it. She wouldn't tell me how she was going to get the money. What if she knew Gil's son was a meth dealer and threatened to tell everyone here about it unless Gil paid her?"

"That's a lot of what ifs. And why blackmail Gil? He didn't do anything wrong. Parents aren't responsible for what their adult kids get into."

"Yeah, but Gil is totally into his all-American, law-and-order image. He's tight with the cops, holds a big Fourth of July barbeque every year. He wouldn't want it known his son is a drug dealer. Would he?"

"No, but is his reputation worth killing someone over?"

She shrugged. "Who knows what some people will do?"

My cell phone rang. It was Garrett. Before I could tell him about Ashley's theory, he said, "I just heard from the Canadian police. They have a man named Gilbert Acevedo, Junior, incarcerated in Calgary. He was the leader of one of the outlaw motorcycle gangs called the Lucifers. He was originally charged with killing a rival gang member in a fight about territory. Apparently, Gil Junior was a big-time meth dealer. The Mounties had been after him for a couple of years."

I stared at Ashley, my mind whirling. Could she be right about Gil? Surely he wouldn't want it known that his only son was a drug dealer. Could he have killed Heather to keep her quiet? Or to keep from having to pay her?

"There's something else," Garrett continued. "When they tried to arrest him, he shot one of the cops."

"Oh, no. Did the cop die?"

"Yes."

I felt sick. Poor Gil. He must be horrified at what his son did. A drug dealer and cop killer? What would Gil do to keep that from getting around? I remembered those nice young cops at the barbeque who were friends of Gil's. What would they think of Gil if they learned his son had killed one of their own? And what would his neighbors think?

Maybe keeping that quiet was enough motivation to kill Heather, especially if she threatened to tell everyone. I also couldn't help wondering what it would be like to be married to a policeman and worry every day he was on the job.

"Ryn? Are you there?"

"I'm here. That's awful. Garrett, are you coming by today? Ashley has something she wants to show you. It's in Heather's journal."

"I can't get away right now. How about tonight? I can meet you at the café after dinner."

"Fine. We'll be waiting for you." I hung up. "Ashley, bring the journal with you tonight. Garrett will meet us at the café after dinner."

She handed me the journal. "My dad's coming to-night. I don't want him to know about any of this. He's freaked out enough."

"Okay. You keep him and your mom busy. I'll show Garrett the journal and tell him your theory." I gazed out the window at the burnt trees. "But even if Gil did kill Heather, why would he try to burn down his own store and his cabin? It makes no sense."

Alma knocked on the door and poked her head in. "Ashley, your father called. He said he's coming down tonight. He sounded upset. Did you talk to him?"

"Yeah. He knows about the arson and about Heather. He wants me to spend the rest of the summer with him. Can he do that? Make me go back with him?"

"No. I have primary custody of you. He knows that. He would have to take me to court and make the case that you're not safe here. By the time the lawyers wrangle about it, the summer will be over, and this will have all blown over. Don't worry about it. I'll handle your father."

"Okay, Mom. Thanks."

"I'm going over to get things ready for dinner. Are you two coming?"

"We'll be right there."

On our way to the café, I noticed Duane lounging by his bike. The other four were playing with a Frisbee, shouting and laughing like a bunch of kids being watched over by their father. I wondered if Duane knew anything about Gil's son and his Canadian gang. I strolled over and watched the men play for a while.

"Want to get in the game?" Duane asked.

"No, thanks. I'm lousy at Frisbee." I sat on the grass beside him. "Duane, I want to ask you something."

"Shoot."

"Have you ever heard of a motorcycle gang called the Lucifers?"

"Oh, yeah. They're one-percenters."

"Have you ever heard of one of their members named Gil Acevedo?"

He thought a moment. "Acevedo. Wasn't he involved in that shootout with the cops up in Canada?'

"Yes. One of them was killed."

"That's right. I remember."

"Did you know his father is Gil from the bait store?"

Sorrow filled his eyes. "I didn't know. That must be hard on him."

I didn't want to mention Heather's journal or our suspicion that Gil might be a murderer. "What's with the names these guys choose for their gangs? Lucifers? What's that all about?"

He plucked a blade of grass and chewed it thoughtfully. "I guess they think they'll frighten people if they associate themselves with the devil. Either that or they actually think of themselves as evil. Beyond redemption, beyond hope with nothing to lose."

Digger's gang, the Sons of Evil, came to mind. "It seems so opposite of the way we're taught to think."

"They do everything opposite of what normal people do. You have to remember that they pride themselves on being outlaws, the one percent of bikers that aren't law-abiding. They wear that identity as a badge of honor. Or dishonor. The gangs try to outdo each other in their evil ways. I think it's their way of thumbing their noses at God. At all authority. And at the rest of society."

I could see how people could be angry with God. I certainly had been for years. But intentionally aligning themselves with evil? I didn't get it. "I'd better get to work," I said, standing up. "Are you guys going to stick around?"

"I'm not sure. We have another couple of weeks before we have to be back for the first semester, and there are parts of Colorado we haven't seen yet. Like Aspen and Vail and the Western slope."

I hadn't visited the ski meccas either, but I knew they were big tourist destinations. Maybe that would be my next stop. Crenshaw couldn't complain about a column about those areas. I left Duane to his relaxing and went back to the café.

Ashley met me at the door and handed Heather's journal to me. "Here. Hide this until Garrett comes. I don't want my parents to see it."

I took the journal from her. "Are you sure you don't want to tell Garrett your theory about senior and junior? After all, it's your discovery. You should take credit for it."

"I could be all wrong. In that case, you can take the credit."

"You're too kind."

We were kept busy throughout the dinner hour, and it was after eight before Garrett came into the café. Alma and Ashley had gone back to the cabin to wait for Ashley's father, leaving me to lock up. Garrett and I sat at his table near the fireplace. I pulled out the journal and explained Ashley's theory about Gil and his son. He listened carefully, turning the pages of the journal as I spoke. I stopped talking and waited for his response.

He was maddeningly slow to respond. Finally, he leaned back and said, "Maybe."

"Maybe?"

"There are still a few things that don't add up. Suppose he did kill her to keep her quiet, why wash her in bleach? Why take out her piercings? The autopsy report said she hadn't been assaulted. So why remove her clothes and throw them in the creek? And why try to burn down the stores and cabins? What does he have to gain by it?"

"We thought of those things, too. But there's no doubt in my mind Heather was blackmailing him about his son. As for the other things—"

He closed the journal. "To tell you the truth, I still

think it's Malone. He has motive. He still wants Alma to sell to him. He is suspected of burning out that farmer in Pennsylvania to get him to sell. He lives north of here and has access to the creek from his property. He could easily have poured the ammonia into the water to kill the fish. You have to admit, business is down since those two events."

"But the same questions exist. Even if he killed Heather to give the place a bad rep, why the piercings and bleach and all that?"

"I have a theory about that. Suppose he wants to give the place a reputation for bizarre or occult activities. That's the kind of thing those people would do, and if Trout Fork got a reputation as an occult hangout, that would drive the tourists away."

I remembered Madam Gauzie telling me there was a strange aura around Trout Fork for the past few years. Occult happenings would certainly explain it. I sat back, greatly encouraged.

If one of them had to be the murderer, I would much rather it was Malone than Gil. If Garrett was right, then Malone killed Heather, poisoned the fish, and started the fire all to get Alma to sell. He stood to make a huge amount of money with the highway going through. It all added up. "Okay, what now?"

"Malone has agreed to come in tomorrow for questioning. I'll let you know what happens."

After Garrett left, I locked the door behind him. I cleared the dishes from the few dirty tables and brought them into the kitchen. As I stood at the sink, I thought over the evidence against both Gil and Malone and decided Garrett was right. It had to be Malone who killed Heather.

I felt a great relief that Gil, who was kind and generous, seemed to be above suspicion. Of course, it was sad that his son had turned out the way he did. But like I told Ashley, parents aren't responsible for what their adult kids do. For that, I was sure my mother was grateful.

CHAPTER 16

Garrett had left early that night, but I stayed in the café finding things to do so that Ashley and her parents would have plenty of time alone to work out their differences. It was after ten when I locked up and turned out the lights. I stood outside the back door breathing in the cool mountain air. A slight rain had fallen earlier in the evening, which served to clean the air of much of the smell from the fire. Now the sky was clear, and the stars, which always seemed so much closer at this altitude, were scattered thickly across the sky, reminding me of a dark blue sequined blanket.

The silence was broken by the sound of raised voices coming from Alma's cabin. I listened for a moment, then realized going in would intrude on the family. I walked along the dark path that ran behind the stores and saw a light coming from the liquor store. Hank was mopping the back step with what smelled a like very strong, caustic cleaner. He splashed some from a bottle and scrubbed it with the mop. Then he went back into his store and closed the door.

What a sad, lonely existence he must lead, I thought, *as he waits for the wife he will never see again. No wonder he drinks.*

I continued on past his store and the bait shop. As I neared the end of the building, the back door of Madam Gauzie's store opened, and she came out carrying a bag of garbage. She shrank back when she saw me. "Oh, Ryn! You scared me half to death. What are you doing out here?"

"I'm sorry. I didn't mean to startle you. I just closed the café and wanted to give Ashley some time alone with her parents."

"Oh, Robert is here? My, my."

"Here, let me put that in for you." She handed me the bag, and I opened the top of the dumpster and tossed it in.

"Thank you, dear. I'll tell you what. Why don't you come to my cabin while you're waiting for the all clear to sound? I'll make us some tea."

I accepted her invitation, and we walked down the path toward her cabin, about fifty yards from Alma's. She held onto my arm to steady herself along the winding path. "Do you know I attended Alma and Robert's wedding?"

"I didn't know that."

"Oh, yes. I've known that family for years. Alma's father was a lovely man. I remember him in his tuxedo walking Alma down the aisle. That must have been, oh, nearly twenty years ago. Seems like yesterday." She unlocked the door of her cabin and flicked on the light switch. The décor was much as I would have expected, old-fashioned and quaint. I half expected a Victorian maid to emerge with a white cap and feather duster.

"Sit down, dear, and make yourself comfortable. I'll put the kettle on."

I sat on the flowered sofa and noticed a large photo album on the coffee table. Leafing through the pages, I saw numerous faded pictures of a laughing girl in the attire and hair style of the 1960s.

"Is this you?" I asked as she put the tea tray next to the album.

She peered at the page I was holding. "Yes. Hard to believe that cute young thing is me, isn't it?" She sat down and began pouring the tea. "That was a long time ago in another life."

"Have you always lived in this area?"

"Always. Oh, I've done my share of traveling, but I always come back to Colorado. There's no place like it. We have the mountains and the plains, the farms in the western valleys, the lakes, and rivers. The only thing we don't have is the ocean. And the seasons! I hope you'll still be here in the fall when the Aspen trees turn gold. It's really something to see."

I thought about future columns, wondering whether I could ever capture that sense of wonder so many Coloradans seemed to have about their state.

I turned more pages in the album and came upon one of a group of people standing in front of Alma's café. I recognized Alma, Madam Gauzie, and Gil in the picture.

"That was taken not long after Alma's father died and left Alma the café and the rest of the property." She pointed to a tall, dark-haired man standing next to Alma. "That's Robert. Handsome, isn't he?"

"Yes. Who's this guy?" I pointed to another young man standing next to Gil.

"Oh, that's Sarge. Do you know him?"

"I've waited on him. How long has he been here?"

"He came back from the Marines about the same time Gil got out of the army. He had been in Vietnam, two tours I believe, and came back with a drug problem. Gil kind of took him under his wing. Felt sorry for him. He stayed with Gil for a while, until he could get himself sorted out, he said, but he's been here ever since. He lives in a tent up in the woods most of the year. I don't know what he does in winter."

I stared at the picture of the man. He looked so different from the old wreck I'd met in the café. "You say he had a drug problem? Did he ever kick it?"

"Maybe, but now that marijuana is legal in this state, who knows? I'm pretty sure Gil is keeping an eye on him. I've seen him giving Sarge food now and then."

That explained the odd smell that hung on the man. Marijuana.

She turned several more pages of photos then leaned back and sighed. "It was all so different then, so calm and peaceful."

I thought she was just reflecting the attitude common to many senior citizens when the world they once knew fades away in the face of new technologies and new ideas. But I decided to humor her. "When did things change? Can you recall? Was it when the motorcycle clubs started showing up?"

"Well, they certainly made things a lot noisier around here. But I don't mean that. Oh, it's hard to explain. It's a feeling I get. Like there's something in the air that's wrong, out of step, you know what I mean?"

I didn't, but I nodded anyway.

She poured a cup of tea from the teapot covered with a knitted cozy and handed it to me. "It's like there's a darkness hovering over Trout Fork, even on the brightest sunny day. You can't see it. You just feel it. I guess you wouldn't notice it since you're new here. But I know one thing. That feeling built to a climax until that girl was killed. Then it went away. But you know, it's starting to build again. I can feel it."

I watched her eyes for signs of the psychosis that would explain her words, but she seemed as sane as anyone I knew.

She grasped my arm, her eyes searching mine. "You will be careful, won't you, dear? When you're alone?"

"Of course," I assured her. "I'm always careful. I'm from New York City, remember?"

I stayed with her until well past midnight then headed back to the cabin. There was no light coming from the living room, so I assumed Robert had left. I was about to open the front door when I heard some shuffling noises coming from the side of the cabin, as though an animal was moving through the pine needles. I froze for a moment, and the sound stopped. I decided it was probably a raccoon. They were notorious for finding their way into buildings that might provide them with an opportunity for food.

I fumbled with the key and heard the sound moving closer. "Is someone there?" I said, loud enough to give the impression I wasn't scared out of my wits. Then I heard an eerie sound somewhere between a moan and a growl. The hair on the back of my neck stood up and blood began to pound in my ears as my trembling hand jammed the key into the lock. I slid into the cabin and slammed and locked the door. I leaned against it, waiting for my pulse to return to normal. I strained my ears in the silence and thought I heard the sound of footsteps running away from the cabin. But it didn't sound like any kind of animal I could think of. It sounded like a person.

❧❧❧

"How did it go last night? With your parents," I asked Ashley as we dressed for work the next morning.

"Great. If you like shouting matches."

She stood before the mirror brushing her hair, and I could see the sorrow reflected in her eyes. Divorce must be hard on kids, especially teenagers. Even with the tragedy in my family, at least my parents had stayed together.

"I'm sorry, Ashley. Did they get anything resolved?"

"Nope. Dad says he's going to talk to his lawyer. Mom says she won't give up without a fight. They make me feel like the rope in a tug-of-war." She turned and looked at me. "If only we could find out who killed Heather and get him arrested, I know Dad would feel better about me living here."

"That would certainly solve a lot of problems. Garrett is bringing Dave Malone in today. Maybe he'll find out something." I pulled out my cell phone. "Tell your mom I'll be right over. I need to call the magazine."

She narrowed her eyes at me. "You're not going to leave, are you?"

"I don't want to, but I may have no choice. That's what I need to talk to my editor about."

She left, the cats padding after her, and I dialed the New York number. I was connected to Crenshaw, who sounded like he was in an unusually good mood. "Good morning, Ryn. How are you?"

"Fine, sir."

"Good. Good. Glad to hear it. Where are you?"

"Still in Trout Fork, sir." Silence on the other end. I cleared my throat. "That's what I'm calling about."

"Oh?"

"Yes, sir. I'd like to stay on here for a while longer." I braced for the explosion. But he said nothing, so I continued. "I have some good ideas for columns about Colorado towns. Resorts are abundant here, ski resorts, golf resorts, health spas. But I need to stay in Trout Fork for the time being. If that's okay."

"Now, Kathryn…"

Uh-oh. He only calls me Kathryn when he's about to lay down the law. I heard him take a deep breath before he continued.

"You know what my doctor tells me? He says I have to avoid stress. Do you know what causes me the most stress?"

I assumed it was me, but I said, "What?"

"What causes most of my stress is unreasonable demands. Like writers who expect me to pay them for not working."

"Oh, no, sir. I wouldn't expect you to pay me until I send you another column. I'll pay my own way until then. But I can't leave here yet."

"This wouldn't have something to do with that murdered girl, would it?"

"How did you know about that?"

"I did some background for your last column. So that's it? You're playing amateur detective?"

"Well…"

"Trying to get yourself killed, that's what. How would I explain that to your parents?"

I felt guilty about stressing him out, but I sensed he was weakening. At least he hadn't given me an ultimatum or threatened to fire me. I heard him take another deep breath. "One more week, Kathryn. That's all I'm giving you. By next Friday, you need to be in another town writing a column. And it damned well better be an improvement over your last one. Got it?"

"Yes, sir. Thank you, sir."

"One week, Kathryn. Seven days. Don't disappoint me."

I hung up and dashed out the door and in the back door of the café. Alma was at the grill flipping pancakes with unusual vigor. Then she would bang the edge of the metal spatula on the grill as though she was decapitating someone with it. I didn't have to wonder who that was. Ashley wasn't the only one upset by last night's conflict with her father.

"Uh, hi, Alma. Sorry I'm late. I had to call the magazine."

"Ashley told me. Everything okay?"

"My editor's giving me one more week here. Then I have to find another place to write about."

"One more week. But you said—"

"Don't worry. I'm not leaving until Heather's killer is found. I think we may be closing in on him. At least that's what Garrett thinks. Then I'll go, but not until then. But I'll have to move on eventually. I have to make a living doing what I do best, and that's writing."

"I understand. That's the life of a single woman, I guess. Of course, if you were…"

"Married? But I'm not. And not likely to be anytime soon."

She gave me a sideways glance. "You never know."

∽∾∽

The breakfast rush kept my mind off my marital prospects, although Garrett kept intruding into my thoughts. Should I tell him about the running footsteps and that weird moaning sound I heard the night before? I decided against it. What could he do about it anyway? Besides, I couldn't be sure it wasn't an animal.

It was nearly noon when I glanced out the window and saw Garrett's pickup pull into the lot. He came in and motioned for me to join him outside. I told Ashley I'd be right back and followed him to the bench in front of Gil's.

We sat down, and he smiled at me. "I've arrested Dave Malone. He confessed."

I gasped. "He killed Heather?"

"No. But he did confess to setting the fire and poisoning the fish. When I told him we knew all about the fire in Pennsylvania and how his consortium made a fortune on that deal, he folded like a cheap suit. Started bawling and everything. He admitted pouring twenty-five gallons of ammonia into the creek upstream near his house to kill the fish so they would float down here where everyone could see them. He also admitted setting fire to the trees behind the café last week. He claims he never intended to hurt anyone. All he wanted was for Alma to sell up and get out. But when I tried to connect him to Heather's murder, he was adamant he had nothing to do with it."

"He's lying."

"I'm afraid his alibi checks out. He was at a planning commission meeting in Denver that night. They were discussing the proposed road through here. I confirmed it with a couple of people who were there. He didn't leave the meeting until nearly eleven."

"Couldn't he have driven down here and killed her after the meeting?"

"That doesn't fit with the time of death. The coroner is pretty sure she died between six and ten that evening."

I leaned back against the wooden bench. "What happens now?"

"He's in jail on the arson charge awaiting arraignment."

"I mean about the murder?"

"We've eliminated Malone, and that just leaves—"

"Gil. Of course. We've been trying so hard to figure out who would kill Heather, poison the fish, and start the fire. But now it turns out it was two different people. Gil is the only one who had a reason to kill her. I hate to think it was him, but it has to be, doesn't it?"

"Not necessarily. I haven't questioned Hank or Zach or even Duane and his friends. Of course, there's the possibility it's someone we haven't even thought of. Like one of the local fishermen. The problem is I can't bring these people in for questioning about a murder out of my jurisdiction. The most I can do is let Jenkins and the Denver PD know about my suspicions, which I have to tell you, seem pretty weak."

Gil came out of his store with a broom and began sweeping the walkway. He nodded to us while I studied his face. He was certainly an enigma. Tight with the cops, but with a son in prison for killing one of them. Such a good neighbor that he treated them to a barbeque each year, yet he was a bit of a hermit who lived alone year round and fished by himself. And he hated the bikers and everything associated with them. We were pretty sure he was being blackmailed by Heather, but what did he do about it? The only way to find out was to ask him. I started to tell Garrett but stopped myself. I knew what his reaction would be.

Duane and his friends came out of the café and headed toward the grassy area where their bikes were parked. They greeted us as they passed by. Gil leaned on his broom and followed them with his eyes. Then he went back into his store.

Garrett stood up. "I'm going to talk to Duane. Then I have to get back to the station. Will you have dinner with me tonight?"

"Sure." I watched him walk away, and I slipped into the bait shop.

Gil was waiting on an older man wearing waders and a cap with a "Fish fear me" logo. Gil looked up when I entered and nodded. I wandered around while I waited for him, fingering the fishing poles and reels, the lures, and other paraphernalia of a sport that was totally foreign to me. I've never been able to understand the attraction of standing hip-deep in freezing water or sitting for hours in a boat waiting for a fish.

The man paid for his purchases and left.

Gil turned to me. "What can I do for you? Have you decided to take up fishing?"

"Not really." I hadn't given much thought to what I would say to him, but that's never stopped me before, so I jumped right in. "Heather was blackmailing you, wasn't she? About your son."

He froze and gaped at me with wide eyes. His tongue flicked across his lips, then his shoulders slumped. "My son," he murmured. "How did you know?"

"Ashley and I found Heather's journal. Heather wrote that she was going to give you one last chance to pay up or she'd tell everyone about Gil Junior. That was her last entry the day she disappeared." I waited a moment to give that time to sink in. "So, what happened? Did she threaten you? And you killed her in anger? Or was it an accident?"

I expected him to blow up and tell me to get out, but instead, his demeanor was one of sadness. He slowly wiped some dust off the glass countertop with a rag. "I didn't kill her. I had nothing to do with it. Yes, she tried to blackmail me, but I never gave her a cent. The first time she came to me was about a week before she disappeared. She told me she had met Gil Junior in Canada and knew he was dealing meth. She said that boyfriend of hers had bought some from him. She said the people in Trout Fork would call me a hypocrite and laugh at me. She came back a few days later with a clipping from a newspaper about my boy being in jail for killing a cop. She asked me what my buddies at the police station would think about that. If I didn't give her a thousand dollars by the next day, she'd 'blow the lid,' as she called it."

"So, what happened?"

"She came here that next evening demanding the

money. I told her to go to hell. She could tell who she liked, but I wasn't giving her any money. She followed me into the back room, squawking about my reputation and laughing like the witch she was. I shoved her out the back door and locked it. That's the last I saw of her. I swear." His eyes pleaded with me.

I thought about Madam Gauzie's interview with the cops the day Jack uncovered Heather's body. She swore she saw Heather leaving Gil's store, heading for the trail. There was no way I could prove what he was saying was true, but I believed him. I wanted to believe him.

CHAPTER 17

I thanked Gil for his honesty and commiserated with him about his son. I left the bait shop and noticed Garrett's truck was gone, so I assumed he'd gone back to the police station. I stood on the walkway thinking about where this left us. If Gil was innocent and Malone had an alibi, who else could it have been? It depressed me to realize we were no closer to Heather's killer than we were two weeks ago.

I strolled past the liquor store and heard Hank laughing with one of his customers. Could it be him? Maybe he got drunk that night and followed Heather to the trail. Maybe he made a pass at her, and she shut him down. He could have killed her in anger. But despite his temper flare-ups, he didn't seem like a killer. Besides, what would be his motive? The only two people with motives had been eliminated.

What about Heather's boyfriend, Digger? Did she have something on him that she was holding over his head? But he wasn't even in Trout Fork at the time. Or was he? He could have come back sometime that night looking for her.

Then there was Zach, a strange little hyper-religious man who lived alone and kept to himself. Maybe he did it. But again, what was the motive? He tried to convert her, and she refused, so he killed her? I shook my head. "Maybe it's time you stopped playing detective and got back to writing," I said out loud, "before you lose your job."

"Who's going to lose their job?" Duane asked with a grin as he approached.

"Probably me. I was giving myself a lecture. What did Garrett have to say?"

"Oh, he was asking about the group that girl came in with. The one that got killed. He asked if I knew much about them. I told him I don't know them at all. We ride in different circles from that crowd."

We stood watching another group of motorcycles pull into the lot. There were about eight of them, all on different types of bikes. Duane waved at them, and they greeted him with smiles and waved back.

"I guess you know those guys?"

"No, but there's a camaraderie among bikers. There are no strangers. Except the one-percenters, of course. They keep to themselves."

I watched the group dismount and stand by their bikes, laughing and chatting. What was it about that lifestyle that produced such free-spirited *joie de vivre*? Whatever it was, I longed for it. "Duane, I'll be leaving in a week or so. Would it be okay to take another ride on your bike?"

His kind hazel eyes found mine, and he sensed my eagerness. "Sure. Why don't we ride into Pineland Park? I'd like to show you something."

"Okay. Let me run in and tell Alma I'll be gone for an hour."

When I came back out, Duane's bike was parked in front of the café, and he was on the rear seat. He handed me the helmet, and I straddled the bike in front of him. I hit the ignition button, and the bike purred to life, like a large cat waiting to pounce on the open road. Maybe what I thought of as the feline nature of the bike was part of its appeal.

We pulled onto the road, and I shifted through the gears like an expert.

"Impressive," Duane said in my ear.

The air was warm, the sun bright on the pavement, and I felt again the thrill of freedom. The twenty miles to Pineland Park flew by as we leaned into the numerous curves on the road.

We passed several groups of motorcycles going in the opposite direction, and Duane waved to each of them. "Why do bikers always wave to one another?" I shouted at him over the sound of the wind rushing by.

"The brotherhood of the road."

Amazing. I'll have to find a place for that concept in one of my columns. Or maybe the novel I've been neglecting for weeks.

Before we got to town, he had me stop and switch places with him. "You don't have your motorcycle license yet, so we better not tempt fate."

We sailed by the police station at the edge of town, and I hoped Garrett wasn't around to see us. While I was flattered by his concern for me, it still irritated me that he sometimes treated me like a child. Duane drove into the parking lot of a Honda dealership, where rows of shiny bikes were parked throughout the lot.

"Are you buying another bike?" I asked as we dismounted and hung our helmets on the hooks on the side of the seat.

"No. I wanted to show you one I think would be perfect for you to buy."

"Me? Oh, no. I couldn't. Do you think I could? What about my car? And my cat?"

He laughed. "One thing at a time. Just look at it. The rest will take care of itself." He led me to a group of smaller bikes and stopped at one in particular. "When I saw this one, I thought of you. It's lighter than mine and the engine is smaller, but it still has plenty of power. And there's room here in front of your seat for your cat. You could secure some kind of carrier here and strap him into it. The windshield will keep him from getting scared by the wind. What do you think?"

I visualized zooming along on the open road with Jack in his goggles and helmet. "Is it expensive?"

"It's used, but only has a few thousand miles on it. If you sold your car, you could pay cash for it and still have money left over."

The money part was certainly appealing. I was trying to temper my enthusiasm by putting obstacles in the way. "I'm planning on staying in Colorado for a while. What about winter? How does that work?"

"Unless the roads are blocked or really icy, all you need to do is bundle up. You probably won't do much joy riding in winter, but you'd still be able to get around on it."

Just then a young man with long blond hair in a ponytail came out of the store and strolled toward us. "Hey, Duane. What's up?"

"Jason. Good to see you. I'm looking at this Honda for my friend here. She's thinking about buying a bike."

Am I really thinking about it?

"Perfect bike for a lady," Ponytail said. "Smooth, lightweight, economical. Gets about eighty miles per gallon. Want to test drive it?"

"I don't have my license yet." *Did I really say "yet"?* I felt like I was being propelled along by a rushing river.

"No problem. You can ride in the back lot. Plenty of room. No cops."

Visions of Garrett's stern face warning me about motorcycles loomed before me, but I dismissed them. After all, it was only a test drive.

☙❧

Dressing for my dinner date with Garrett that night, I wondered how I was going to break the news to him that I was now the owner of a Honda motorcycle. Maybe I would wait until I had completed the sale of my car and gotten my motorcycle license. Then I could drive it to his house with Jack secured on the front of it.

I heard Alma greet Garrett in the living room and joined them. "I hope this is okay," I said. "I wasn't sure where we were going, so I didn't know how to dress." I was wearing another of Ashley's tops and her gray sling-back shoes.

Garrett wore a sports jacket and slacks. "You look great," he said, his eyes appraising me.

"Where are we going?"

"There's a new Italian place I've been wanting to try. Borelli's."

"Oh, I've heard the food there is wonderful," Alma said as she ushered us to the door. "I want a full report. Now, Garrett, don't keep her out too late. She has to work the breakfast shift alone tomorrow. Ashley is spending a few days with her father."

I hoped that meant there might be a reconciliation in the offing. "I guess you'll be alone this evening? Just you and the cats."

Alma smiled. "Well, not exactly. I'm—"

She was cut off by a knock at the door. I opened it to find Hank on the doorstep, his bushy red hair and beard neatly combed and wearing a smart-looking shirt very different from his usual scruffy attire. He was holding a bottle of wine and a single red rose. I stammered something incoherent and stepped aside to let him in. I looked at Alma and actually saw her blush. Garrett's gaze met mine, and his eyebrows shot up. Hank greeted us and shook Garrett's hand sheepishly.

"Well," Garrett said, "I guess we'll be going. Have a nice evening, you two."

We slipped out the front door and waited until we were a few feet from the cabin before we both burst out laughing.

"Do you believe that?" I asked between giggles. "Alma and Hank?"

Garrett took my elbow and propelled me away from the cabin. "Shh, they'll hear you."

"Did you see the rose? I had no idea he was a romantic."

"Well, I think it's great. Two lonely people who've known each other for years getting together at last. I'm all for romance."

I took his arm. "You play the hard detective, but you're really an old softie, aren't you?"

We drove through Pineland Park on the way to the restaurant and passed the Honda dealership. I could see my bike had been removed from the lot to be prepared for delivery to its new owner.

Duane said he would lend me his bike for the driving test I would have to take. I would have to think about how to sell my car, too. Maybe an ad on Craigslist would be the way to go. I grimaced to myself at the thought of keeping a secret from Garrett. He was becoming too important in my life for that. I would have to tell him. "Uh, Garrett?"

"Hmm?"

"I bought a motorcycle today." I cringed inwardly, waiting for his response.

He looked over at me. "You did?"

"Yes. I'm going to sell my car and take my motorcycle test in a couple of days."

He was quiet, and I stole a sideways glance at him. His eyes were fixed on the road. I expected the usual lecture about how dangerous motorcycles are, but he didn't mention it.

"I guess that means you'll be heading down the road on your new bike pretty soon."

I hadn't planned to tell him quite yet that I had been given only one more week in Trout Fork, but I decided there was no sense in keeping it from him. "I talked to my editor this morning. He's giving me until next Wednesday. If I'm not writing a column from somewhere else by then, I lose my job." More silence. "At least there's one good thing. I've convinced him to let me stay in Colorado and write on some of the resorts here. For the time being anyway." I saw Garrett's shoulders and jaw relax a bit. "Say something," I said.

"What can I say? If you're going, you're going."

"I don't see what choice I have."

He looked over at me. "Don't you?"

His deep blue eyes were inviting and disconcerting, but I knew what he was hinting at wasn't going to happen. I ignored the question, and we drove the rest of the way in silence until we pulled into the parking lot of Borelli's. Our table by a window was waiting, complete with candles and a view of the mountains. We chatted about the menu, ordered wine, and settled on chicken piccata for him and pasta primavera for me. We sipped our wine while we watched the sunset over the mountains, and I knew I would miss this place desperately when I left.

"By the way," I said, trying to sound nonchalant. "I talked to Gil today about Heather blackmailing him."

He narrowed his eyes at me. "You did what?"

"Now don't go all paternal on me. It was fine. He admitted she tried to get money out of him by threatening to tell everyone about his son. He refused and told her to get lost."

"You shouldn't have. You were questioning a potential killer. Do you know that?"

"He's innocent, Garrett. I'm sure of it. Why don't you question him yourself? You'll see what I mean."

"Oh, you're giving me permission to do my job? Thanks very much." He started stabbing at the salad the waiter had set before him.

"I didn't mean it like that." *What is it with men and their egos?* "I just mean you'll satisfy yourself that he's innocent. Don't be angry with me."

He put down his fork and looked at me steadily, his eyes boring into mine. "You don't get it, Ryn. I'm not angry with you. I'm afraid for you. You do rash things. I've seen too many murders and too many murder victims. It scares me when you put yourself in danger like that. I don't want to lose you." He hesitated for a moment then reached for my hand and squeezed it gently. "I may be falling in love with you."

I was not entirely surprised by his revelation, but I wasn't sure how to respond, so I poked at my salad with my fork. Even if I could feel as he did, what would it mean? I gazed out the window at the pink and golden streaks the setting sun had left in the sky. Italian opera was playing softly through the room. Pavarotti's voice was crooning "Nessun Dorma," and Garrett hummed softly along with him. I remembered his vast opera collection, so incongruous for a police detective.

"What do the words mean?" I asked.

"He is singing to his love. He says 'no one shall sleep, even you, oh, princess, in your cold room.'"

"How sad."

"Not really. At the end of the song, he sings 'I will win.' So he's hopeful it will all turn out, and he and his love will be together."

I would have had to be a complete dunce not to see where this was going. I bit my lip and pulled back a little.

He reached for my hand again. "Ryn—"

"Don't, Garrett," I whispered, looking down. "I'm not ready."

He relaxed and poured more wine into my glass. As usual, there was an unspoken understanding between us. As much as I loved that connection, anything more at this point had to be out of the question.

"All right. I won't press you. But before you leave, we'll have to talk about the future."

I nodded, not sure whether I looked forward to that conversation or dreaded it.

We had a lovely dinner, and Garrett was true to his promise to Alma to bring me home early.

Alma was in the living room alone watching TV when I came in. "Hi," she said. "How was your date?"

I plopped on the sofa next to her. "Fine. How was yours?"

"I don't know if it was a date exactly."

"A bottle of wine and a red rose? Looked like a date to me."

At the sound of my voice, Jack trotted in from the bedroom with Sasha close behind. They both jumped up on the sofa and paced back and forth across our laps, meowing for our attention.

"Poor Sasha. She misses Ashley," Alma said, stroking the cat. "I miss her too." Tears began to form in her eyes, and her voice became husky. "Did you know Robert wants to take me to court and try to get custody of Ashley?"

I put my arm around her shoulders. "I know. That won't happen."

"I'm not so sure. He claims making her live here with a killer on the loose is irresponsible of me. Not something a fit parent would do."

"Oh, please. If that were the case, all the parents in New York City would be unfit."

"Still. He said something about three women living here alone not being safe."

"Is that what the date with Hank is about? Are you looking to get married again?"

"What? Oh, no. I like Hank. He's good company. When he's sober, that is. We're just friends."

I thought of that single red rose. "I'm not sure he sees it that way."

"Hank is still pining for his wife. He's just lonely."

I stroked Jack and hesitated, wondering if I should say what I was thinking. "Alma, how much do you know about Hank's past?"

She wrinkled her brow. "What do you mean?"

"Garrett told me he and Gil got into a knife fight with a couple of Hell's Angels. They put two of them in the hospital. And there's that temper of his. I've seen his Jekyll and Hyde act. It's pretty ugly."

"I know all about that fight. There are no secrets in Trout Fork. As for his temper, it's not all that bad."

"Then you don't think he could have—"

"You're not thinking he killed Heather, are you? 'Cause that's just crazy."

"Well, somebody killed her. And we're running out of suspects."

"Honestly, I don't think it was anyone in Trout Fork.

I know these people. There's no one here that's capable of killing."

"Maybe you're right. Maybe it was a drifter or someone passing through."

"Let's not talk about it. How are you and Garrett getting along?"

"Tonight he told me he's falling in love with me."

She raised one eyebrow. "Oh, ho. What did you say?"

I scratched behind Jack's ears, and he flopped over for a belly rub. "I told him I didn't want to discuss it. How can I commit to him? Even if I want to, it's too early. I barely know him. It's all so confusing."

She patted my hand. "I know. But consider this. Men like Garrett don't come along every day. If you leave here and lose him, you may regret it."

"But if I stay, I'll lose my job. Then what? Stay here and wait on tables? How long before I regret that decision?"

She looked at me with the motherly affection I had never seen in my mother's eyes. "I'm sure you'll do the right thing, dear. Whatever you decide."

I lay in bed that night with both cats purring by my side and felt safe and very much at home, more at home than I'd ever felt in my large, smartly-furnished bedroom in New York. I pulled the curtain aside to let the moonlight stream in and felt the cool breeze waft across the bed. Would I really do the right thing in the end as Alma said? I wasn't even sure what the right thing was. Stay here and see where my relationship with Garrett would lead? Or keep my job and move on? I was determined not to leave here until Heather's killer was found, but the likelihood of that was becoming more remote each day. One by one the pool of suspects was drying up. It could be years before the murderer was brought to justice. If ever. What was I doing with my life?

CHAPTER 18

The smell of coffee woke me the next morning, and the first thing that came to mind was how I would survive without Alma's strong coffee once I left Trout Fork. A melancholy feeling came over me as I realized I would miss more about Alma than simply her coffee. She had provided the warm, accepting mother figure I had longed for all my life.

I opened the bedroom door, and the cats scurried toward the kitchen for their breakfast. I showered and changed, and by the time I joined them, Alma was putting my coffee cup on the table. "How did you sleep, dear?"

"Really well."

"Problems always seem smaller after a good night's sleep, don't you think?"

I smiled at her and sipped the coffee. "You really should write a book, you know. You could call it *Aunt Alma's Advice for All Occasions*."

She chuckled. "You're the writer in the family. I'm just the cook."

In the family. What a lovely thought.

She plunked a plate of hot buttered toast in front of me. "Now have some toast. I'm going over to fire up the grills. See you in a bit."

Without Ashley to help, it took me longer than usual to get the café ready for breakfast. I unlocked the front door to find Zach and his parents standing there waiting first in line, his father impatiently tapping his foot on the walkway. He managed a chilly "Good morning," and led his family to the patio where they found a table in the shade. I followed with the menus.

Zach pulled out a chair for his mother and sat close to her. They reminded me of two rabbits huddled in the corner of their cage, quivering at the sound of a ferocious dog growling nearby. I tried to engage them in conversation, but Zach's father interrupted with a command for orange juice and a few minutes to peruse the menu. Zach gave me a small apologetic smile and asked quietly for coffee. His mother, who spoke barely above a whisper, said, "Tea, please."

When I returned with the drinks, I couldn't help noticing that Zach kept his hands in his lap, even after I set his coffee before him. When he did reach for his cup, I saw small red stains dotting the cuffs of his long-sleeved white shirt. He pulled the cuffs down when he saw me staring at them and folded his arms, hiding his hands in his armpits.

His father pushed a menu closer to Zach. "We need to order, Zachary. We have a long journey ahead of us today."

"Oh, you're leaving us?" I smiled at Zach's mother. "I hope your stay was a pleasant one."

She directed her gaze at her husband, as though waiting for his permission to answer a simple question. He ignored her, so she peeked up at me and nodded. As I waited to take their order, I had a fleeting thought about how many unhappy marriages I had seen lately. My own parents barely spoke to one another, keeping a chilly distance enabled by their wealth and social status. My brother and his wife were now separated. Alma and her husband were wrangling about their only child. Hank was pining for a wife who'd left him years ago. Now here were two people who appeared to be completely incompatible, trying to keep up appearances. The possibility Garrett and I could rush into something and be as miserable as so many others caused a shiver to go down my back.

Zach ordered his usual pancakes and bacon, despite the frown from his father who ordered sensible, healthy breakfasts for his wife and himself. He gave me the menus and dismissed me with a wave of his hand. As I moved away, I heard him start in on Zach. I tried to focus on taking orders from the customers at a nearby table, but I couldn't help overhearing the man's overbearing tone.

"Well, Zachary, have you decided to come to your senses and return home with us?"

Zach's voice was barely audible. "I want to stay here."

"For what? You accomplish nothing here. God is not pleased with sluggards. You need to be about his work. You've wasted enough time in this place."

"I do work. At the church—"

The older man scoffed. "That little church isn't growing. You admitted as much. If a church isn't moving forward, it's moving backward. In no time, it will close. You need to be in a place where you can do more. Have you given any more thought to the mission field?"

I took the orders back to the kitchen, so I didn't hear Zach's response, but a less likely missionary than Zach was hard to imagine. As I waited for the coffee to finish brewing, the door opened, and Duane came in with two of his friends. They waved as they headed for the patio.

"I think we'll sit outside today, Ryn," Duane said. "Lovely day. Bring us three coffees, will you?"

I followed them with the coffeepot and cups as they sat at the table next to Zach and his parents. Zach's father examined their leathers and gray ponytails with a furrowed brow, nodding stiffly to their cheerful "Good morning."

"Just the three of you today?" I asked Duane.

"Yep. The three bachelors. Alan and Ron had to get back to their families."

As I took their orders, I heard Mr. Wayland say quietly, "How long do you expect to be living on those disability checks, Zachary? Isn't it about time you weaned yourself from them? I hope at least you're tithing to the church from them."

I stole a glance at Zach, who was huddled in his chair, his eyes glued to his coffee cup.

"Disgraceful," his father muttered to himself.

I saw Duane regarding the two men with sadness in his eyes. I strolled over and asked Zach if he needed a refill, but he didn't respond.

I brought the Waylands' breakfasts to them and left their check on the table. The inside diners kept me busy, and when I came back to the patio, Zach and his parents had left and were standing near their car. They had left money on the table to pay their check, with a very small tip included. As I cleared the table, an angry shouting match ensued in the parking lot, loud enough to attract the attention of everyone on the patio.

Zach had abandoned his timidity and was resisting his father's orders and instructions. "I won't," he shouted. "You can't make me." He stood with his hands pressed against his ears, rocking back and forth while his mother tried her best to be invisible.

His father drew himself up. "If that's your final decision, I wash my hands of you. Let's go, Margaret."

The woman hesitated for a moment, her eyes on her

son, and then got into the car. Zach stood alone, watching them go, and I felt terribly sorry for him. What must it have been like growing up in that home? No wonder he moved two thousand miles away from them.

Duane called me over and asked if I was free that afternoon to take my motorcycle test.

"I need to practice on your bike a little more, if that's okay. Besides, I can't leave the café. I'm the only one here until Ashley gets back."

"Okay. Whenever you're ready."

❦❦❦

Alma closed the café a bit early that night for the poker game. Hank came in first, spruced up and clear-eyed. He smiled at Alma in a way that told me there was more than friendship between them, at least on his part. Madam Gauzie followed him with trays of homemade cookies and sandwiches cut into dainty quarters. Gil came in behind her.

We all sat at the table, and as he dealt the first hand, Gil began berating the bikers. "Did you see that lazy bunch over in the field? They actually put up a tent. Why do you let them camp there, Alma? I'd have the cops run them off."

Alma patted his arm. "Now, Gil, they're not hurting anyone. Leave them be."

"Biker scum," he muttered.

I felt my face flush. "They're not scum. And they're hardly lazy. They're all college professors."

Gil gaped at me, and I nearly laughed out loud at his expression. "You're kidding."

"Nope. They teach math, English, economics, and philosophy."

"I don't believe it."

"Honest. They ride around during the summer and go back to teaching in the fall."

"See there, Gil," Alma chided. "You shouldn't judge people." She picked up her hand. "I'll take two, please. Did anyone hear Zach and his father arguing today?"

"I heard them all the way down in my store," Hank said. "What was that all about?"

"His father wants him to go back to Georgia," I said. "Zach refused, and the old boy nearly had a coronary over it. He said something about Zach taking disability checks, too. Do you know anything about that, Alma?"

Alma leaned back thoughtfully. "I do remember him telling me something years ago. Oh, what was it…something about a breakdown. That's it. A nervous breakdown. I think that's why he came to Colorado in the first place."

Madam Gauzie sat nearby listening, her arms folded in front of her. "Humph. That father of his would give anyone a nervous breakdown. Such a prune face I never saw."

Alma snickered. "Prune face. Good one, Madam G."

"Well, I mean, honestly. Did you ever see a more disagreeable man? And that wife of his. She looks like a strong breeze would knock her over. But, of course, she has been beaten down by her husband. I don't mean physically. How does a woman live with such a man? Now my Edgar was a wonderful man. Never an unkind word from him. He was a saint."

Gil interrupted her before she could really get going. "I hear they arrested that Malone character for starting the fire. They should have charged him with attempted murder. He could have killed us all."

Alma shook her head. "And all because I didn't want to sell. The things people will do for money."

"I was so sure he was the one who killed Heather," I said, "but Garrett says his alibi is tight."

"I still think it was one of her biker buddies on a drug high," Gil said.

I saw Hank cast shy glances at Alma. "What do you think, Hank?" I asked.

"Huh? What? Sorry. I wasn't listening."

That confirmed it in my mind. There was definitely something going on in his mind with regard to Alma.

We played for about two hours, taking a break to eat some of Madam Gauzie's delicacies. At about ten, we heard the sound of a car pulling up and saw the lights on the wall. Then the back door opened, and Ashley came in lugging her suitcase. She greeted us and gave her mother a hug.

"I thought you were staying up there for the weekend," Alma said.

"I came back early. I think Dad's ticked at me for wanting to come home." She plopped down in an empty chair. "It's so boring up there in the burbs. Nothing to do."

"Is he still threatening to sue me for custody?"

"Nah. He was just bluffing. He likes to make a fuss, but he's a good guy." She got up and grabbed a cookie. "I'm going over to the cabin. I need to unpack."

"All right, dear. We won't be long."

Ashley looked at me. "How's Sasha?"

"Fine. Jack keeps her company. They sleep together on your bed during the day and with me at night."

"Sasha's going to miss Jack when you go...where are you going anyway?"

"I'm not sure. I've talked to my editor about some of the ski resorts. Maybe I'll be going to one of them. I have to do some more research."

"There's more than the ski resorts," Gil said.

"There's health resorts, golf resorts, all kinds. Even dude ranches."

Alma patted my arm. "Wherever you end up, I hope you'll keep in touch."

"Of course I will. I'll never forget Trout Fork." Gil dealt again, and I picked up my next hand then tossed it on the table. "I can't even open. I guess this isn't my night. I think I'll go with Ashley. I can use an early night."

Ashley and I headed back to the cabin, carrying her suitcase between us. She chattered away about her father and his home in a Denver suburb. The air was cool and crisp, with just a hint of autumn and the winter that comes early in the mountains. As we approached the door, I heard a noise coming from the side of the cabin.

I stopped and grabbed Ashley's arm. "Shh."

"What?" she whispered.

"I thought I heard something." We stood still for a moment. "I guess not." I unlocked the door, and we went in. "Ash, you want to be extra careful when you're out at night."

She frowned at me. "You're starting to sound like Madam Gauzie. She sees spooks around every corner."

"I heard something near the side of the cabin the night your dad was here. Footsteps. They ran away when I opened the door."

"It was probably a critter of some sort."

"Maybe. Just promise me you'll be careful."

"Yes, Mother."

At the sound of our voices, Jack and Sasha came trotting out of the bedroom, meowing their greeting.

Ashley stooped down and picked Sasha up, covering her with strokes and kisses. "Oh, Sash. I've missed you."

Jack paced back and forth, rubbing himself along my legs until I picked him up as well. We carried the suitcase into the bedroom, and Ashley began to unpack. I sat on my bed with my laptop.

"You won't believe it," Ashley said. "Dad had a date last night."

"Well, he's divorced, so it's natural for him to date. What's she like?"

"She's like twenty years younger than him. It's gross."

"Does your mom know?"

"No. And I'm not gonna tell her. I don't want to make her feel bad about being alone."

"She may not be as alone as you think. She had a date the other night."

Ashley stopped and gaped at me. "No way. With who?"

"Hank. He showed up with a bottle of wine and a single red rose. Is that romantic or what?"

She came over and sat on my bed, her eyes gleaming. "Oh. My. God. I don't believe it. Hank? He's like a hundred."

"He's a few years older than she is, but hardly a hundred." I opened my laptop. "I need to sell my car. I'm buying a motorcycle."

Ashley's mouth opened even wider.

I was certainly dumping a lot on her at once.

"A motorcycle? No way. Does Garrett know?"

"Yeah. I thought he'd give me the lecture about the danger, but all he said was he knew it meant I'd be leaving soon."

"Everything is changing," she burst out. "I don't like it. Why can't things stay the same?" Tears began to form in her eyes.

I put the laptop aside and hugged her. "I know. But it will be okay. Your parents will always love you, no matter what changes occur in their lives. I love you, too.

You're like a sister to me. But you know I can't stay here forever. I have to make a living." I gave her a tissue to wipe her eyes. "My editor gave me a week to find another place to write about. I'm staying in Colorado, though, so we will still see each other. I promise."

She tried to smile and be brave, but I could see the sadness in her eyes. I remembered what it was like to be fifteen, a time when even the smallest change could trigger intense emotions. She sighed and went back to her unpacking. "Oh, hey, I took the journal with me, and I found something." She brought the journal over and sat on my bed again. "Look at this."

She showed me an entry toward the end of the book in Heather's bizarre shorthand. It read, "r gives me the creeps. no fun ragging on him anymore. he scares me."

"It has to be Zach, don't you think? He's the only one she ever teased that I know of."

"So the 'r' stands for rev? Is that what she called him?"

"I'm not sure. Before this entry, mostly she called him things like 'weirdo' and 'freak.' But who else could 'r' be? It has to be Zach."

I stroked Jack and looked out the window. "So at some point he started to give her the creeps."

"Well, he gives me the creeps. Him and his Bible quoting."

"Does the journal mention anything about Sarge? Any reference to him at all."

"I haven't seen anything yet. Why?"

"Remember that day at the barbeque when thought he was waiting for you outside the bathroom?"

"I don't know for sure he was waiting for me."

"No, but you said it felt weird, whatever he was doing."

She got up and went back to her suitcase.

I turned back to the journal, leafing through the pages, looking for any reference to Sarge, which I didn't find. *So she was starting to fear Zach. Could he possibly be a killer?* I remembered him cowering before his father like a whipped dog. It was hard to imagine he would have the nerve to murder someone, and in such a personal way, removing the piercings and washing her in bleach. For what purpose?

I tossed the journal aside and went back to the laptop. I pulled up the Craigslist website and typed in an ad for my car on the Pineland Park page. I would start there. Used Corollas were always in demand, so I had no doubt I could get cash for it. Then I could pay for the bike and plan my next move.

I finished posting the ad and closed the computer. The night breeze came through the open window, carrying the sounds of crickets and the rustling of the pines. An owl hooted in the distance. I watched Ashley unpacking and playing with Sasha, who kept crawling into the suitcase. That familiar feeling of melancholy came over me in a rush. I had been so focused on finding out who killed Heather that I hadn't allowed myself to process the sense of loss I would feel leaving this place and these people. I promised myself I'd keep in touch, but as Ashley was finding out, nothing stays the same. What changes would occur in Trout Fork over the next few months or a year? What about Garrett? He said he was falling in love with me. How long could I expect him to remain alone and single while he waited for me to make up my mind about him?

CHAPTER 19

The next morning, Ashley and I ate breakfast in the cabin where Alma spoiled us with French toast and sausages. The cats prowled at our feet, sniffing the air and meowing. But we knew the greasy sausage meat wasn't good for them, so we filled their bowls with cat food. They sniffed at it, and Sasha began to eat while Jack glared at us reproachfully.

"So, Mom, what's this I hear about you and Hank?" Ashley asked, chewing a mouthful of sausage.

"Don't talk with your mouth full, dear," Alma said, giving me a withering look which I pretended not to see.

Ashley swallowed loudly. "I hear he gave you a red rose. So romantic." She uttered a loud sigh, and I couldn't tell if she was being sarcastic.

"We're just friends, so don't go jumping to conclusions."

"Hmm." Ashley gave me a sideways glance. "Friends."

"Yes. Don't make more of it than it is. We like to keep each other company sometimes." She furrowed her brows at me. "No matter what you've heard."

I couldn't help grinning at her, and she punched me lightly on the arm.

"I'm going over. Now don't dawdle, you two." She folded her apron. "You know how busy Saturdays always are."

After she left, Ashley and I speculated on the possible future of Hank and Alma.

"I hope they don't get married or anything," Ashley said. "That would be too weird. He drinks too much. Besides, he's OCD about germs. The other day he actually asked me if I washed my hands before I brought his food to him."

"You know, he seems to have stopped drinking. At least he always looks sober lately. But alcoholism is a dreadful disease, and many people find it impossible to kick the habit."

"What's up with you and Garrett? Still going strong?"

I leaned back in the chair. "I don't know. We seem to argue a lot lately. But he did say he thinks he's falling in love with me."

Her fork stopped in midair. "Seriously? That's awesome. How about you?"

"I honestly don't know what I'm feeling. Love is such a big thing, and it leads to bigger things. I'm not ready for any of it. I've only known him a few weeks."

"Well, we've known him for years, and he's a good guy."

"No doubt. But is he the *right* good guy for me? That's the question."

She got up and put the dishes in the sink. "You know what they say. Love is like fishing. It's all about the one that got away."

I got up from the table. "I'll keep that in mind. Tell your mom I'll be right over. I need to make a phone call."

Ashley left for the café, and I went to sit on my bed with Jack. I took my phone off its charger, dialed the

number, and waited to hear Mother's voice. I wasn't sure
how I was going to approach her with the latest news, but
it had to be done.

"Hello. Lowell residence," her cool voice answered.

"Hi, Mother."

"Oh, Kathryn. Your father and I were just talking
about you. He asked where you are and where you will be
going. I told him I didn't know."

There was that subtle implied criticism again. "I'm
still in Trout Fork."

"Oh, yes. I read your column in the magazine." I
waited for editorial comment, but there was none forth-
coming. "Where will you be going next, dear?"

"I'm not sure yet, Mother. There are some things
here I need to wrap up before I leave."

"Like what?"

I took a deep breath. "I'm selling my car. I'm buying
a motorcycle." Silence. "I need you to call the insurance
agent and take the Corolla off the policy and add the bike.
I'll email you the details, if that's okay." More silence.
"Mother? Are you still there?"

She sighed. "I'm still here. I'll let your father know
so he can call the agent."

"Thanks."

"Anything else you need to tell me?" I could imagine
her fanning herself with today's copy of *The New York
Times*.

"Mr. Crenshaw has allowed me to stay a bit longer.
Then I have to find another locale to write about. I'm
thinking of one of the ski resorts."

"Vail is lovely this time of year. The Bransons have
a home there."

"I'm thinking of doing the column on one of the
smaller resorts. People are often looking for less crowded, less touristy resorts. There are a couple fairly close

by, and anyway I'd like to stay in the area. I've made some close friends here that I don't want to lose touch with."

"Does that mean you're dating someone?"

"I do have a friend I see now and then. But it's not serious."

"What kind of man could you meet in Colorado? Is he suitable?" I knew exactly what she meant by suitable—wealthy and socially connected. "What does he do?"

"He's a detective with the local police department."

I heard her sniff disdainfully. "A detective? Really, Kathryn—"

I could feel my anger beginning to take hold. "Now, don't start, Mother. You should know by now I have no interest in New York society or the men I've met there. Besides, Garrett and I are really only friends."

"Garrett?"

"Garrett Easterbrook." I could imagine her reaching for the social register to look up the Easterbrooks.

I heard her exhale into the phone. "Well, as your father says, it's your life."

"I need to go to work, so I'll say good-bye. Give my love to Dad."

"I will, dear. Please, please be careful on that motorcycle."

I hung up and leaned back against my pillow, and Alma's voice echoed in my mind. *'It's not easy being a mother. You girls have no idea.'*

ɛↄɛↄ

It was nearly ten o'clock before the crowd in the café thinned out. I was cleaning the patio tables when Duane came in.

"Are you up for some practice on my bike? Not that you really need it. Then we could go into town for your driver's test."

"I don't know. Do you think I'm ready?"

"Yes, I do." He shuffled his feet. "The thing is, we have to leave today. We have meetings at the college on Monday that have been moved up a couple of weeks."

I made one last swipe at the table I was cleaning. "Then today it is. Let me tell Alma I'll be gone. How long should it take?"

"You'll probably be back by noon."

"Perfect. I'll meet you in the parking lot."

On my way to the kitchen, I glanced at the table in the corner where Garrett usually sat, wondering why I hadn't heard from him in three days, since that night at Borelli's. Was he still annoyed with me about the bike and about talking to Gil? Or was he just giving me some time to react to his saying he was falling in love with me? Whatever it was, it was depressing to think I might have to spend my last few days here without him.

Duane was sitting on the backseat of his bike waiting for me. "Let's go to the Honda dealer. You can practice on their lot."

I drove the bike along the road to town, glancing briefly down Garrett's driveway as we flew by. The cabin looked at once inviting and lonely. It was a lovely little house, and I remembered how much I had enjoyed living there those few days after the fire. But would I enjoy living there permanently?

Duane yelled in my ear over the sound of the wind. "When you've had some practice, we can go to the DMV, and you can take the tests. There's a written test and a driving skills test. You have a Colorado driver's license, don't you?"

"Yes. My New York license expired, and I wasn't about to go back there to renew it."

"And you've studied the manual I gave you?"

"Yes."

"Then it should be easy. Let's hope it's not too crowded."

We pulled into the Honda dealership, and I directed the bike to the back lot where I practiced steering around cones, stopping, starting, and shifting through the gears. Duane was right. It really was easy, and I seemed to take to it naturally. We left there and pulled into the DMV down the street. Fortunately, there were few people waiting to take driving tests, so after I passed the written exam, Duane and I took seats near the door to the test lot with two other people.

"Duane," I said as we waited for the examiner to call me, "did you hear Zach and his father this morning?"

"It was impossible not to hear them."

"Did you know his father is a pastor of a church in Georgia?"

He shook his head sadly. "I didn't know that, but it doesn't surprise me."

"How much of their conversation did you hear?"

He looked at me, his eyes seeming to pierce into my soul. "What is it you're trying to say, Ryn?"

"I've been thinking about what you said about do-do religion, and I want to know what effect that has on a person. I mean, psychologically."

"Depends on the person. Why?"

"Well, Zach's father was pretty rough on him. What caught my attention was when he said Zach had to do more, that it was what God expected of him. That reminded me of what you said about it. And Alma said Zach had some kind of nervous breakdown in the past. Could the two things be related?"

"You mean can a person have a breakdown because of the pressure his religion puts on him? If the pressure is extreme, then certainly. That pressure can lead to all kinds of things. It can even cause someone to blow themselves up or hijack an airplane full of innocent people and fly it into a building. It's all about the perceived need to sacrifice and prove oneself to God. That can have a devastating effect on the human psyche."

"Could it drive someone to kill? I don't mean the radical Muslims. I mean regular people."

Duane was quiet for a moment. "I've certainly had murderous thoughts."

"You? I don't believe it."

"Believe it. Like Zach, I was raised in a legalistic church. I was taught that God can't accomplish anything without our help, which seemed pretty lame to me. But I bought into it until one day I couldn't stand it anymore. I grew more and more angry until I was ready to strangle someone. That's when I knew it was time to get out. So I chucked the whole scene and joined the Hell's Angels."

I gasped. "What? No."

"Yes. They seemed to me to be as far from the whole God scene as I could get. I blamed God for putting unreasonable demands on me when, in fact, it was the man-made religion that did that, not God. So I rebelled and went the opposite way for a time. I became a bonafide one-percenter." He chuckled at the expression that must have been on my face. "You see, it was as far as I could get from everything I'd been taught all my life."

"What made you leave the Hell's Angels?"

"For one thing, I had no peace there. I thought, at first, it was the guilt that had been ingrained in me all those years. But after a while, I really began to detest that life. It was just as restricting as the church life, only in a different way. So I lit out on my own and rode my bike, hundreds, thousands of miles, simply riding and enjoying the scenery. That's when God started speaking to me, not in an audible voice, but through what I was seeing. That's when I realized what the do-do system misses—God didn't need our help to create the world. He didn't need us then, and he doesn't need us now. He will accomplish what he wants to accomplish, with or without us. It was a relief to get that burden off my back."

"What about those who don't come to that conclusion?"

"Most stay in the do-do system. A few of them convince themselves they're doing the great things they're supposed to do, which makes them arrogant and proud. The rest just struggle along under the burden until they either give up and chuck it all, like I did, or they develop a kind of neurosis from trying to hide their failures from one another. I suspect that's where Zach is and what caused his breakdown. Sad."

I sat there pondering all that Duane had said and wondering about Zach. Could he have killed Heather as his way of proving himself to God? Or was he so angry and frustrated that he was ready to lash out at anyone, and she got in his way? Could that sad little man really be a killer and if not, who else could it be? I would have to talk to Garrett about him.

The examiner came to the door and called, "Kathryn Lowell."

I got up to follow him. "Wish me luck."

eɔeɔ

Just as Duane had predicted, I breezed through both the written and driving tests and had the motorcycle endorsement added to my license. We stopped at the Honda dealership where I talked to the manager and assured him that as soon as I sold my car, I would be back to finish paying for the bike. As I drove us back to Trout Fork, it began to really sink in that my time here was almost over, and I was overwhelmed with a sense of loss. There was a sense of failure, too, to think I might be leaving without finding out who killed Heather.

As I pulled the bike into the parking lot in front of the café, there was Garrett's gray truck. We dismounted, and I handed the helmet to Duane and hugged him. "Thanks for everything, Duane. I'll never forget you. I hope to meet you again someday. Have a good trip home."

He laid a hand on my shoulder. "Enjoy your bike. I hope your cat takes to it."

I smiled at the thought of Jack in the little helmet and goggles I would buy for him. "I'm sure he will. He's up for pretty much anything."

I watched Duane drive the bike slowly toward the field where his two friends were packed up and waiting for him. They all waved to me as they pulled out of the lot together. I stood watching them until the sound of their engines died in the distance, and the same melancholy feeling of loss washed over me. Ashley was right. Everything was changing, and I didn't like it any more than she did.

When I turned toward the café, I saw Garrett sitting on the patio watching me. I joined him at his table.

"You missed lunch. Ashley was wondering where you were." He seemed a little peeved. Could he be jealous of Duane?

"Let me go in and tell Alma I'm back. Then I want to talk to you about something." I left him and headed for the kitchen where I found Alma and Ashley. As I passed the cash register, I noticed that the Help Wanted sign had been put up again.

I guess they've accepted that I'm really going, I thought.

"Did you get your license?" Alma asked.

"Piece of cake. Duane is a good teacher. He and his buddies are on their way home. They just now left. Could I sit with Garrett for a while?"

"Sure. We're not busy."

I went back to the patio to Garrett's table.

"I have a theory," I said to him as I sat down, "and I want you to tell me if I'm crazy."

"Okay."

"Do you think Zach could be the killer? Ashley read in Heather's journal that it was no fun teasing him anymore and that he was giving her the creeps."

Garrett sipped his coffee. "That hardly makes him a murderer."

I pulled my chair closer to him. "Let's think about some things. We know Heather was starting to be afraid of him. And I know someone has been hanging around Alma's cabin at night. I've seen him twice. Well, once I only heard him. But I think he's been looking in the windows. Maybe at Ashley. Or me."

"Did you see him looking in the windows?"

"No, but who else could it be? We've eliminated Malone, and I'm sure it's not Gil."

"You're sure. I'm not. He's the one Heather was blackmailing. Zach has no motive. Even if he was stalking Ashley and looking in the windows at you girls, that makes him a pervert or a voyeur, not a killer. And suppose it was him, why didn't he assault her? All he did was take out the piercings, wash her in bleach, and put her in a white sheet. Those aren't the actions of a sexual predator."

I didn't know what to say to that. If Duane was right,

and Zach was being driven crazy by his father's religion, that still didn't provide a motive for murder. I sat back and realized how far-fetched my theory sounded. "Then who was it? If not Gil or Malone or Zach, who's the killer?"

"The only one with an alibi we can confirm is Malone," Garrett said. "Gil hasn't been eliminated, and neither has Hank. Not in my mind. Then there's Sarge. I'd like to find out more about his time in the Marines, but it's not easy to get that information." He watched me for a moment. "Not to change the subject, but where did you and Duane go?"

"He took me to get my motorcycle license. I passed both the tests."

He stirred his coffee in silence. "Now you'll be getting your bike and be on your way."

I reached for his hand and held it. "I can't stay here, Garrett. I have a job, and I can't afford to lose it."

"Are you sure that's the reason you're leaving? Or does it have something to do with what I told you the other night? Did that scare you away?"

"No. If I'm honest with myself, I have to admit I'm developing the same feelings for you."

He looked at me hopefully.

"But I can't quit my job and stay here, hoping it might work out between us. What happens if it doesn't? Then I'm out of a job and have no choice but to go back to New York. I can't take that chance. Someday something might happen between us, but not now. There's just no time."

His deep blue eyes pleaded with me. "Then stay here, and we'll have that time. You can find a job in Pineland Park. That will give us the time we need."

"A job doing what? Working at Walmart? Or brewing coffee at Starbucks? I can't do that. I'm a writer, and that means I have to go where the work is. Right now, the only work I have is writing a column about resorts in Colorado. Pineland Park isn't a resort. Try to understand. At least I won't be far away. We can still see each other, even if it's only once a week or so."

His cell phone rang, and he answered. "Yes, sir. Right away." He got up. "I have to go. Have dinner with me tonight?"

I nodded and reluctantly let go of his hand.

છ∕ગલ∕ગ

Garrett and I sat at his dining room table in what seemed to be a re-creation of our first date. The candles glowed, the wineglasses were kept full and the score of Gounod's opera, *Romeo and Juliet*, played softly in the background. It seemed like a last-ditch effort to woo me with romance. I had to admit, I was tempted to stay, but something told me if I jumped into a relationship with him too early, I would ruin it. If it was meant to be, it would survive a separation of a few months or a year. We sat together on the sofa.

"How's your novel coming along?" he asked as he poured more wine into my glass.

I leaned back. "I haven't written anything on it since I've been here."

"I guess your detective work keeps you busy," he said with a sideways glance.

"Very funny. Actually, writing a novel involves more than purely the writing part. There's the background research, character development, thinking up plots. Most of it goes on in your head before your fingers ever hit the keys."

"That does sound a lot like detective work, come to think of it. The leg work is all done before the arrest. It's like solving a puzzle. That's what appeals to me about it."

"I can see that. I guess we're a lot alike. We both analyze people, me so I can write about them, and you so you can find the criminals. Take Madam Gauzie, for instance. How would you analyze her?"

He raised an eyebrow. "Tell me you're not thinking she's the killer."

"Of course not. But she will definitely wind up in my novel somewhere. A truly unique person. She's always warning me to be careful at night and lock my doors. She told me there has been something sinister lurking around Trout Fork. She says she can feel it."

"Does she think she's psychic?"

"Maybe. Don't the police use psychics sometimes?"

"Some do. But they've proven to be wrong as often as they're right, so they're not of much use."

We were interrupted by Garrett's cell phone ringing. "Now who can that be?" He went into his bedroom to retrieve the phone, and I could hear him talking, but all I could make out were the words "stay calm." He came back to the table, and his expression told me it was something serious.

"Who was that?"

"It was Alma. Ashley is missing."

CHAPTER 20

As we raced along the road back to Trout Fork, my stomach was in knots and my throat dry. I gripped the handle above the passenger's side door until realized I was cutting off the circulation to my arm. My only thought was the devastation that would be caused if anything happened to Ashley. *First Heather and now Ashley. How will Alma ever survive it?*

Garrett was on his phone with the police at his station. He sounded calm and in control, which seemed inconceivable to me. He disconnected and laid his phone on the seat.

My eyes desperately sought his. "Are they coming?"

He reached over and took my hand. "They're contacting the CBI, Colorado Bureau of Investigation, to ask them to issue an Amber Alert. If she has been abducted, the public will be on the lookout for her. In the meantime, the captain says I'm to take charge of the search here until he notifies the Denver PD." He stroked my hand. "Don't worry. We'll find her."

The possibility she might be found the same way Heather was found terrified me. I tried not to envision Ashley buried in a shallow grave, wrapped in a white sheet, and smelling of bleach, but the images of that awful day pummeled my brain without mercy.

We skidded to a stop in front of the café which was blazing with light. The residents of Trout Fork were gathered outside, some with flashlights and even a few with rifles. Hank, Gil, and Zach stood huddled together talking. Gil had a sidearm in a holster on his belt.

Alma burst out of the café, tears streaming down her face. She ran toward us, Madam Gauzie following closely behind, her disheveled gray hair flying.

"Thank God you're here!" Alma cried. She hung onto Garrett's arm as he got out of the truck. "What should we do? Everyone is ready to help look for her."

"Come inside, all of you." Garrett's commanding tone and authority seemed to be reassuring to Alma.

I put my arm around her shoulders, and we followed Garrett into the café. The rest of the group trooped in and stood along the walls of the dining room. There was a good deal of angry muttering among the residents. Garrett stood near the table where Madam Gauzie and I had deposited Alma. He leaned over with his hand on her shoulder. "When did you see her last, Alma?"

"At about eight." Her voice trembled. "I was finishing up in the kitchen, and she left for the cabin. She said she was tired and wanted to take a shower. She worked so hard today. She's such a good girl." Tears filled her eyes, and her lower lip quivered. Madam Gauzie held her hand, her eyes beseeching Garrett to do something.

"She wasn't in the cabin when you got there?"

She shook her head. "I thought maybe she had gone to visit Madam Gauzie or took a walk. When she didn't come back, I checked with Madam Gauzie. Then I called you. Madam Gauzie called Gil, and he brought the rest of the folks." A sob escaped from her throat.

Garrett patted her shoulder and straightened up. He looked at his watch and cleared his throat. "Attention, please. Ashley has been missing since eight o'clock. It's now ten-thirty. Has anyone else seen her in that time?"

No one responded.

"Did anyone see anything suspicious? Like a stranger hanging around?"

Again, no response.

"All right. There will be an Amber Alert issued for her, but in the meantime, we're going to search every inch of the area. We'll start with the cabins. Gil, you and Hank and Zach knock on every door and ask to look in all the rooms. Report to me anyone who won't cooperate or who asks for a search warrant."

"We can't wait around for a search warrant," Gil growled, gripping the handle of his holstered revolver.

"Now look, Gil," Garrett said sternly. "There will be none of that. You're not law enforcement. If you are turned away at any door, you must come directly to me. Are we clear?"

Gil nodded, but there was fire in his eyes.

The three men left, and Garrett turned to the others. "The rest of you search the area. Begin at Alma's cabin and work your way out in a circle. Look for tracks or any kind of suspicious marks. Keep calling her name and listen carefully for any sound. If you see or hear anything, and I mean anything, stay where you are and call me. Put my cell number into your phones."

They all pulled out their phones, and he repeated his number slowly.

"Now let's go."

The men filed out, and Garrett turned to Alma. "I'd like to look at her room now, if that's all right."

She nodded dumbly, and I could see that shock was beginning to set in, stunting her ability to speak or move.

"I'll stay with her," Madam Gauzie said, hugging her protectively.

"Thank you. Ryn, come with me."

We went to the cabin where Garrett looked carefully at the steps and peered closely at the surrounding ground, shining his flashlight in all directions. The concrete walk that led to the steps offered no clue. Neither did the gravel around the walk. If she went with someone or was dragged or carried, there was no trace of it here. Standing at the door, I thought about the footsteps I had heard the other night. Was it the same person? Was he just waiting for an opportunity to grab one of us? A shiver went down my spine.

"Let's go in," Garrett said. "But don't touch anything."

We walked through the cabin's small living room into the bedroom I shared with Ashley. Jack and Sasha were lying together on Ashley's bed. They looked up and squinted at us when we switched on the light. Jack hopped off the bed and came to me, rubbing on my legs and meowing for attention. I picked him up and held him in my arms, grateful for the warm comfort he provided.

"Does anything look different?" Garrett asked.

I looked around at my clothes on the bed, my hairbrush and makeup on the dresser. "Nothing. It looks exactly like it did when you picked me up this evening."

"She hasn't been here. That means she disappeared somewhere between the back door of the café and the front door of the cabin. Let's go back to the café."

Leaving the cabin, we could see the beams from the flashlights flickering in the woods around the cabin and heard voices calling Ashley's name. We stood on the darkened front step for a moment, and I was struck by the irony of the beautiful summer night on which this horror had occurred. The sky was covered in stars, and a soft breeze caressed my face. An owl hooted a lonely call from a nearby treetop.

We went back to the café where Alma sat quietly weeping with her arms wrapped around her. Madam Gauzie offered what comfort she could, but Alma was inconsolable. I was furious with myself. Hadn't I promised to find the lunatic that killed Heather? If I had kept my promise, Alma wouldn't be going through this hell now.

Garrett checked his phone every few minutes, and at one point, he said, "Damn."

"What? What is it?" Alma demanded, her expression one of hope mixed with fear.

"Phone service cut out. Oh, wait, it's back now."

Alma was frantic, her red-rimmed eyes silently begging us to end this terrible night. I felt completely helpless. All I could do was sit with her and rub her shoulders.

Garrett sat down next to her. "Have you tried calling her?"

"Yes. It goes right to voice mail. It must be turned off. I called her father to let him know. He hasn't heard from her. He's on his way down. Oh, my God."

The tension was unbearable.

At one point, I said, "Isn't there something we can do? We can't just sit here and wait."

"Unfortunately, that's all we can do until morning. The CBI will be here then with their forensics team. Hopefully, one of the searchers will find her before then." He grasped my hand. "This is the hardest part." He looked at Alma. "Why don't you go back to the cabin and try to rest. There's nothing you can do here. If she comes back on her own, the cabin is where she'll go. You'll want to be there."

Alma nodded and stood, weaving unsteadily in her shock and fear. "I'll take her," Madam Gauzie said, and the two of them left through the back door.

I searched Garrett's face. "You don't really think she'll come back on her own, do you?"

He shrugged his shoulders and ran his hand across his eyes. "When teenagers run away, they often do come back on their own."

"But this isn't a runaway."

"We don't know that for sure. Didn't you tell me she was upset about her parents arguing?"

"Yes, but Ashley is too level-headed to run off. That's just not her."

The rest of that awful night dragged slowly. I made a pot of coffee, and we drank it as we waited for news from the searchers. Each time a team had searched a cabin, they notified Garrett, and he checked it off the list we'd made of the residents of Trout Fork. Once the cabins were all cleared, the teams were told to spread out along the trail in both directions, heeding Garrett's instructions to shine their flashlights along both shores of the creek and into the water.

At one point, Hank called Garrett to say he thought he'd found something.

"Where are you?" Garrett asked. "Okay. Stay there. I'm on my way."

"What is it?" I was almost afraid of the answer.

"A cloth of some kind. It could be clothing."

My heart sank as I remembered the Pink Floyd T-shirt that had started me down this nightmare trail, and I prayed silently that God, if he was listening, would spare Ashley's life.

It was after four a.m. when Garrett finally returned. "False alarm. It couldn't be Ashley's. It had been there too long."

I exhaled for what seemed like the first time in hours. "I can't stand anymore of this. I'm going over to check on Alma."

In the cabin, I found Alma and Robert holding one another on the sofa. Madam Gauzie dozed in the chair. Ashley's father's face was ashen gray. They both looked up hopefully as I came in.

"Any news?" Alma asked.

I shook my head. "Nothing so far."

Their faces reflected both relief and fear. I went into the bedroom and was overwhelmed with sorrow at the sight of Ashley's empty bed. I sat down on my bed and stroked Jack. My muscles were tight and sore from the night's tension, and despite my fatigue, a jog along the trail seemed very appealing. Maybe I could help look for Ashley. I changed quickly and slipped out the back door without disturbing the grieving parents.

I switched on my phone's flashlight and jogged slowly along behind the cabins before sunrise. There was a faint pink glow in the sky to the east, but the path was shrouded in near darkness. I could still hear voices calling for Ashley, but they were far away and very faint. The pre-dawn air was crisp and cool, and I breathed deeply to clear my head.

As the trail led me past the place where I had seen Zach the day before, I thought I heard a muffled cry coming from the direction of his cabin. I stopped and listened, not sure whether it was an animal or a bird. It came again, a little louder and sounding more frantic this time, followed by the sound of a man's voice. Then silence. I climbed quietly up the hillside toward the cabin, sidled up to one of the back windows, and peeked in. My heart leapt into my throat when I saw Ashley slumped in a corner of the room, wearing only her underwear. Her hands were tied in front of her, and a piece of duct tape was across her mouth. There was abject terror in her eyes as she stared at the man standing over her.

"Now you'll have to put this on," Zach was saying in

a wheedling tone, holding up a long white garment. "I got rid of all those nasty clothes you had on. They were Satan's handiwork. Not suitable for what we're going to do."

Ashley struggled frantically against her bonds, her terrified screams dying in her throat. Her eyes darted to the corner of the room where a thick wooden beam in the shape of a cross leaned against the wall. Zach hauled her up by the arms and began to pull the white robe over her head. She continued to struggle, trying to kick him in the groin until he gave her a vicious smack across the face. She collapsed with a whimper, but he held her up. "My child, despise not thou the chastening of the Lord, nor faint when thou art rebuked of him. Hebrews twelve, five," he intoned.

He forced the white garment over her head and dragged her toward the corner. He threw her onto the floor and picked up a huge hunting knife which he began to sharpen on a stone. I gasped as the reality of what he was about to do became clear to me. My head was spinning, and my hands shook violently as I pulled out my phone and hit the button that auto-dialed Garrett's number. But it went right to voice mail. Damn! He must be talking to someone. Even if I ran to get help, it would be too late for that poor girl being prepared for a ritual slaughter. I whispered a frantic message to his voice mail. "Come to Zach's cabin. He has Ashley. Hurry!"

I dashed around to the front door of the cabin and saw my hand trembling as I reached for the doorknob. I bit my lip and tightened my hand around the knob. It wouldn't budge. I took a deep breath and began pounding on the door. After what seemed like an eternity, Zach opened the door. His cherubic face was wreathed in a beatific smile. "Well, good morning, Ryn," he said cheerfully. "What brings you out so early?"

I stared at him mutely. He was so calm, so normal. Had I imagined the whole horrible scene in the bedroom?

"I saw you," I said, trying to keep my voice from shaking. "Through the window. I know what you're doing." I straightened my shoulders and tried to appear taller than I was. "You have to let her go."

His smile never faded, and he spoke softly and evenly. "Oh, I see. You've made a mistake. It's not what you think. Come in and talk to her." He held open the door and ushered me in with extreme courtesy.

I stepped into the cabin tentatively, being careful to keep him in front of me and an eye on his hands. I didn't have a plan, but perhaps if I could free Ashley somehow, she and I together could overpower him.

"You're to be commended for your concern," he said with a crooked smile. "Like the Good Samaritan. But you'll see there is nothing to worry about. Come and see for yourself."

He led me to the bedroom and opened the door. The powerful smell of bleach permeated the air in the small room. Ashley was still on the floor, her terror-filled eyes pleading with me to help her. I started to run toward her, but as I passed Zach, he grabbed me from behind, his arm like a vise around my neck. He held me close to him, his hot breath next to my ear.

"Thank you, Lord, for sending thy servant another sacrifice," he whispered as he dragged me to the bed and pushed me down. I jumped up again and was met with a terrific blow to the head. Tiny lights appeared before my eyes as I fell back down. I tried not to pass out, telling myself to remain calm and keep my wits about me. I was no match for his strength, but I knew his mental state was fragile. If I could only keep him talking, I might have a chance.

He bent down and began to bind my feet together,

rocking back and forth and mumbling. He glanced out the window. "Almost dawn. It has to be now. Has to be at dawn."

I spoke softly and tried to reason with him. "Zach, you don't want to do this. You've known Ashley since she was a little girl. Why would you want to hurt her?"

He ignored me and began to tie my hands together in front of me.

"And what about Alma? She's been your good friend for years. Can you imagine the pain you'll be inflicting on her if you kill her only child?"

He looked up at me, his eyes dilated and frenzied. Then he picked up the knife which he drew across his sleeve, still mumbling in a sort of trance-like state.

"Are you going to sacrifice us to God?"

He continued ignoring me, so I tried another tack. "God must be very pleased with your faith."

He shook his head vehemently. "Even so faith, if it hath not works, is dead, being alone. James two, seventeen."

"Your work is to sacrifice innocent girls like Heather and Ashley? That will please God?"

He looked at me with a fearful expression. "No. No. He's not pleased with me. I made a mistake. I did it wrong the first time. With that other one. Don't you understand?"

My mouth was so dry I could barely speak. "No, I really don't. But I want to. Can you explain it to me?" I tried to sound genuinely interested in his warped theology, anything to keep him talking.

"The other one wasn't innocent. She was one of them."

"One of who?"

His buggy eyes blazed with fury behind his thick lenses. "The harlots," he shouted. "They're Satan's temptation sent to try us. Every day she flaunted herself in front of me. Tempting me, laughing at me. I stopped her."

"You sacrificed her. You tied her to that cross you built, didn't you?"

"Of course," he said with a lopsided grin. "That's the way it has to be done." He leaned in close to me, his foul breath causing me to turn my head. "But she wasn't good enough. It has to be a lamb without blemish. Not a harlot." He lurched over to Ashley, who was staring at us in terror. He stroked her hair. "This one," he crooned. "This one is the lamb without a blemish. Not that other one. I tried to clean her. I took out those ugly piercings and threw away her worldly clothes. But it wasn't enough."

"You washed her in the bleach, didn't you?" I said, trying to keep him talking until Garrett could get my message.

"Yes! But it wasn't enough. She wasn't good enough. Not a perfect lamb. This one. This one will release me."

"Release you from what?"

He came close to me and squinted. "You don't know what it's like. It's like a fire in my veins. A consuming fire. I've tried to stop it. I moved here. I got rid of my computer. The internet is the devil's playground with all those evil websites. Evil. Evil everywhere."

"You mean the porn sites."

"Yes! But I couldn't get away from the images in my mind." He began pounding his head with his fist. "And those women that come in with the bikers. Half naked with their painted faces. Evil. Harlots, all of them. I tried not to look at them. I hid my eyes from them. Until that other one showed up."

"Heather."

He paced back and forth in front of me, waving the knife. "She moved in with Ashley, and she was there all the time. Always tempting me. I couldn't stop watching her."

"You were watching them through their window. And then you watched us. It was you I heard running from the cabin that night."

He stared at me frantically. "Yes! Yes! I couldn't stop it. I watched you all. Oh, I knew it was wrong. I had to punish myself every time. See what I did?"

He put down the knife and pulled up his long sleeves, a wild, almost proud look in his eyes. I gasped at the sight of the deep wounds cut into his arms and wrists, some fresh and oozing blood and some old enough to have produced white scars. "But it wasn't enough. It's never good enough," he whined. "Never. But this one will be good enough." He appraised Ashley with an al-most affectionate gaze.

"But what if it's not? What do you do then? Keep killing? Kill Ashley then kill me? What then? You can't kill every female on the planet. The bikers will keep com-ing with their women. There will always be another wait-ress, another girl to tempt you. You can't kill us all. Don't you see? It's not us. We're not the problem. It's in your mind. In your heart."

He furrowed his brow at me, his eyes widening as my words seemed to stop him. He glared at me, as if facing the devils of his own soul, all those devils of torment and doubt which had plagued him since adolescence, the ones he had tried, and failed, to keep strictly under control. He shook his head as if to shake away my words and what they meant. "Stop it. *Stop it*." He raised the knife to my neck, his hand trembling, and pressed the blade into my throat.

I turned my head and waited for the end. Then his manner became frenzied, and he began to pound the blade of the knife into his hand, opening up cuts with each stroke. His red-rimmed eyes stared at the wall, seeing nothing. Saliva dripped from his mouth. "In my heart," he mumbled over and over. "In my heart, *my* heart." Sweat was running down his face and defeat seemed to be in the depths of his soul. He suddenly staggered away from me and stood in the middle of the room in a queer half-stupor, chin sunk onto his chest, staring at the floor.

I watched in horror as suddenly, with one hideous scream, he plunged the knife into his own neck. Blood spurted all over from his severed jugular vein. He collapsed to the floor, shuddered for a moment, then was still, his thick glasses lying askew on his face and his lifeless eyes staring.

CHAPTER 21

The silence was palpable. The only sound was the drip, drip of his blood slowly seeping from the wound in his neck and pooling on the wooden floor. Ashley and I stared at each other in disbelief. My pulse began to slow, and the pounding in my ears diminished, allowing the night sounds to fill the room—the crickets and frogs, the breeze whispering through the pines, a dog barking in the distance.

The scene felt so surreal that it seemed any movement would break the spell and the horror would begin again. But the sound of Ashley quietly weeping brought me back to reality. I slipped off the bed and, kneeling down next to Zach, pulled the bloody knife from his hand, and began to saw at the rope around my ankles. It was time-consuming and difficult to do with my wrists bound together, and I had a fleeting thought about how quick and easy it always seemed when done in a movie.

Once my feet were free, I stumbled over to Ashley, who was still lying crumpled on the floor, and together we cut through the ropes binding our hands. Then I threw the knife on the floor, and we fell into each other's arms, sobbing with relief.

The crash of the front door being broken in was followed by Garrett and Gil bursting into the bedroom where Ashley and I were staggering to our feet. The two men stood transfixed by the scene.

Then Garrett came to us and gently gathered us into his arms. "I'm so sorry," he whispered to me. "I just heard your message. Are you two all right?"

We nodded. "He killed himself," Ashley whispered.

Gil was standing over Zach's body. Then he looked up at us, his hands spread wide, a look of horror on his face. "She was here all the time. I should have insisted. But we all agreed we'd be wasting time to search each other's cabins. We could've found her. I should have—"

"Don't blame yourself, Gil," Garrett interrupted. "Thank God, Ryn found her in time." He held me at arm's length. "How did you know?"

"I didn't. I was jogging along the trail and heard a noise. I came up to the cabin to see what it was and looked in that window. That's when I saw Ashley." My eyes searched his face, trying to find a sane explanation for insanity. "He was going to crucify her. At dawn. The same as he did to Heather. Not with nails. With ropes on her wrists and ankles. He was going to hang her on that cross and kill her. That's what he did to Heather."

Ashley's knees buckled, and Garrett sat her down on the bed. I stood with Garrett as he pulled out his phone and dialed. "Alma? We found her. Yes, she's all right. Just scared. We're in Zach's cabin. Come over." Then he dialed another number, and I heard him talking to the coroner as he walked around Zach's body. He hung up and began taking charge of the scene. "Gil, stand by the front door, will you? Don't let anyone in except her parents and the men from the coroner's office."

Gil nodded and left the room. I watched Garrett squat down next to Zach's body and begin to take pictures with his phone. He lifted one arm and took a picture of the wounds on his wrist. He looked up at me. "He's been self-mutilating. See here? It's very common in cases like this. They cut themselves as punishment. Guilt drives them to it." He shook his head sadly.

As he worked, he asked questions of Ashley. In a trembling voice, she told us that the last thing she remembered was trying to unlock the door to her cabin. She heard a noise and saw Zach standing in the shadows, smiling at her. He came toward her with a green cloth in his hand which he put up to her face. She remembered struggling, and the next thing she knew, she woke up in this room with her hands and feet tied. Her clothes were in the corner, and he was putting her in the white sheet she had on now. Then she heard me come in.

Garrett picked up a green cloth next to the body and sniffed it. "He used chloroform. He must have made his own. All it takes is ammonia and bleach. That's why there was no record of him buying it."

"His father did say something about him being a chemistry major in college," I said.

Garrett nodded. "That explains the bleach bottles with no fingerprints." He picked up the knife with his handkerchief and turned it, examining it from several angles. "This must be what he used on Heather. It's about the right size."

Alma rushed in with Robert, their ashen gray faces terror-stricken, and went to Ashley. The three of them hugged and cried together. How different that little family scene was from the one I remembered after Davey's death.

My mother and father sat in opposite chairs in the hospital waiting room, lost and isolated in their shared grief, unable to comfort one another. Or me.

e/ɔe/ɔ

Five days later, I woke for the last time in the bedroom I shared with Ashley. I pulled the lace curtain away from the window and surveyed the scene. The fire-blackened trees stood stark and lonely on the hillside. I wondered how long it would take for the forest to reseed itself and whether I would ever return to see it. But this was Friday, and the extra time Crenshaw had given me here was up.

Jack rose from my side and stretched. Then he sat down, staring at me. Somehow, he seemed to sense we would be on the move again soon. The whirlwind of activity in the past few days had alerted him to a change in the routine. The ride he took on my new Honda motorcycle had been met with his usual cool composure.

I smiled at the memory of him secured in the basket in front of me, the wind whipping his fur as he raised his nose to sniff at it.

While some cats would be terrified by such an experience, Jack seemed to take it in stride. At one point, he even curled up in the basket and snoozed.

Ashley turned over and mumbled something in her sleep. I hoped she wasn't having nightmares about her experience. But she seemed to be immune to any repercussions. In fact, she had been unusually buoyant these past few days, but that could be attributed to the new relationship her parents seemed to be developing. If, as Alma had said, their divorce was due to their having been too young when they married, maybe this experience would give them the opportunity to start again. The three of them seemed to have grown very close since Sunday. I hoped it would continue.

I got up quietly and went out to the kitchen. Alma and Robert sat at the kitchen table, she in her bathrobe and he with his hair mussed and sleep in his eyes. So he had spent the night. Well, good for them.

Alma got up when she saw me. "Good morning, dear. Did you sleep well?"

"Very well."

She filled a coffee cup for me. "Are you really leaving us today?"

"I'm afraid so."

"Will you see Garrett before you go?"

"He said he would come by before going to work."

"Where's your next stop?" Robert asked.

"I've booked a room at the Above the Clouds golf resort. It's a small place farther up in the mountains. There's a golf course, restaurant, hotel, and spa. That should make an interesting column."

Alma patted my arm. "Well, let's just hope it turns out to be quieter than Trout Fork. I bet you'll be glad to see us in your rearview mirror."

I hugged her tightly. "On the contrary. I'll miss you all terribly. It's been a wonderful few weeks, in spite of…everything. I hope you'll keep in touch. I want to know how things work out." I nodded slightly toward Robert, who was wolfing down some toast with Alma's homemade wild berry jam.

She blushed slightly. "Well, Madam Gauzie still hasn't forgiven you for not letting her plan a going-away party."

"She's such a sweetheart. I'll miss her too." A lump was growing in my throat, so I made the excuse that I had to pack, afraid my emotions would overwhelm me.

Ashley came into the kitchen with Sasha on her shoulder.

"Good morning, princess," Robert said. "Have some breakfast?"

Ashley hugged her father. "Thanks, Daddy."

I hadn't heard her use that endearment toward Robert before. I left the three of them chatting and enjoying each other's company. As I packed, I felt the excitement of a new adventure, tinged with that old aching loneliness that left me wondering how long it would be before this nomadic lifestyle would begin to wear on me.

After I showered and changed, I took my suitcase and laptop out to the bike to secure them on the back rack. I gazed around at the scenery for the last time. The early morning sun filtering through the trees created moving patterns on the pavement. The only sound was the gurgling of the creek across the street, the same sound I heard that day I pulled into Trout Fork for the first time.

I was securing Jack's basket on the bike when Garrett's pickup pulled slowly into the lot. Our date the night before had been bittersweet. We had sat for hours in front of the fire he had built. His excuse was that the nights were becoming chilly, but I had a feeling it was a last-ditch effort to get me to change my mind. And it nearly worked. Tearing myself away from him had been difficult.

He came to me. "You're on your way."

I nodded, unable to meet his eyes. *Don't start crying,* I warned myself. *Just don't.*

"Is the café open yet?"

"No. Alma is late today. She and Robert and Ashley are having breakfast together. You know, I think Alma and Robert may be getting back together."

"That's great. I hope it works out for them." He touched my elbow and led me toward the bench in front of Gil's. "Let's sit down for a few minutes." We sat quietly, watching a squirrel searching for food around the trash can on the walkway. "I spoke to Zach's parents yesterday. Did I mention that?"

"No."

"It seems he was troubled most of his life. He was on disability for his mental problems."

"That's sad. But I still don't understand what made him do it."

Garrett took a deep breath. "From what you told me about his last few minutes, it sounds to me like a problem with lust that he couldn't conquer. His upbringing convinced him it was wrong and that he had to get rid of the source of it, so he killed the girls who tempted him. Then when you reminded him he couldn't kill all the women in the world, it sent him over the edge in despair. I guess, in the end, he decided the only way out was to kill himself. His father didn't seem particularly surprised by what happened. He sounded cold and distant."

"Parents can really screw up their kids, can't they? It's a wonder any of us survive."

Garrett put his arm around my shoulders. "It's not as bad as all that. You turned out pretty well."

I leaned against him. "Thanks."

"What happens now, Ryn? Do you just ride off into the sunset and forget? Doesn't our time together mean anything to you?"

I turned to him. "Of course it does, Garrett. Look, I'll only be an hour from here. It's not like I'm going to China."

"But you'll only be there long enough to write the article for your column. Then what? Another town? Another Trout Fork somewhere?"

I gazed into his intense blue eyes. "I just don't know. You're asking me questions I have no answers for."

We watched Hank come out of his store and begin to sweep the walkway. He looked a little sad to me, but his eyes were clear, and his face had lost that blotchy, bloated look. Maybe his short romance with Alma had renewed his self-esteem. Whatever it was, I hoped he had come out of a long night of sorrow and regret over his wife to now look forward to the future.

He waved at Gil who came whistling up the path from the creek in waders, carrying his fishing pole and a basket of trout. "Here you go, Hank," he said opening the basket. "Enough for a week." They divided the fish between them, and Gil unlocked the door of his bait shop.

Hank leaned on his broom. "Getting lazy in your old age, Gil? I've never known you to open up late," he teased.

"Life's too short for schedules, my friend. Much too short." Gil opened the door and went inside, still whistling.

I stood up and turned to Garrett. There was nothing left to say, and we both knew it. He hugged me and kissed my cheek. Then he got into his pickup and drove slowly out of the lot onto the main road. Watching him go, there was an ache in my heart. I knew how much I would miss him.

I went back to the cabin and said my good-byes to Ashley and her parents. They made me promise to call as soon as I was settled. We hugged, and I whispered to Ashley, "Let me know how it goes with your mom and dad."

She smiled at me, tears beginning to fill her eyes. "I'll never forget you. You saved my life. I wish you could stay forever."

"I'll only be an hour away. I'll call you." I patted her shoulder and went to the bedroom. I pulled on my jacket and put Jack over my shoulder. Sasha looked wistfully at us, and I wondered if her heart was breaking like mine.

On the way to the door, I turned to Alma. "Oh, I forgot." I pulled a piece of paper from my jacket pocket. "I wrote this. You might want to consider posting it on the bulletin board outside the café. If you want to, I mean. Don't feel obligated."

"What is it?"

"An obituary. For Zach."

Alma took the paper and read out loud: "Zachary 'Rev' Wayland, fifty-one, a member of the Trout Fork community, passed away on July fifteenth. Born in Atlanta, Georgia, he moved to Colorado in 2001 and settled in Trout Fork the same year. Zach was the only child of Pastor and Mrs. Aaron Wayland of Atlanta. He was a member of Pineland Park Community Church, where he sang tenor in the choir. 'Rev' loved fishing and the outdoor life. He will always be remembered by the Trout Fork community. May he rest in peace."

Alma turned to me. "Very nice, considering what you could have written."

I shrugged. "Everyone deserves a kind word when they die."

As I closed the door behind me, I smiled as I heard Alma say, "Let's get going, Ashley. There will be a line of hungry people outside the café."

I was fastening Jack into his basket on the bike when an old beat-up Ford chugged into the parking lot, belching black smoke out of its tailpipe. It pulled up next to me, then the engine coughed once and shuddered to a stop.

A girl got out of the car and smiled at me. "Whew. I never thought this old wreck would make it." She was about eighteen, short and stocky with bright green eyes and slightly sunburned skin. Her strawberry blonde hair was pulled back neatly and woven into one long braid down her back. "Oh, how sweet," she exclaimed when she saw Jack in his basket. "Does he really ride with you?"

"He really does."

"Awesome. Do you live around here?"

"I've only been here a few weeks. What brings you to Trout Fork?"

She pulled a folded newspaper page from her pocket. "I saw this ad in the Pineland Park paper. It says there's a café here that's looking for a waitress." She looked up at the sign above Alma's. "This must be the place."

"This is it. The owner's name is Alma. She's in the kitchen. You'll like working here, if you decide to stay, I mean."

She surveyed the stores and the surrounding area. "Not much to look at though, is it? Hard to see how a café can do much business here."

"You'd be surprised how busy it can get, especially now. The summer tourist season sees a lot of action."

"Well, I'm only looking to work for the rest of the summer until I make enough money to get my car fixed. Is there any place to say here?"

"No. The waitress rooms with Alma and her daughter, Ashley. She's fifteen."

She gave a shrug that told me she would be up for pretty much anything. "Oh. Okay, thanks." She started toward the front door. I mounted the Honda and switched on the ignition.

The girl turned back, shading her eyes with her hand against the morning sun. "What's it like around here? I mean, is it safe for a girl on her own?"

I thought of the day I found that Pink Floyd T-shirt in the water, of the night we fled from the fire as it raced toward us, and of that horrible day in Zach's cabin. But Dave Malone and Zach were gone now, and Trout Fork had returned to normal.

I buckled the strap on my helmet. "Yes, I think you'll find that it's quite safe."

Madam Gauzie strode up the walk from her store, her necklaces jangling and her diaphanous attire wafting in the breeze. "Oh, Ryn," she called. "I'm glad I caught you. Are you just leaving? Oh, dear. How we're going to miss you." She came to the bike and flung her arms around my neck. "You will call to let us know how you get on."

I returned her embrace. "Of course I will. And I'll see you again before you know it."

She cast a suspicious eye at the young girl still standing near the door to the café. "Who might that be?" she asked quietly.

"She's here to apply for my job."

"Humph. Well, we'll see about that." She moved toward the girl, her rapid stride belying her age. "Young lady? I presume you're looking for Alma?"

"Yes," the girl said tentatively.

Madam Gauzie held the café door open for her. "Let me introduce you to her. I've known Alma for years, even before Ashley was born. You'll like Ashley. She's about your age. I think you'll enjoy working here. Of course, it's not the same as it used to be. Not at all. I do hope you like cats."

THE END

About the Author

DM O'Byrne's first job was as a waitress. Now she's a writer of mystery novels. In between, jobs included English teacher, racehorse exerciser, jockey, accountant, golf resort assistant manager, writer, and editor. Her places of residence ranged from the Jersey shore to a lengthy sojourn in California and finally to the Colorado Rockies. Each profession, each location was rife with life lessons, fascinating characters, potential plot lines, and wide-ranging experiences. Sooner or later, they will all end up on the written page. O'Byrne is the author of *Dangerous Turf* and the sequel, *Three to One Odds*.